T0279172

WE'RE *NEVER* GETTING HOME

ALSO BY TRACY BADUA

This Is Not a Personal Statement

WE'RE NEVER GETTING HOME

TRACY BADUA

Quill Tree Books
An Imprint of HarperCollinsPublishers

Quill Tree Books is an imprint of HarperCollins Publishers.

We're Never Getting Home
Copyright © 2024 by Tracy Badua
All rights reserved. Printed in the United States of America.
No part of this book may be used or reproduced in any manner whatsoever
without written permission except in the case of brief quotations embodied
in critical articles and reviews. For information address HarperCollins
Children's Books, a division of HarperCollins Publishers, 195 Broadway,
New York, NY 10007.
www.epicreads.com

Library of Congress Control Number: 2023936861
ISBN 978-0-06-321780-5

Typography by Erin Fitzsimmons and Laura Mock
24 25 26 27 28 LBC 5 4 3 2 1
First Edition

For my Girlstrip friends
You can't get rid of me that easily

ONE

SATURDAY, APRIL 23
2 pm

I 've never quite reached that high note of the Newcomers and Goers' latest. I try anyway as I sweep on another coat of ultra-black waterproof mascara. My lips mold to the words, my pulse matches the beat of the drums. And this is just what a tinny online stream does to me. I may self-combust when I see my favorite band in person tonight, in all their eardrum-splitting, heart-stopping, latex-pantsed glory.

"Can you turn that down?" Mom's voice cuts through the music.

The interruption makes me jump, and I smudge my carefully applied mascara. I bite back a curse word—not about to catch an earful of lecturing from Mom today, of all long-awaited days—and reach for the speaker on my dresser. I tap the volume down.

"Better?" I ask. I peer at her reflection in the dresser mirror. Mom leans against the doorframe and smiles at me. She's in black leggings and a mid-thigh-length denim tunic, virtually the mom uniform in our suburban neighborhood.

"Much. That glitter eyeshadow is a nice touch," she says, "but are you sure that's safe? It won't mess up your contact lenses?"

I try my best to repair the mascara damage with my pinkie, and it comes away dusted with the glitter eyeshadow Mom's already skeptical of. "I'll only be at the Orchards for a couple hours. I'll be home with plenty of time to wipe all this off, put on my nice, safe glasses, and pick up Dad."

Mom sighs knowingly. She was the one who fought for me to be able to go to the Orchards Music Festival out in the San Bernardino foothills, nearly two hours away. A year ago, a car accident landed her in the hospital for a week, and though she's mostly recovered, it shifted her perspective on life; losing 40 percent of your blood leaves room for something fresh, I guess. After she was discharged, she became all about eating dessert before dinner, filling the gas tank without worrying about prices, and generally enjoying our time on this planet responsibly.

That "responsibly" is where Dad swooped in. To their combined "yes," he added, "Fine, but you're coming home right after the set." To which I countered with staying a little later—I didn't want to be racing from the stage to the parking lot the second the music ended—in exchange for picking him up from his work retreat.

And this was after I proved I could come up with the two hundred dollars for the one-day ticket myself.

With a card-shark-like flip of her hand, Mom reveals a small stack of ten-dollar bills. "Buy yourself a band T-shirt or some overpriced bottled waters at least."

I open my mouth to graciously protest but she silences me with a shush.

She reaches for my tan leather mini-backpack. "No arguments. It's my money; I get to decide what to do with it. You think I fought with our health insurance for fun? I earned this hundred bucks." She stuffs the cash in the front pocket. "Consider it compensation for you picking up my last-minute refills from the doctor last week during rush hour."

I've performed my one requisite protest, so I'm not going to turn down her offer again.

"Thanks, Mom."

"You're welcome, Jana. I know how hard you worked for this." Her smile wavers, no doubt at the memory of my extra late-night and weekend shifts behind the cash register at Callaway Drug. I had to cram in school, homework, extracurriculars, and—somewhere between all of that—sleep too. I needed to scrape up every last penny for this Orchards ticket though.

Mom shifting to part-time remote teaching was the best move for her health; she couldn't do the long drives to her full-time job in the city anymore. But according to Dad, this was perhaps not the best move for our family finances. The money for any "fun" stuff, from this festival to any of the paid events the Samuels High Associated Student Body set up for graduation to even the drops of gas that exceed my to-school-and-work-and-back commute, comes out of my pocket. But it was worth it for a chance to see our favorite band.

My chest tightens. I mean *my* favorite band. *Our* would imply that I'm still going with my usually best friend, Maddy, but she's going with her boyfriend, Tyler, instead. We've been off-balance since our fight earlier this week.

"What time is Nathan picking you up?" Mom asks.

Maddy was supposed to be my ride, until our plans crumbled. I refuse to let this ticket go to waste, so I hitched a ride with Nathan Clark, my friend from church. I didn't fill Mom in on the reason for the switch, but she knows the Clarks well enough that she convinced Dad it was fine for us to have a night out—within those responsible limits, of course.

"Any time now," I say, zipping up my backpack. "You're tutoring tonight, right?"

Mom nods. "A three-hour Business English immersion class for a couple execs in Indonesia. Don't worry about me—I've got some leftover pizza and a FaceTime date with your sister later. And you're sure you're all set to pick up your dad from his work retreat?"

"Ah, the glamorous life of an accountant: a whole Saturday in a conference room, a forced awards dinner, then your teenage daughter as your designated driver." I'd meant my words to come off lighthearted, but Mom frowns, so I add, "Yes, I'll be home in time to grab the car and pick him up."

Mom hasn't driven late at night since the car accident, and it's a sore enough spot that none of us have wanted to press her on it. It's easier for me to haul myself back from the concert and make the forty-minute trek to the conference resort than it is for us to make Mom claw through the fear that's set into her bones.

My phone buzzes on top of my dresser. "That must be Nathan."

"Maddy's meeting you there then?"

I lower my gaze to my phone so she doesn't see the slight frown that flits across my face at the mention of Maddy. Mom and I don't have that kind of made-for-TV-movie relationship where I dish to her every bit of drama about friends, love interests, or bodily changes. Before my sister, Jackie, went off to college, she and I used to scoff together at movie scenes where the gorgeous teen and her mother have a heart-to-heart about having sex for the first time (a topic that would be mortifying for us to detail to our mom) all while sitting on their perfectly made beds with their gross shoes on (equally mortifying).

"Yeah, she'll be at the Orchards. With Tyler." The truth, even if it paints an incomplete picture.

I do wonder whether Mom somehow knows something's up between me and my best friend lately. She might've noticed that Maddy hasn't shown up at our house for snacks—Mom *always* feeds her—and homework help as often. But that was true even before this latest fight. All that free time belongs to the boyfriend now.

Something rumbles into our driveway, and I know it's time to leave. Sheer energy shoots through me at the prospect of kicking off the best night of my life.

With one last stop at my dresser mirror bordered by band photos and reminder sticky notes, I swipe a stray dot of glitter off my cheek and test my orchid-pink long-lasting lipstick. I tug down my denim cutoffs to hide where my dark brown tan shifts abruptly into sunless beige, then rearrange the straps of my loose white-and-turquoise tank. Mom hands me my backpack and a satiny fuchsia bomber jacket as she follows me to the front door.

"I put the phone numbers for Nathan's cell and his mom's cell on the fridge," I say. No way my parents could ever say I didn't fulfill the conditions of my release tonight. Our household is built on rules—the only way for us to sort through the chaos of Jackie's mid-semester return and departure, Dad's ever-expanding work hours, and Mom's health—and I'm not giving my parents any reason to question their teenage daughter's excursion to one of the biggest music festivals in Southern California. "CoGo is on at eight, and their set's about an hour long."

Mom raises an eyebrow. "CoGo?"

"You know, the Newcomers and Goers? CoGo?"

Mom tips her chin up, suppressing a smile. "Ah, of course. Sorry I'm not as cool as you."

My phone buzzes again. I yell a "I'll be right there!" toward the front door before offering a few more reassurances to Mom that yes, I have my wallet and my cell phone.

"And midnight, okay, CinderJana?" Mom says, adjusting the strap of my tank top.

I nod. "I know. I'll be home on time to get Dad so he doesn't panic and assume he has yet another rebel daughter who'll threaten to live at home forever."

Mom shakes her head. "Don't pick on your sister. She was going through a lot at school."

I bite my tongue. Honestly, who isn't going through a lot at any given time? As if anyone's existence these days is worry-free and daffodil-filled. But whatever Jackie went through in her first tumultuous year at college somehow led her to leave half-way through the first semester this academic year. This meant her moving back home into the shared room that was supposed to be finally all mine. Her posters and photos of high school friends had been long gone by the time she'd dropped her duffel next to the closet. This also meant extra pressure for me to stay the remaining "good" daughter, hardworking and focused always.

"You two need to get along," she continues. "You're sisters."

The issue isn't Jackie and me getting along. It's that I'm now scrutinized through the same cracked lenses they judge Jackie's every move with, even though I haven't done anything to warrant that.

With Nathan idling in our driveway, I don't have time for a deep conversation or, more accurately, a monologue from me on all the reasons why my sister can sometimes be the worst. She's not even physically around—she moved back to campus to start afresh at the beginning of this semester—so this is a battle I can delay.

Instead, I spout out another assurance I'll be home on time and remind Mom to call her pharmacist back—that sticky note has been next to the landline phone for a week. Then I double-check my backpack, drape my jacket over my arm, and practically leap out the front door.

To my horror, the promised ride to the Orchards in our driveway is a gray minivan with cloudy headlights, dirt-crusted dark-tinted windows, and a rust-dotted bumper held up with duct tape. The whole thing looks like it could fall apart at any minute.

When Nathan told me he'd also gotten tickets to CoGo and could drive me, I'd jumped at the possibility that my own Orchards ticket wouldn't go to waste. Never mind that CoGo has been the soundtrack of my and Maddy's friendship ever since the band's music drifted into our ears one carpool ride home in junior high. Music doesn't belong to anyone. It's as much mine as it is Maddy's and Nathan's, even if it speaks to us in different ways.

But now I'm going to spend the next eight to ten hours with a guy from my confirmation class at church, whose mom is in a book club with mine, in a sad minivan that seems one too-fast speed bump away from petering out. If I'd known that there was more of a chance of me pushing this vehicle than riding in it, I would've reconsidered.

I stalk toward the minivan. Nathan has his driver's-side window open and is trying to reshape the short faux-hawk he's tried to mold his flat brown hair into.

"Hey, Mrs. Rubio!" he shouts to my mom. He has a palm-tree-print tank top on, and the muscles in his shoulders and arms pop from all those club sports hours as he waves.

Mom waves back, but her slightly pinched face looks as nervous about this jalopy as mine must look. "Hi, Nathan. Tell your mom I said hello," she calls out. "And drive safe, all right? You've got precious cargo there."

"Don't worry, Mrs. Rubio. This thing doesn't really go past seventy anyway," Nathan answers.

He likely means that to be reassuring, but that little fact about this dilapidated van only makes me more worried about hopping inside.

"And home by midnight, Jana," Mom calls after me, as if I need reminding. As if I'm not the one who plasters gently nagging sticky notes all over the house for everyone.

Once I'm close enough to the driver's side, I ask in a low voice, "What—what is this? I thought you had one of those new Priuses. I could've sworn you'd pulled up next to us in the church parking lot in that supersilent hybrid dozens of times."

Nathan shrugs casually as if he didn't just perform a huge bait and switch. "Parents needed it this weekend, but luckily we've got this beauty." He slaps a hand on the driver's-side door, and I swear it creaks like the metal's about to give way. I nearly jump back, lest the side mirror pop off and crash on the concrete at my feet. "Hop in!"

It's fine, I tell myself. I'm going to see my favorite band ever, at the epic Orchards Music Festival, no less: a once-in-a-lifetime experience. If Nathan is confident this minivan will get us there and back, then I'm happy for the ride. I'm not going to let this one minor surprise dampen my good mood.

I round the front of the van toward the front passenger seat, but someone is already sitting there.

"Everett?" I say. Another unwelcome surprise: Nathan's fifteen-year-old brother, who usually waits outside our confirmation class doing his homework, taking selfies, or live streaming his skateboard tricks. "What are you doing here?"

Everett pushes a button to slide down the window a little more. He's a lankier version of Nathan, with a messy mop of curly hair instead of Nathan's straighter strands. He's in a red long-sleeved plaid shirt that I've seen sported by a dozen social media influencers in the past week. "Um, did Nathan not tell you I'm coming? My parents wouldn't let him take Stampy the minivan here unless he took me too."

My jaw drops. We're going to be stuck babysitting his little brother. At a wild, possibly drug-scattered music festival. With a dilapidated minivan they've affectionately nicknamed Stampy.

My stomach gurgles with preemptive stress. This is not the beginning of the grand adventure I expected, but I tamp down the anger that's starting to bubble up. I'd planned all this out, down to the penny. Mom's cash was a good surprise, but everything since then is decidedly not.

I force my shoulders to relax. Sure, I'm not happy to have a minor tagging along, but I'm not letting this get in the way of what's sure to be *the* concert of my life. I can deal with this. Or at least I have to pretend to, because Mom is watching me and I really don't want to give anyone reasons for me not to go, not after how hard I fought to go to the Orchards at all.

I beam a wide smile at Everett, exaggerating a show for Mom so she and Dad won't worry about me tonight. "Great. That means I'll have the whole back to stretch out then."

Nathan nods. "Well, you'll have to share with—"

I heave open the sliding door behind Everett's seat. My heart sputters to a halt in my chest.

"Us," Maddy finishes from the back seat.

I actually tilt my head like a confused cocker spaniel. This I didn't expect whatsoever. My hitching a ride with Nathan is evidence of me going to extraordinary lengths to put a little cooling-off time and distance between Maddy and me. I'd even hoped to avoid her all day at the Orchards: it's that big of a festival.

She still hasn't apologized for ruining last weekend or for any of the other times she's second-placed me. We hadn't even spoken since our blowup a few days ago.

So how Maddy and Tyler managed to squeeze into this particular carpool with Nathan, of the hundreds of cars trekking to the San Bernardino foothills today, is beyond me.

"Oh, embarrassing," Maddy says before forcing a laugh. She moves to brush her hair away from her face like she always does when she's feeling nervous. Except that she's got her blond hair pulled back in a fishtail braid and her fingers graze nothing.

From her words, I'm hopeful she's admitting how awkward this is. Maybe she's ready to apologize and this forced hangout won't be totally tense.

Next to her, Tyler, his brown eyes hidden behind orange-lensed reflective sunglasses that match his neon orange T-shirt, laughs and points at me in a way that seems shallower than what had been going through my own mind. "Whoa, Jana! You and Mads have the same shirt!"

I peer down and, sure enough, we sport the same exact white-and-turquoise tank. Where mine is loose and billowy at my hips, she has the bottom hem of hers tied in a knot, exposing a sliver of pale pink-peach midriff above her wide-legged jeans. Peeking out of her waistband is the faded scar on her hip from when we rode—and crashed—shopping carts in the drugstore parking lot after hours last summer. As we patched up the nasty scratch with a decade-old first aid travel kit, CoGo's surprise album release blared out of the speakers of Maddy's white Civic, the same car that I assumed she was going to drive to the Orchards today.

Shock and sheer annoyance root me to the driveway. I painstakingly arranged everything to avoid going to the CoGo concert with Maddy, and now I have to spend the whole day with her, in matching outfits?

My options float before me. I could give up on my grand plans that have been so frustratingly wrecked. I could admit to myself that all these unwelcome surprises got to me, give up the thrill of this live concert I've been looking forward to for months, and instead stream the CoGo set from my room, alone. My two-hundred-dollar ticket won't have bought me a highlight-of-my-life experience: it will have bought me a password to a website with choppy video and subpar sound.

Or I could go. Nathan seems confident enough about the minivan, and his little brother is his little problem. And Maddy is the one in the wrong, after all. She should be bothered by our forced proximity, not me. I can put on a smile and rock out to my favorite band how I planned, more or less.

I angle back toward the house, conflicted. Then Mom, her hand already on the front door as if to close it behind me, waves. "Have fun! Text me when you get there."

Mom's platitudes about enjoying life, living and laughing and loving or whatever, come flooding in. I'm not about to let Maddy Parsons ruin this night for me. She doesn't deserve that kind of space in my head right now. Especially not after everything I've gone through to secure this one night of carefree, music-filled freedom.

Nathan adjusts his rearview mirror. "Hurry up, Jana. Traffic's getting worse every second."

And now I don't even have time to go change shirts. I slide my backpack off and toss it onto a seat. Maddy's lips press into a tight line, the way they do when she accidentally eats something with cilantro but doesn't want to make a big deal out of her hatred of it. I think she says something, but I can't hear her over the unsettling metallic sound of Nathan putting Stampy the minivan into reverse.

I buckle myself in, then twist my head to cast a "Hey" over my shoulder to her and Tyler. I can at least be civil if we're going to be stuck in here for two hours.

"Hey," Maddy says, leaning forward toward my seat. "Nathan is Tyler's friend from rec soccer. I didn't know he was yours too."

Her explanation needles me in a way she probably didn't mean it to. "That really goes to show how well you know me then, doesn't it?"

"Come on, Jana. Chill. Let's just have fun today."

"That's exactly what I'm planning to do." I dig into my backpack and tug out my earbuds. I push them in, tuning out the rising debate over what music to play on the Stampy stereo, and stare out the fingerprint-smudged window, waiting for our surroundings to go from concrete and stucco to greenery.

Maddy leans back and talks to Tyler instead. He uh-huhs almost absentmindedly as he teases up his straight black hair that he's gelled into short spikes for the festival.

In a few hours, I'll be screaming along with CoGo, the band whose music has an eerie way of echoing my soul. And even though I'll be one of thousands in the crowd at the Orchards, I can pretend that they're singing to me and only me, that I'm the most important person in the world to someone, for at least a moment.

SIX MONTHS AGO
October 27

I wiggle one last cord into the already crowded power strip jut-ting out from the wall, and I'm rewarded with that *ping* sound announcing that my phone is charging.

"Isn't that a fire hazard or something?" Maddy says, eyeing me between the laptop and tablet she has set up on my bed. One hot-pink-manicured hand taps the tablet screen to refresh the Orchards ticket purchase web page. The other reaches for a handful of crinkle-cut potato chips we've been demolishing in our stress over navigating the purchase process.

I rise and back away from the power strip, as if walking slowly will somehow make it safer. No sparks. So far, so good. "Prob-ably, but we need all the juice we can get. I'm not missing out on CoGo tickets because my phone or laptop dies in the middle of the transaction."

Maddy's apprehension vanishes at the horror of my suggested worst-case scenario. She agrees: What's a little fire if it means we get to see our favorite band ever?

I resume my place on Jackie's twin bed, pushed up against the wall on the opposite side of the room from mine. Her wall is painted a deep, moody purple, and there are thumbtack holes from where her decorations used to hang. She hadn't bothered to put any of them back up when she came home for the summer to take some general ed classes at the community college. She moved back into the dorms in August to start her second year, but for some reason, Mom and Dad still won't let me clear out her stuff. So now I've just started taking over the empty bed, dresser, and desk I'm not allowed to move or sell, like vines creeping over an abandoned house as it returns to nature.

Dragging my laptop onto my legs, I click to refresh my browser, then gasp at the new screen. A bright white *Welcome* in swirly font tops a lengthy disclaimer, with an *Enter* button at the bottom of the page. "I'm in the waiting room!"

The Orchards ticket purchase process involves a series of registrations, waiting rooms, and luck, and I've just crawled over a major hurdle.

Maddy throws a chip-crumb-covered air-five in my direction. "So between us, we've got two devices in the waiting room, two others trying to get in. I like our chances here."

"Me too. Can you imagine? Capping off senior year with—" A *ping* from Maddy's phone interrupts me. My eyes widen. "What was that? Did you get another device in?"

Maddy smiles but shakes her head, her blond ponytail swishing gently at her back. "No. You know that sports photographer for the school paper?"

"Tyler Su? The one from our English class? He's always getting passes to skip out mid-class to make it to a practice or game or something, right?"

"Yeah, that's him. He covered one of our competitions and needed to verify some names and spellings. He's"—her smile widens as she reads whatever's on her phone—"nice."

I refresh my other browser again. "That's good. You deserve 'nice' after Concession Stand Dan."

We both laugh at the nickname we'd come up with for her last crush. I'm relieved at the thought of her moving on. Her entire being is governed by her heart, with her brain relegated to backseat driver status. No matter how much I and her brain told her that her last crush was a dud, Maddy was going to do what her heart wanted to do. It's that big difference between us that keeps our friendship interesting and, to be honest, extremely frustrating sometimes.

Our laughter is cut short by another tone ringing out, this time from my computer.

I sit up. "I'm in! It's letting me make a purchase. Quick, the card!"

Maddy springs into action. Deftly leaping off the bed, she bounds over to my side, her dad's silver credit card gleaming in her hand. He took some convincing to let us use it, but after we detailed the purchase process for him and how it's practically a requirement that we use a card—unless he wants us to go meet some random ticket seller in a parking lot, with a bagful of cash—he handed it over. But not until after we both promised to pay him back.

I scooch over as Maddy types in the billing information, and Jackie's bed creaks beneath our weight. Seeing the final total, which includes my own two-hundred-dollar ticket, plus fees, makes me wheeze. It'll be worth it, I tell myself. This will be unforgettable.

At the top of the web page, a timer clicks down. "Hurry up, Maddy, we only have ten minutes to buy these things or we get kicked back into the waiting room!"

She pauses her typing to side-eye me. "And you nagging me helps how?"

"Point taken." I slide off Jackie's bed and start to pace across the worn gray carpet. It's only when I see Maddy's shoulders relax that I dare to speak again. "So?"

Her smile beams with sunshine and music. "We're going to the Orchards, Jana!"

I rush over to hug her, and we set my phone to blare out our *Maddy and Jana's Intro to Newcomers and Goers Playlist* in celebration. We dance to the folky pop rhythms as we pack up our laptops and wind up our charging cords, all the while discussing our big ambitions for the night of our lives six months from now. Rides, outfits, songs we hope they play.

"You think we'll get to meet them?" she asks, ever the dreamer.

"That'd be amazing, but realistic-me says probably not."

She rolls her eyes playfully. "Realistic-you is a buzzkill."

"And dreamer-you needs to listen to some logic. It'll be a huge venue with tons of people dying to meet them too."

She zips up her backpack and slides the straps onto her shoulders. "All right, I gotta get to cheer practice."

"Isn't it kind of late?"

"I told them I had an appointment I couldn't miss. But what I didn't tell them was that this was an appointment"—she paints on a mischievous grin—"with destiny!"

I snort at her over-the-top joke and close my laptop. I'm not about to argue with whatever way she managed to clear her schedule this afternoon for our hangout. It's been a while since she's come over for more than a snack and some homework help, and it was nice to have a little throwback into how our friendship used to be, before we both got impossibly busy.

"I'll call you tonight so we can plan our grand adventure?" Maddy asks.

"I picked up an extra shift at Callaway from six until close, so afterward maybe, if that's not too late. Then you can tell me about this photographer guy and how done you are with Concession Stand Dan."

"I can always FaceTime you during some tosses," she says, making her way to the door.

"Um, please don't. No wild flying stunts and breaking your neck. You know these tickets are nontransferable, and I did not just shell out two hundred dollars to see CoGo alone."

She laughs then as she digs her car keys out of her pocket. "Ha. Like you'd ever get rid of me that easily."

TWO

Wake up, Jana. We're here!" Nathan's too-cheery voice booms in my ears.

I'd fallen asleep to some eighties music—Tyler had won the battle of the minivan playlist—and my brain slowly registers the shift back into wakefulness. When I remember I'm stuck in a halfway-to-the-junkyard minivan with unexpected company including a best friend who hasn't apologized yet, I keep my eyes half-closed. I'm in no hurry to announce my return to this closed space full of cheap cologne and social awkwardness.

In the front seat, Everett snickers. "She fell asleep before we even got onto the 10 freeway. No wonder she asked you to drive." Everett reaches over to smack Nathan on the upper arm, which I guess is something brothers do. Jackie and I rarely punctuate our conversation with lighthearted, physical violence.

"You don't think it had something to do with Nathan's stunningly good looks?" Tyler calls out from the back.

"Wait, is this why you rushed out to get a haircut last night?" Everett adds.

Pretending to still be asleep was the right decision. I'd had enough of Mom and Dad prying into why Nathan, of all people, was driving me to the Orchards while dodging any questions about Maddy.

Why, is he your boyfriend?

You're too young to be dating.

Do we need to have, um, a talk?

To which all my replies were a resounding "Oh god, no! Please stop!"

As if my only motivation tonight was to run off with a no-good rebel (whose family we know from church, so it's anyone's guess where my parents' sudden suspicion comes from) and forever live outside the bounds of respectable society. Never mind I've been blasting CoGo music nonstop for the past month. They should know how excited I am about seeing this band.

Don't get me wrong—Nathan's fun and nice, and he gets his share of eyelash-batting looks and folks shoving their way into our conversations at church events. I've known him for years, before he put on the muscle and realized a bowl-shaped hairstyle doesn't work for his square-jawed face shape. Maybe I do have the tiniest of crushes on him. But with the end of senior year coming up fast, and the friendship between Maddy and me at its messiest, I don't have a single extra brain cell to devote to figuring out anything else.

"Shut up, both of you," Nathan says. I pry one eye open just enough to catch his reflection in the rearview mirror and notice the pink spreading across his cheeks. "And it's not a crime to get a haircut at nine at night. It's the only time my barber was available."

I finally force my eyes wide open and dab at a tiny dot of drool that's escaped onto my chin.

We've exited the freeway into a line of vehicles stretching a mile ahead on a road bordered by brown-green shrubs and tall, dry grass. Everything from motorcycles to camper vans to limousines crawl toward the entrance of the Orchards, a high, temporary gate made up to look like apple trees worthy of tempting Adam and Eve.

I sit up as the adrenaline starts to stream through me. I'm here, about to see my favorite band ever. We're still probably not going to meet CoGo, but I'm dead set on getting as close to the stage as I can.

The muscles in my neck and back have tensed from a long two hours of uncomfortable car sleep, and I stretch and twist to loosen them. Over my shoulder, I see Tyler drum on an empty can of Pringles. Maddy digs through her purse for something.

Part of me wants to squeal with her "we're here!" to recapture the same sparkle from that afternoon we bought the tickets and danced to our jointly created playlist. But what would that fix? We'll just go right back to me waiting for an apology from someone who doesn't even recognize when she does something wrong. As if totally ditching your best friend is some low-level crime like taking the last French fry.

I'm determined to have the best time tonight, apology or not, and it starts with me fully waking up and getting into the festival hype. "Everett, can you turn up the volume?"

From the times our families have hung out together at church functions, Everett has always seemed a good kid, eager to please. And he doesn't disappoint.

"Ah, the princess is awake!"

He's sure growing into this unique brand of annoying though. "Volume. Please."

He twists the grime-caked knob on the dash before lightheartedly spouting, in a cringe-worthy attempt at a British accent, "Is that to Her Royal Highness's satisfaction?"

Nathan meets my gaze in the rearview mirror, and we exchange a knowing eye roll at his little brother's behavior.

A bass-heavy beat drowns out the low conversation of Maddy and Tyler behind me. It even covers his Pringles drumming. "Yup. It's perfect."

Six songs later, we pass the Orchards main gate and get directed into a packed-dirt parking spot. My heart starts to pump the second I force open the minivan door—with an unsettling creak—and plant my feet on the ground. The adrenaline only grows through the multiple levels of security and ticket checks.

People swirl around me, chattering and laughing as they head to the various stages. The air is earthy with dust and pine, and the wild, unnatural hint of stale beer and perfume. In the distance, I catch a glimpse of the famous Forest Wheel, the Orchards' signature neon green Ferris wheel that features prominently in the background of most selfies and videos taken here. Clusters of food and souvenir trucks and tents dot the grounds, and a whole corner nearby is bright blue with a line of porta-potties.

While I wait for the others to get their bags inspected by the Orchards' renowned, no-nonsense security, I channel my restless energy into fulfilling one of those parental conditions for attendance. I find a decent safe-looking background, a wooden signpost decorated in an old-timey saloon font directing festivalgoers to the different stages, and text them a picture of me smiling.

Me to Mom and Dad:

Just got here! Plenty of security and cleanish bathrooms.

Mom to the group:

Have fun! Scream extra loud at CooGoo for me

Dad to the group:

Resort driveway is easy to miss. Call if you can't find it or if you need anything else

Me to the group:

More money? (Relax, I'm joking. Sort of)

When I finally tuck my phone into my back pocket, the last in our group, Everett, practically skips over to join us.

"This is so cool!" He bounces in place from excitement.

"Stay close, Ev," Nathan says. He analyzes the signpost behind me. "All right, looks like there are five stages: Gala Apple Main Stage, Avocado Stage, Date Tent, Almond Tent, and Walnut Tent."

We collectively sweep our gaze around, and I swear there's even an awed sigh we release in unison. This place feels massive, monumental.

"CoGo's playing at Avocado," I say.

"That direction," Tyler says. He gestures northwest toward a stage looming large behind a row of lit-up food trucks.

"Not until eight though," Maddy cuts in. She threads her arm through Tyler's, like she's Dorothy about to skip down a yellow brick road with the scarecrow. Tyler's other shoulder balances the strap of Maddy's purse. "So we've got time to explore, right?"

I don't have to stick by her and her pretending-everything's-fine this whole time? That sounds damn delightful. "Yup! See you all at eight by Avocado!"

The enthusiasm in my voice must tip her off because her mouth dips into the slightest frown. Is she finally ready to deal with how broken we left things? Her behavior since I climbed into the van has been so *normal*—I doubt anyone can even tell we're on bad terms—and it's frustrating, like we're all swimming but I'm the only one having trouble keeping their head above water. But because they can see me, they assume I'm fine, that I'm not in danger of disappearing under at any moment.

Anyone else would probably call for help or latch on to the nearest person. But that's not my style. With everything that's happened at home, I've had to become the strong, silent type. Why add to the chaos with my own screaming?

Maddy knows this about me. She's an expert at reading my moments of quiet, my odd changes in tone. But this time, she doesn't dig further.

"I want to hit up the Almond Tent," Tyler says. He mentions a rapper famous for his thirty-second flows on the Clippity app, and Maddy nods along.

"Anyone want to come?" she asks the rest of us. I suspect she's purposely not making eye contact with me.

"No, you two go ahead. I'll stick with these guys." I jut a thumb at Nathan and Everett.

Tyler lightly tugs her arm. "Come on, Mads. We'll meet up with them later. I only get you in person for a couple more months. You and Jana are going to be living it up at Santa Clarita without me in the fall!"

"Tyler," Maddy snaps, a thinly veiled warning in her voice. So maybe someone does know that we're not getting along right now. I should've known she'd tell Tyler. Her voice is infuriatingly back to normal when she speaks again. "So which way to the Almond Tent?"

Soon, I find myself wandering off in the direction of the Date Tent with Nathan and Everett. They're dying to catch a glimpse of a celebrity DJ known for their fast-paced electronic hits, and I don't have any grand plans other than seeing CoGo.

The sheer number of people and amount of bare skin is exhilarating. Late April here means 70- or rare 80-degree temperatures during the day, and the non-locals visiting must be loving this delightful weather (meanwhile, I'm thankful I brought my bomber jacket. I find even 70 degrees in the shade chilly).

Music winds through the air from stages near and far, and amid the performances, festivalgoers, and vendors, there isn't a millisecond of silence. It's only Day Two of this festival, but the dirt hardened beneath me looks like it's been trod on by thousands of feet.

As we stroll by an art installation of metal and wire trees, a swift movement to my right catches my eye: Everett, slapping something onto a red clay art piece molded to look like a huge agave. When he moves his hand, in its place is a shiny, circular black sticker of a clown face with an *e* as one eye and a tiny QR code as the other.

I lean in to look at it. "What is that?"

The poor kid jumps like I've caught him doing something bad. Which I actually may have done. I'm pretty sure you can't go throwing stickers on everything here without getting some sort of permission.

"It's my logo," he explains with a sheepish smile. He pulls a thick stack of stickers out of the neon yellow fanny pack at his hip. "Trying to go viral. People scan that QR code right there and it leads them to my Clippity page, where they can watch all my videos. Pretty cool, right?"

Nathan groans. "Not this again, Ev. I told you to leave those at home."

"How'd you even get those past security?" I ask. My mints

and water bottle are one thing, but there aren't too many ways to explain away a hundred stickers that mysteriously end up all over the venue.

"Hid them in my boxers. Clever, right?"

I scrunch my nose. "Or disgusting. Adds new meaning to the phrase 'going viral,' am I right?"

Nathan laughs in his too-loud way that made him the bane of our confirmation teacher's existence every Thursday evening. I learned early on in our friendship that there is no such thing as a quiet conversation or joke with him. The sheer volume of his laugh gave away any kind of amusing whispers or passed notes that would secretly circulate in the church pews or classrooms. It can be embarrassing but also a little endearing, the thought that he's unafraid to express unabashed joy like that.

Everett's pale cheeks redden. "The stickers are clean, I swear. And I have hand sanitizer in here." He points down to his neon fanny pack.

I suppress my own laughter. I may have been annoyed at Everett tagging along at first, but like with his brother, his enthusiasm for everything is so genuine it's refreshing.

"You really have thought of everything."

"Well, one of us has to. Someone"—Everett glances at his brother—"almost forgot his wallet before we left the house. If not for me, he'd—" His words fade and his eyes widen as a busty brown-haired girl in a formfitting crocheted dress struts by.

Nathan literally reaches out and lifts his brother's jaw up, cartoon-style. "Keep it in your pants with those stickers, Ev."

Everett twists away. "Um, yeah. I'll . . . I'll see you guys later. I'm going to go make some friends, build my brand. I'll call you and—" He lifts his phone in the air and squints. "Huh. My cell service is spotty. You?"

I fish out my own phone and see that my last text to my parents wasn't delivered. "One bar, on and off. Maybe the mountains are messing with the reception?"

My stomach squirms at the thought that I might not be reachable to my family. Not that I didn't fight for this one night of independence, but I'd hate to miss a call from my parents about where I am—the length I take to respond is directly proportional to Dad's anger—or a question on where Mom's medicine is, despite the trail of sticky notes I left.

Nathan checks his phone too and gives a firm shake of his head. "Same. So no way you're going out on your own, Everett, especially if I'm not able to text you to get your butt back to the minivan."

"We can just pick a spot and a time and meet there after."

"Sounds reasonable to me," I say, mostly because I still have no interest in being responsible for a minor amid the madness of this festival. The kid's got hand sanitizer in his fanny pack—how much trouble can he get himself into though? Then again, to our right, a sun-wrinkled white guy in his sixties shotguns a beer and smashes the can against his head, to the cheers of his twenty-year-old friends.

Nathan shakes his head. "If there's anything more unreliable than the cell phone service right now, it's my brother being when and where he's supposed to be."

"Come on, we're at the Orchards!" Everett whines. It doesn't help his case. It actually makes him sound younger. "Jana likes my plan! She said it was reasonable!"

"No. You're not going to run off and find a girlfriend here," Nathan says, "and you're not going to go viral and get endorsements and free stuff. Whatever plans you've got in that head of yours, stop it. We're here for CoGo, then we're co-going home."

Everett grumbles something that sounds like assent, but there's a glint in his eye that worries me. Maybe I was right to be wary when I saw him in Stampy's front seat. He's out to make trouble, and the way he's casually vandalizing everything with his stickers and sighing longingly after a passing blonde in a halter top proves it.

So I of course do the responsible thing. Well, responsible for a newly turned eighteen-year-old on the best night of her life.

I turn to Nathan. "Not it!"

Nathan grimaces. "Wait, what do you mean, 'not it!'? We're all here together!"

I pat Everett on the shoulder. "Yup, but he's *your* brother, Nathan. I'm staying out of this little power struggle you're having."

He gives me a pouty, puppy-dog-eye look that some of the more heart-eyed folks in our confirmation class would snap and make their phone backgrounds. "Some friend you are."

His words echo something Maddy said days ago, and the guilt slinks in, even though we're joking. "Tell you what. I'll buy everyone Red Vines when we hit up the gas station on the way back. Still friends?"

"Make it Red Vines and a slushie and you have a deal."

"How do you seriously ingest that much sugar and look so—" My words fade as the blood rises to my cheeks. I wasn't about to straight-out call him hot, was I?

Everett grins. "Look so what, Jana? What were you going to say, hm?"

With a killer glare in his direction, I mentally double down on my "not it!" when it comes to Everett.

Thankfully, Nathan spares me having to finish my sentence. "Hey, I think that's the Date Tent over there. Looks like the DJ hasn't come on yet. Everett, any other stuff you want to check out in the meantime? And not slap stickers on?"

Everett chuckles and the two immediately launch into prioritizing which artists they want to see. If only mending the rifts between Maddy and me was this easy.

We explore the grounds, dance to the celebrity DJ's hypnotically repetitive beats, and have time to check out another set and a half. Everett also manages to lay down a dozen more stickers when he thinks Nathan and I aren't looking. The sun begins to set, and fluorescent lights flicker on throughout the venue. We make our way over to a fifteen-foot-high avocado statue to meet up with Tyler and Maddy. As we approach, the sound of the crew prepping for CoGo makes my heart pump to a different rhythm.

I push away every other worry—the cell phone reception, my

curfew, the tense vibe with my best friend—and focus on what I'm here for: the music. I point to the side of the stage, by a metal barrier. "There, we can squeeze in and get closer to the stage."

"You think they'll play 'Say Something Interesting'? Or maybe 'Forget Her Name'?" Nathan asks.

I smile. Those are two of CoGo's older songs, from when they exclusively played small, dark venues around their Bay Area home-towns. Nathan is a true fan. He knows CoGo's discography as well as I do. Yes, I'm here to see the band, but it's nice to have someone to share it with, especially when my original plans were smashed to bits. Being lonely in the middle of a crowd is no fun.

"I hope so," I say, matching his excitement. "And if they play 'Your Move,' I'm going to lose it."

The excitement dips then when a memory flits into my head. "Your Move" got me through plenty of rough patches in the past few years. I used it to drown out Mom and Dad's arguments with the insurance company, any number of Jackie's tantrums during her time at home, even the crushing late-night silence when we all lay in bed pretending we were asleep so we didn't have to talk.

But the most recent memory was a good one: Maddy and I sitting on the curb outside the hoagie place by school last month. We had one earbud from the same pair in, blasting "Your Move" as we split our regular #3 combo, with an upgrade to a straw-berry milkshake. We'd both gotten our acceptances to UC Santa Clarita and were celebrating and planning out our next four years together. We'd be roommates, of course, and I'd be perfectly content with an easily accessible bottom bunk while cheerleader supreme Maddy would vault in and out of that top bunk with her eyes closed. This memory shines golden, though tarnished a little now by the throwdown we'd just had.

"Everett, cool it with the stickers!" Nathan suddenly snaps. "You're going to get us in trouble."

Everett zips his fanny pack. "There's like a hundred thousand people here! No way are they going to waste their time on me instead of the many, many drunk people around."

As if speaking it into the universe made it happen, a guy near us vomits into a trash can, then takes another swig of his lime-flavored hard seltzer.

Nathan whirls in the other direction, plants his hands on his thighs, and pales. "Sorry. I'm a sympathy vomiter."

I almost laugh but he looks so miserable. "And you thought coming to a music festival was a great idea?"

Everett pats his brother on the back. "This is why it's such a good thing you have looks, because the brains . . ."

"Shut up, Ev," Nathan says, still hunched over.

"Let's go find Maddy and Tyler and try to get up near the stage," I say. "Hopefully there'll be fewer vomiters there."

At the giant fiberglass avocado west of us, Maddy and Tyler are mid-makeout when we walk up. They have the decency to pry their lips apart when they notice us.

"Check out any cool bands?" Tyler asks. He might be asking me directly, but I honestly can't tell who he's looking at behind those reflective orange sunglasses.

I shrug. "That heavy metal band, Fuzzy Jacket Crew, was

pretty good. But CoGo's the main event." And because I'm civil and not at all petty about my friend ditching me for her boyfriend, again, I add, "How about you?"

Tyler launches into a whole, enthusiastic rundown of their visit to every stage, which means that they must've booked it across the Orchards grounds without spending more than a few minutes at each place. And because I know Maddy hates walking—she will literally wait for her mom to get home so she can borrow her car to get their mail from the group mailbox at the end of the street—I send her a sympathetic smile without thinking.

Her blue eyes meet mine, and for a moment, the ice is on the verge of thawing.

Then a "Hello, San Bernardino!" booming through the speakers and into our eardrums stops everything.

Maddy and Jana's Intro to Newcomers and Goers Playlist
Created three years ago
30 minutes of the best music by the best band, curated by two die-hard fans

1. Your Move: This is a song of new beginnings and celebration! Pairs well with strawberry milkshakes and hope.
2. Josie: We don't know who Josie is, but whew, did you ruin someone in CoGo's life. Shame on you. Then again, it probably means one of them is single now.
3. Dive In: An anthem of fearlessness. Great before a football game or cramming for that test tomorrow you forgot about.
4. Calibrate and Commiserate: Okay, "misery loves company and we're a corporation" sounds like boring lawyer talk, but that beat is amazing.
5. Say Something Interesting: For all those times you've been a victim of mansplaining, listen to this song and eat a cookie.
6. You'll Feel the Love Tonight: Not to be confused with the song from The Lion King, at all. Turn down the volume if you're listening to this around your parents or literally anyone you'd be embarrassed sitting through pretty graphic sex scenes with. You're welcome.
7. Homer Simpson Dad Bod: We're not even sure what this song is about, but have you heard that guitar solo? It's like someone took the thrill of a roller coaster ride and turned it into notes. You'll either want to go again or throw up.

8. Forget Her Name: This will make you feel like you just went through a breakup, so be careful projecting your angst on a real-life love interest.

Like this user-created playlist? Log in now to listen and share!

THREE

SATURDAY, APRIL 23
8:02 pm

The voice emanating from the speakers is so familiar. It draws to mind a hundred memories at once. Speeding in the car with the windows down, the whipping wind threatening to drown out the song. Falling asleep with earbuds in, tuning out the rest of the messy world. Shedding a tear to a heartache vocalized in a somber tune when you haven't even spoken of your pain aloud to anyone else.

The husky, captivating voice of the lead singer of the Newcomers and Goers is one that earned hours of our listening, memorizing, and dreaming. The music of CoGo can swing from synth-heavy dance pop to soulful, hand-wringing ballads set against orchestras and electric guitars, but that voice is the common gleaming thread in it all. Our group instinctively turns toward the stage.

To say the crowd began to crush to the front like sardines would be an insult to the orderliness of sardines. We bump, wriggle, shoulder our way as far up as we can get, eventually settling into a corner where I, in all my five-foot-and-change glory, can actually glimpse the top of the band's heads, more if I lift up on my toes.

Keaton, the nonbinary lead singer, rocks a brown leather vest, holey jeans, and a whole lot of gold body glitter dusting their deep brown skin. Even with as much as they change their look, I'd recognize them anywhere.

"We're the Newcomers and Goers," Keaton croons to the backdrop of riotous applause. "And we are so, so glad to be here."

For the first time tonight, so am I. A massive speaker faces our group, and each word, each breath reverberates out of it, through the ground itself, and into our bones as if we're onstage too. I may not meet CoGo in person tonight, but this massive open-air venue somehow has the intimacy of a jam session in a cramped garage. One quick look at Nathan, Everett, Maddy, and Tyler confirms that they're as utterly entranced as I am.

With a "One, two, three, four!" Derrick the drummer kicks it off. The stage bursts into sheer, visceral energy. Turquoise and magenta lights crisscross the darkening sky and the crowd, blending the line between earth and humanity. Everything that seemed so serious and important moments ago falls away.

No tense household teetering on an easily crushed foundation of "normalcy," whatever that is.

No friendship ties pulled taut, yet again.

No fierce need to hold it all together like fine sand in the wind.

It's just me and my favorite band and the applause that muffles my screaming along of the lyrics: exactly how I want it.

Every now and then, a bold fan gets pulled onstage or a crowd-surfer lifts their head above the fray for a brief moment in the starlight. Within seconds, a uniformed Orchards security guard materializes to usher non–band members offstage. Among the crowd-surfers, the majority vanish down into the masses after someone fails to pick up their weight, but they always pop up sweaty and smiling and singing. I'd never do something like that, but I can see the appeal: getting caught up in the crowd's energy, being propelled toward our idols or the heavens.

Unforgettable chords ring out, and I recognize the first CoGo song I ever heard, a pop-punky song about heartbreak that somehow felt so relatable even though I, a seventh grader then, hadn't experienced more than a distant, one-sided crush. But I remember Maddy and I begging her dad to turn up the radio when those first notes rang out—not only to drown out her little brother's whining, but because we somehow knew even then that this sound would change our lives.

At the chorus, a wave of loneliness hits me so unexpectedly that I whirl around to try to find a fix. This is an amazing moment, and I want to share it with someone. But Maddy stands in front of Tyler, his arms around her, her eyes starry as she mouths the lyrics. As outgoing as she is, she's never loved singing in front of people, though it's unlikely anyone will hear her here. I rip my eyes away from them, feeling like an intruder in a private moment.

Instead, I cast my arm around Everett's bony shoulders, not only to have a duet partner, but to keep him from drifting off after a petite, pixie-cut brunette who keeps batting her false eyelashes in his direction. Next to me, Nathan is lost in the music too, bobbing his head so hard he'll get whiplash, his carefully styled faux-hawk a sweat-dampened mess. We sing together until the final note, then drag in quick breaths to steady our racing pulses.

I release my grip on Everett once the brunette is out of our line of sight and instead turn to Nathan.

"I can't believe we're here!" I yell a little too loudly: a side effect from the damage these speakers are doing to our hearing.

"Me neither!" he says. His face is flushed from dancing, perspiration dotting his temples and forehead.

"I've wanted to see them play live for so long. Being here, like this? It's a dream."

And something about the way Nathan's rough "yeah" ends quietly feels loaded, like we're talking about two different dreams entirely. His gaze meets mine head-on then, those colorful stage lights reflecting in the dark brown of his eyes. There's something charged about it, now that there isn't an added layer of rearview mirror or walkway between desks in a crowded religious education classroom. Just us standing too close, the electricity of the moment making messes of us both.

"We should do this again," he says after a second.

We've been friends for years, us circling each other at church and every other function our families rope us into, and he decides that now—near the end of senior year, in the middle of a packed concert—is somehow the ideal time to suggest more time together?

It's suddenly impossible to miss how close we're standing, as if the crowd, the band, and the whole universe conspired to shove us together.

Doesn't the universe realize high school is over in a couple of months? Then I'm off to Santa Clarita with Maddy, and he's off to the Naval Academy all the way on the other side of the country. I don't have a better answer to his invitation, especially not one that could be cut off by an eardrum-shattering song at any second. These sobering thoughts make me break eye contact and return my focus to the stage, where Keaton cradles the mic with both hands.

Keaton gives a teasing smirk. "I feel like the energy's a little low here. You know we're at the Orchards and not your grandmother's basement, right?"

I and the crowd scream our answer. It's a much simpler question to respond to than whatever Nathan was trying to pose. I have to admit though that part of me is a little curious and sad at the prospect of where it could've gone, if we'd only had the time.

"Then show me you're having a blast!" Keaton yells before the drummer throws out another beat to launch the next tune.

Despite the pain and drama of the past minutes, days, and years, I am having a good time. Better than good, actually. This may be the best night in ages, like I thought it would be. The more I sing along, the more I feel weightless, like nothing is holding me down. I can float, drift where I please. I am free. Nothing is going to ruin this.

I think I actually scream that aloud at some point, but I can no longer hear myself above the crowd and the boom from the speakers.

When CoGo launches into "Say Something Interesting," Nathan flashes a look at me so full of unabashed excitement that he practically glows. He turns then to Tyler, and before I know it, Tyler hoists Nathan up, with Everett's help. Up and over shoulders Nathan goes, singing along with the lyrics of his favorite song as he crowd-surfs.

"Be careful!" I don't even know why I yell that. No way he can hear me. And even if he could, who am I to tell him what to do? I'm simply a friend, a girl he knows from church: despite whatever sparks we might feel tonight, I've made sure to keep things at surface level.

Hands surge up to catch Nathan, and he bobs and twists over shoulders and outstretched arms. Tyler, Everett, Maddy, and I clap and cheer him on. He and I lock eyes again for a moment, and any lingering awkwardness from earlier has vanished. Instead, his thrill is contagious. I find myself grinning wide to match him. He makes it about thirty feet away before someone ducks away instead of bracing him, and Nathan disappears into the dancing crowd.

A song passes, and he still hasn't come back to our group. "I don't see him," I tell Everett in the momentary calm. "Do you?"

Everett shakes his head. "He knows where we are. He'll find us."

I nod, ignoring the squirm of worry in my gut. Something doesn't feel right, but I forget it as soon as Derrick and Keaton start telling a story about how they wrote the next song. It involves churros, staying up until dawn, and a unicorn-shaped pool floatie, to my surprise.

Nathan doesn't find us until three whole songs later. His palm-tree tank top is rumpled, and his face is scrunched in a way that doesn't immediately say "I had a great time crowd-surfing."

"Took you long enough," I start to tease, but then I catch his unnatural stance. "Hey, are you all right?" I put a hand on his arm to steady him.

"My knee. Again," he says to all of us.

"Again?" Maddy asks, eyebrow raised. Some strands of hair have come loose from her fishtail braid, and I'm sure we all look the worse for wear after our haphazard dancing.

"The soccer injury?" Everett manages to cut in through the thump of the music. He takes my place next to his brother: a relief, because the height difference made it tough for me to reliably carry any of his weight.

Nathan nods in response, his mouth set in a frown.

Tyler leans in. "Should we get out of here? I can drive."

Nathan's face somehow goes even more sour, so at odds with the happy, fast-paced beat and light show swirling around us. And somehow, in that pain-induced wince, I catch a hint of something else: Guilt? What is he hiding?

The notes suddenly ring off-key, Keaton's voice strained, the lights too bright and glaring. My shoulders tense unwittingly, like when you see lightning rip across the sky and your body braces for the crack of thunder.

"About that," Nathan says. He flinches as if speaking the next words will hurt more than his knee. "I—I lost the minivan keys."

"Mother—" The big finale note of CoGo's latest hit covers up the obscenity I screech into the night air.

FOUR

Deep breath," someone commands. Actually, I might have been the one who said it. I'm almost hyperventilating. My heartbeat races in a way completely unrelated to the music: Nathan lost the keys to our sole, rickety method of transportation, and we are nearly two hours away from home.

Up onstage, CoGo takes a minute for a guitar change due to a broken string. Because when one thing breaks, of course everything else has to as well. That sums up my life for the past few years.

Maddy sweeps back the wisps of hair that escaped her braid. "Nathan, when did you lose the keys?"

"When I was crowd-surfing. I felt them fall out."

My jaw drops. "You've got to be kidding me. You could've asked any one of us to hold the keys for you, Nathan! I could've put them in my backpack. Even Everett's got a damn zip-up fanny pack!"

Everett angles to plant himself between me and his brother.

"Hey, too late for that. Guess we gotta stay and find them, right?"

For a second, I think he's being sensible, then I catch his split-second glance at the pixie-cut brunette, who has reappeared. His motives to stay at the Orchards clash with the fact that I need to be home by midnight. Otherwise, Dad will be stranded at the work conference resort, all thanks to my wheeling and dealing to spend more time at the festival. He hitched a ride to his conference with his work best friend and his wife, and they and the rest of their colleagues are staying the night. Our family budget couldn't stretch to cover the exorbitant luxury resort stay, which also means that it wouldn't cover an exorbitant taxi or rideshare all the way home. If I'm not there to pick him up like I promised, Dad will explode, the nuclear fallout of which will taint the landscape for years.

"You don't have a spare somewhere in that pack of yours, Everett?" I ask, although I already suspect I know the answer. The likelihood of him carrying a key when he doesn't even drive is low, especially when he's got a ton of other useless items crammed into that fanny pack.

Everett shakes his head, predictably.

"I—I'm sorry," Nathan says.

The others spout out perfunctory it's-okays.

I drag in a breath and close my eyes instead. This never would've happened if Maddy and I had come here together like we were supposed to. But for us to rewind that far, we'd have to undo the fight, the silence, and the distance too. I'm not the one who lost the keys, but somehow I feel every bit as responsible for getting myself in this mess.

Despite how much I want to have this one fun, carefree night out, it looks like it's going to fall on me to find the keys and get us home on time. Nathan is in no shape to run around the Orchards, Everett is a flight risk thanks to his crush-seeking eye, and Maddy and Tyler are so wrapped up in each other that prying them apart for some deep strategizing seems impossible.

CoGo starts their next song, a slower one. The melody ebbs and flows like waves lapping at the coast, bringing me a tiny bit of calm.

When I open my eyes, Maddy is staring at me as if she wants to say something. She tears her gaze away and speaks to Tyler instead. Another closed door. Even with everything going wrong, I find myself disappointed at this too.

I beckon everyone closer so they can hear me. "There's no battling our way out of this crowd now," I say, gesturing to the throngs of concertgoers packing us in, "so stay through the end of this set? Two, three more songs, right?"

Tyler nods. "Sounds right. CoGo's on for an hour, then the stage has to get ready for the next performer."

"So once the crowd thins, we search." I turn to Nathan. "But not you. Sit this out because of your knee." *And because this is all your fault, you dolt.* I don't add that last, unhelpful part. Judging by the slouch of his shoulders and dip of his chin, he feels bad enough already. I may be livid, but I'm not about to kick him when he's down.

Nathan's brow pinches. "But I can help. I can walk it off and—"

"Nuh-uh," Tyler says with a firm shake of his head. "Coach would kill me if I let you mess up your knee more."

"I'll take care of this," I say. Words I've said a thousand times when Mom needs something from the pharmacy or when Dad's shoving a red shirt into a light-colors-only load for the laundry machine while simultaneously trying to dial into a conference call. Taking on this search for the keys means one thing, in my experience: I can count on me to get the job done.

"*We* can take care of this," Maddy adds, in a not-so-subtle correction.

I bristle at her comment. I can't tell if she genuinely wants to help or if she just wants to take credit for being a team player, but I'm the one always left fixing things. Lately, she's been the one breaking them.

Nathan's jaw tightens. "All right. I'll hang by the Lost and Found tent we saw by the entrance. Someone might turn them in."

Tyler slides the reflective orange sunglasses up and rests them on the top of his head. "Okay, you can text us when—huh. Bad cell reception," he says, scowling at his phone. "Anyone else having problems too?"

"I tried to send a bunch of pictures to my brother. I keep getting errors," Maddy says.

"Same, with the reception," Everett yells over the start of the next song. "What a bust on going viral."

"Meet at that Lost and Found tent, ten at the latest," Nathan suggests to the group, but with a pointed glare at his brother.

The music swells, and we turn our attention back to the reason for being here: CoGo. We try to enjoy the last few songs of the set, but I can tell that the night has lost its luster for all of us. Like the cosmetic glitter on my face, it all just feels messy and over the top now. Every lyric turns into a judgment.

Who am I without you?

You, as in the keys? Without you, I'm stranded at the Orchards, with the blade of a midnight deadline hanging over my neck.

We had it so good, baby. And now it's over.

You can sing that again, Keaton. The last time I truly had it good seems like ages ago, as distant as when I got my braces off or my fifth-grade spelling bee.

Standing around moping won't help. It's my personal mission to get those keys back and get us home on time.

Maddy accused me months ago of being a little bit of a control freak. But this is what happens when I let up for even a moment. We veer wildly off course. The only way I can make it through most days with any semblance of happiness is if I carefully manage it all, keeping the engine greased and tanks full. With my family, I balance everything from staying on Jackie's fickle good side to making sure Mom's various appointments are marked well ahead of time on our family calendar. It's exhausting, but no way am I going to let other people's misguided whims and general sloppiness destroy everything.

Keaton blows a dramatic kiss to the audience. "Thank you, San Bernardino! You've been wonderful!"

As sad as I am to see CoGo's set over, this means that we can start looking for those keys. Building in time to search the spot where Nathan fell, get back to Stampy the minivan, and weave our way out of the parking lot, I should be home in time to chug something caffeinated, trade my contacts for glasses, and pick up Dad from his conference as promised. I can avert a "you're going wild, just like your sister" showdown with my parents and live to see the rest of my senior year.

I face the group, scooting aside as folks shuffle past me on their way to the porta-potties or their next stages.

"What kind of keys are we looking for?" Tyler asks Nathan.

"A key ring with our Honda key, a house key, and a Lakers photo souvenir bottle opener—it's got a picture of Everett and me from five years ago."

"Small groups to cover more ground?" I suggest. "In case the keys got kicked around a little."

My eyes drift to Maddy. I don't particularly want to spend one-on-one time with her right now if she hasn't yet worked her way up to apologizing, but I'm willing to do it to find those minivan keys.

Maddy grabs her boyfriend's hand. "Tyler and I will take the left side of the space. From the center of the stage to that line of porta-potties."

"Oh." Why did I automatically assume she was going to pair up with me even when we're fighting? She has Tyler now. That's part of what got us into this weird not-speaking-but-kind-of situation.

I'm surprised, though I shouldn't have been.

No one else seems to think anything of her quick decision. Of course they wouldn't. For all they know, we're still best-friends-forever Maddy and Jana, so inseparable we're rooming in the Santa Clarita dorms together and probably bulk-buying matching sets of pajamas.

Everett zips his hand sanitizer back into his fanny pack and waves at me. "We'll check out that area on the right then. Cool?"

I sigh, Maddy and Tyler already scanning the ground and excuse-me-ing away from us. "Cool."

Nathan squints into the distance, in the direction of the Lost and Found tent. "All right. I'll try to text once I get there. Here's hoping our reception holds up."

"Otherwise, ten pm," I say with a sigh.

"Your mom said midnight, didn't she?" Nathan says.

I blink. I didn't realize he'd been paying that close attention in those brief seconds I'd tread across our driveway, horrified at the sight of Stampy. "Yeah. It's cutting it close to that deadline, but we should still make it on time if we find the keys soon. I'm supposed to pick up my dad from a work thing."

Nathan's eyebrow rises. "That late at night?"

I sigh. "I know, I know. But I swore I'd do it, part of me show-ing that I'm so responsible that they should let me come to the Orchards. They said midnight, but I bet my dad will be more understanding if the alternative to picking him up a couple min-utes behind schedule is both of us not coming home at all."

I couldn't ask Mom to drive out to the conference resort that late, not since the accident. It took hours and hours of therapy for her to even get comfortable behind the wheel during the bright hours of day again.

I can't imagine how livid Dad would be if my failure to live up to my promise resulted in him sleeping in the resort lobby. I would rather find a way to rough out a life in these foothills than have Dad chew me out on the phone in front of everyone here, then again at home.

Nathan winces as he shifts his weight around, and the movement draws my attention back to the world around me.

"Well, once you find those keys, I'll drive extra fast," he says. "Can't have you getting grounded for the rest of your life."

He knows my parents well enough: missing this curfew and utterly failing to keep my promise to Dad could mean any number of "privileges" being denied. Those hangouts he hinted at us doing more often earlier? Those would probably be the first to go. To my surprise, the idea deflates me a little, even though the expiration date on our time in the same town, before we head off to college, is approaching anyway.

"You need help getting to the lost and found?" I offer.

He waves me off. "No need. You two focus on the keys. Tyler's awesome and all, but I really don't trust him to keep his head on straight with your friend around."

"So I'm not the only one who isn't a card-carrying fan of TyDy," I joke.

Everett tilts his head. "Tidy? What is—"

"Tyler and Maddy. It's a portmanteau," Nathan says, to my and Everett's shock that he knows such a big word. "Come on, like in Lewis Carroll's *Through the Looking-Glass*? Slithy? Mimsy? Never mind."

Why did I always peg him as a brainless jock? Then again, I guess we didn't chat all that much about the etymology of Cronuts and Froyo in Bible study.

Nathan semi-hops in the direction of the Lost and Found tent, and I lower my gaze to the ground to start the search. I twist past a few people exiting while I approach the stage, and I get the distinct image of being a salmon struggling to swim up a solid, sweaty stream.

It's not a lovely feeling.

"Wow, people really don't like to hold on to their gum wrappers, do they?" Everett says. From his too-wide smile, I can tell he's trying to lighten the mood. Yes, I'm grumpy, but it's not his fault.

So I throw a joke right back at him. "Says the guy littering the festival with his stickers."

Everett snorts, hopping over a half-crushed beer can. "It's not littering. It's art."

"It's a clown face and a QR code. How is that art?"

He rolls his eyes. "You and my brother, jeez. I don't have to explain my art to you. But hey, when I get famous, maybe I won't sue you when you do your tell-all book about how you know me."

Despite the grumpiness, I laugh.

My phone buzzes and I peer down at a new group text.

Nathan to Maddy, Tyler, Everett, and me:

No keys at lost and found, any luck on your end? Did this text even work?

I purse my lips as I respond.

Me to the group:

It worked. But no, no luck.

If I had any luck to my name, we wouldn't have lost the keys and, better yet, I wouldn't be in this mess at all. I'd have enjoyed the show, then been so energized on the way home I wouldn't have fallen asleep, for once. Then maybe all the good vibes from the show would spur Maddy to realize what a bad friend she's being. She'd finally apologize to me and we'd be back to normal: planning the layout of our shared dorm room in the fall.

As much as she's managing to keep her distance tonight, Maddy needs me there with her at Santa Clarita. She likes to joke that I'm her Emotional Support Jana, a title I sincerely earned after pushing her to try out for cheer after her mom suggested she wasn't the right "size" for it, as if there's anything wrong with having a double-digit dress size. Maddy has said before that she wouldn't be the daring, confident person she is today without cheer, which ultimately means she wouldn't be that person without me standing solidly at her side. It's why all our Santa Clarita plans center on us being together. But even that brief imagining of this future rubs me the wrong way right now, and I'm too focused on this key search to pinpoint why.

The crowd has thinned considerably by the time I look up from my phone. A few groups mill around, chatting or vaping or both. I glance around for Everett, and he's drifting toward a group of girls in varying shades of denim cutoffs, taking kissy-face selfies.

I grab his arm. "No. Your brother didn't crowd-surf anywhere near there. And they look like they're in their twenties. Not going to happen. Focus, Everett."

"But you're the one who said the keys might've gotten kicked around! They might have gotten all the way to where that hot girl in the flower crown is. It's worth a shot, don't you think?"

"Everett," I push out through a tight jaw. "Focus!"

He glares at me like he's going to argue but sighs instead. The group of girls has finished taking photos and is already walking away.

"Way to kill my vibe, Jana."

He smiles as he says it, but the tone cuts in a way I don't think he intends. It reminds me of another fight I'd had with Maddy.

It's like you don't even know how to have fun anymore.

I swallow down the odd emotion that's bubbled up. "I . . . sorry."

"Eh, it's fine, really. Plenty of fish and all that. And the Orchards is basically an aquarium. A big musical aquarium full of sexy fish."

"That is . . . an interesting choice of analogy there, Everett."

"You know what I mean," he says, but not before a pinch of pink brightens his cheeks. He and his brother share the same shade of embarrassment.

We shuffle slowly around the space, our eyes to the ground. To our benefit, the stage lights up bright white as the crew works. CoGo is likely long gone, chugging water or whatever else was handed to them as they strolled offstage.

It's then that I catch a tiny glint of metal up ahead. Not a discarded beer can or dropped purse, but a set of keys lies half-buried in the dirt, perhaps.

"There!" I point, my feet moving as fast as my pulse.

FIVE

SATURDAY, APRIL 23
9:17 pm

I dive for the pocket-size mess of metal and plastic. My fingers wrap around them and I thrust them into the air like they're some magical talisman. Maybe they are: they're going to transport me home, and I can hopefully forget about the off-key parts of what was supposed to be one of my best nights. This is still salvageable.

Footsteps thump to a stop by me, kicking up a small cloud of dust. "Good eye, Jana! Let me see." Everett reaches for the keys in my hand but somehow I'm not holding them anymore.

Next to me stands six and a half feet of beefy, neon-muscle-tank-wearing drunk guy, clutching the keys I found.

"Heythoseare mine," he slurs. Then he actually burps and tosses back another gulp from his can of alcoholic energy drink that I'm pretty sure was outlawed a decade ago.

I shake my head. "No, they're ours." I force my voice to sound confident, though I don't know for sure. It's not *my* Stampy the minivan that got us here, and I'm only vaguely aware of what

Nathan's set looks like thanks to his brief, verbal description.

"They've got to be," I add, more for myself than for Muscle Tank. I need them to be ours. I can't even bear to think of how much worse this night could get if these aren't the keys to the minivan or if we don't find them soon. "I mean, what are the chances that we'd both lose our keys in the same spot?"

Muscle Tank hiccups. "Pretty highactually. Look around. This place was packed. CoGo rocks!" He pumps a fist in the air in emphasis.

I frown. I hate to say it, but Muscle Tank has a couple of good points.

First, this festival isn't exactly known for being a hotbed of responsibility. Nathan, cute church family friend and surprise portmanteau expert that he is, is a prime example of that.

And second, CoGo does rock. There's a reason I threw all my money and hopes into this night. CoGo's music is the soundtrack of moments with shared earbuds with Maddy as we waited too long for her parents to pick us up after school, an auditory set of arms holding me together as Mom evaded questions about how she was truly doing after the accident.

Catching CoGo live is like an eclipse: celestial bodies have to line up just right, band members can't be on solo projects, their record label can't be disputing their rights to their own written-and-performed music. Tonight is CoGo's last stop on the West Coast before they leave for the Asia leg of their tour and are out of reach for at least another year.

I deserve this. I worked hard and played by every single one of my parents' rules to get here. I proved myself responsible time and time again. But if I mess up tonight, this mistake is all they're going to focus on: Dad will have the whole night at the conference resort to dwell on it.

I try again. "From a fellow fan to another, can we take a look?" I throw in a sugary smile to get Muscle Tank's guard down.

"Yeah, I'll know if they're ours or not," Everett cuts in.

Muscle Tank's eyes narrow, like he's trying to figure out if we're scamming him. Or maybe he's trying not to pass out standing up. Maybe both.

Everett groans impatiently. "Come on, dude. I'm not going to run off with them. I'm getting a D in PE. Just let me take a look."

Muscle Tank doesn't hand them over, but he does dangle them in front of us like they're candy. I hold my breath as Everett stretches up to see them up close.

With the slight, disappointed shake of his head, my hopes crumble.

"Not ours, Jana. He's right," Everett says.

My brain refuses to accept that answer. "Are you sure? Like one hundred percent those won't unlock the minivan?"

"They're not ours. That's a Honda key, but it looks like it's for something newer than Stampy. And there's no Lakers photo bottle opener."

"But it could've fallen off." I grasp for something, anything, to magically spin this in our favor. I need to be on my way home soon to keep up my end of the bargain and hopefully keep Mount Dad from erupting.

Dad never used to be this intense, but that all changed after the car crash and more so after Jackie revealed that her grades at her prestigious East Coast university dipped far enough that an academic counselor suggested she take a voluntary leave of absence to "get her priorities in order and come back fresh." Everything we relied on as fact—that Mom was fine, that Jackie was doing well in school—collapsed and cast us adrift. Each of us struggled to get back to some semblance of stability after. But that means that now, the slightest change in plan or display of general being-a-teen high jinks on my end somehow signifies the coming of the apocalypse to Dad.

As much as Mom harps about the value of living our fullest, most wonderful lives, she still backs up Dad doing everything in his power to make sure I don't follow my sister's winding path. And lately, that's meant further demands for high grades and the imposition of stricter curfews with social-life-ending and joy-destroying punishments. The man changed every password to our streaming services when he saw I got a C+ on an uninspired English paper on *The Brothers Karamazov*, to help me "focus." Brutal.

It may just look like a promised ride home, something simple that wouldn't be a big deal to anyone else. But I wasn't there when my family needed me most, and I can't bear to be the cause of any more heartache.

I angle to analyze the set of keys Muscle Tank still holds above my head. As Everett had pointed out, there's no Lakers bottle opener or broken links or any signs showing that something had been there but is now missing.

Then Everett juts his pointer finger at a fuzzy pink key chain dangling from the set. "And see that rabbit's foot?"

A memory clicks in place: Nathan and Everett's mom bringing their own plant-based burger patties to a barbecue. "Your parents . . . they're vegan."

"Right. Real or not, no way my parents would have one of those." He turns to Muscle Tank. "Sorry about the mix-up, dude. You're welcome for finding your keys though."

Muscle Tank's reaction is half smile, half sneer. "No problem, I guess. But keep your little girlfriend in check though, bro. She's killing the vibes here."

"I am not his girlfriend and I don't kill vibes!" I screech, which only makes Muscle Tank literally bellow out a laugh like some video game orc and Everett turn that familiar shade of pink.

Muscle Tank pockets the rabbit-foot set, puts the energy drink can to his lips, and wanders away. I glare after him with a whole lot of anger and a teensy bit of jealousy that those weren't our life-saving keys.

Everett lets out a long sigh. "Next time we have to partner up, I'm going with someone else. Pretty sure you're chasing away the ladies."

I roll my eyes. "Um, I think you're chasing the ladies away on your own."

"No way. Who can resist this?" He sweeps a hand toward his lanky frame, neon fanny pack and all, and I bite my lip to keep from laughing.

Between the disappointment and the lingering adrenaline, my

brain isn't working at its usual capacity. I drag in a deep breath through my nostrils, but the extra oxygen doesn't clear the fog. The glaring lights from the stage aren't calming either. It's then I realize how dark it is. I haven't eaten since I left home.

"I hate to delay our search, but I need food. I'm feeling a little loopy."

"I might have a granola bar in my pack somewhere," Everett says. He starts to unzip it before I remember that he'd hidden his stickers in his pants to get past security.

"No! I mean, no, thank you," I correct. "Let's see if we can find a food cart nearby."

"Lead the way, milady," he says in that overembellished fake British accent again, "and I'll text the others. If we haven't found the keys, maybe they're having better luck."

"Or better yet, maybe someone's turning them over to the lost and found as we speak."

"You really must be loopy if you're holding out hope for good non-drunk Samaritans here. Let's get your blood sugar back up. Where to?"

I scan the nearest food trucks. To my chagrin, Muscle Tank and his friends are at the gourmet hot dog one whose smell is wafting alluringly in our direction. The chili truck next to it just doesn't seem like a great idea before—hopefully—a bumpy two-hour car ride home. But next to it is a gleaming purple truck with twinkling white lights draped like icicles over it. My stomach grumbles a resounding "Yes, that one!"

"There," I say. "Hello Hello Halo Halo."

"What does that mean?"

"It's a dessert. Quick sugar, quick energy, quick finding-those-damn-keys."

"Huh. Haven't had it before."

I waver. "Oh. It's shaved ice with ice cream and sometimes flan on top, but sometimes there's coconut and beans and other stuff in there too. Some people don't really like it. My sister actually only eats the ice cream and flan parts. But we can try something else if you—"

"Nah." He waves a dismissive hand. "What fun is life if you stick to the same old stuff all the time?"

He starts walking, leaving me standing there slightly in awe of the fact that I just got life knowledge dropped on me by someone nearly a whole three years younger than me.

Was everyone else out living their lives while I carefully stayed still and made sure everything went to non-family-member-enraging plan? Nathan becoming a literary device expert? Maddy linking up with Tyler? Everett doing—whatever it is Everett does?

I let the thought go before it sours my night further. My brain must be short-circuiting from the lack of sustenance.

Ahead, Everett has already planted himself at the back of the truck's line and is lifting his phone high in the air, looking for a cell phone signal.

I trudge toward the truck, leaving those messy thoughts in the dust behind me and hoping flan will fill the void.

EIGHT YEARS AGO
Thursday, November 12

Jana's Journal: KEEP OUT, JACKIE. I mean it.

We got a new girl in our class today, which is weird, right? Who starts at a new school on a Thursday? If it were me, I'd ask Mom and Dad to just let me hang out at home for the long weekend and show up on Monday. Then I wouldn't have to stand and introduce myself in front of a bunch of fifth graders. The whole class was already super cranky because of our big social studies test tomorrow. (I know, I should be studying, but I needed this break!)

Her name is Madeline Parsons. I think that's how it's spelled? She goes by Maddy and she's from Arizona. She had a high blond ponytail and this gray sweater that I think was from her old school. Maybe she's not that happy she had to move here. She said her dad got

a new job at an airline based out of LAX. Ms. Keen
made her sit at the empty desk at the back of the
classroom, next to the garter snake tank: the worst
seat in the whole classroom. Because you know what
garter snakes eat? Yup. Living, breathing critters.
And you have to be sitting RIGHT THERE when it's
happening.

Then after school, when I go to the parking lot, Mom's
talking to this high-blond-ponytail lady. It's Maddy's
mom. They're complaining about broken stuff at
Maddy's new house, and somehow the conversation
turns into Mom saying they live really close to us and
hey maybe we can carpool! They traded phone numbers
while Maddy and I just stood there. So awkward.

I guess we might carpool next Monday, the day this
girl should've started school if her parents weren't
weird about this Thursday first-day thing.

I really hope I don't have to hear about the classroom
snake when we're stuck in the car together.

SIX

SATURDAY, APRIL 23
9:25 pm

The halo halo truck beams like a lighthouse in a storm. As with every other food vendor here, a long line of festivalgoers snakes in front. Only the chili truck has a shorter line, but that's probably for the best: folks are rightfully saving the chili for after the mosh pits.

It takes a few minutes for Everett and me to get close enough to see the menus printed on the side of the truck. As we wait, I periodically pull out my phone and check my messages for anything from Nathan, Maddy, Tyler, or even my family. Nothing. Next to me, Everett gives a play-by-play to his phone of what kinds of food trucks are around.

I wait until he's done recording. "You getting any signal?" If he's actively streaming, then he at least has enough bars for us to reach out to the rest of the group for updates.

"Nah," he says, crushing my hopes. "I'm saving it in my drafts. Will post it later if I remember."

We're one customer away from the front, and I sift through

my mini-backpack for my wallet. According to the hand-lettered signs to the sides of the ordering window, Hello Hello Halo Halo specializes in artisan, locally sourced halo halo. Though I don't know where around here they would locally source jackfruit and purple yam from. Even the ice wouldn't be locally sourced—a lot of the water here comes from up north. My stomach grumbles, as if hurrying me up, and I realize something, anything would suffice, grown nearby or on a mountain across the world or concocted in a lab.

When we finally make it up to the ordering window, I immediately shoot out an "I'll take the deluxe."

A pointed cough sounds next to me. Everett dons a sheepish smile that makes me immediately suspect he's up to something. A quick scan of the truck at least shows me he hasn't slathered his stickers all over it. Yet.

"What's up?" I ask.

He rubs the back of his neck. "Think you can spot me? Nathan's holding all my cash."

"Seriously? What do you even have that fanny pack for then?"

"I told you: the stickers! And hand sanitizer. And my medicated lip balm." He rattles off this list with a straight face, like I'm the one who's weird for asking why he has all those big, functional pockets seemingly standard in men's pants and not a single bit of cash in any of them.

Maddy would laugh about this with me, and I almost want to peer around to see if there's anyone else who'd find this funny. But she's off with Tyler still. If Nathan were nearby, he probably wouldn't be in the mood to joke after that busted knee.

I run my fingers over the blue trim of my wallet.

Every penny matters to me after this two-hundred-dollar festival ticket, but then I remember Mom even gave me a little extra. To have fun, she said. Well, that fun ship has sailed, hit an iceberg, and sunk to the bottom of the ocean. I can still afford to be generous though. Plus, this kid is less likely to get in trouble if he's standing in front of me, chowing down on dessert, rather than wandering the grounds by himself.

"All right, go ahead and order. But I'm not paying for that party fishbowl size."

Everett thanks me and steps up to the ordering window. I'm tugging a ratty twenty-dollar bill out of my wallet when I catch the noticeable change in his tone. His voice sounds forcibly deeper, like he's trying to come off as older.

"So, what do you recommend . . . Kayla, is it?" he asks the girl at the cash register.

He has his elbow propped up on the windowsill, his stance oozing so much artificial casualness that I actually wince from secondhand embarrassment.

Oh no, is he hitting on the halo halo girl?

She looks about sixteen years old and the roundness of her face and flatness of her nose match the two burly guys in the back, assembling the desserts. Siblings, maybe? But that's where the similarities end. While the brothers are in no-nonsense white tees with *Hello Hello Halo Halo* airbrushed on the back and faded cargo shorts, the girl—Kayla, according to the handwritten paper name tag slapped on her chest—sports a neon pink crop top and the kind of baggy jeans that someone must've spent serious time and energy making all the right, fashionable holes in. Her hip-length hair has been dyed a vibrant purple that almost matches the exterior of the truck.

The whole look tells me that Kayla of Hello Hello Halo Halo is way cooler than Everett, but the poor kid doesn't seem to recognize it.

"My favorite is the Classic, with mango ice cream instead of ube," she says. "Or if you're a leche flan fan, you can get the deluxe for an extra dollar. The deluxe is what your"—she angles to smile at me—"friend got."

"Oh psh, that's just Jana. We know her from church. My brother likes her," Everett says, jutting a thumb back at me.

"What the—" I nearly choke on my own spit. First of all, how dare he implicate me in this scheme to prove he's single and ready to mingle with this new, purple-haired love interest? Second, how can he drop unexpected "my brother likes her" news in a throwaway line like that?

The logical part of my brain kicks into overdrive. *Focus on getting food, getting keys, and getting your butt home, Jana.*

I nudge Everett's shoe with my own. "Can you hurry up and order already?"

The woman standing behind us in line mutters a "yeah" in agreement, but Everett doesn't budge from his place.

Instead, he leans in closer, like she's Juliet in the window. I swear, if he breaks into some "It is the east, and Kayla of the Hello

Hello Halo Halo food truck is the sun" talk, I may drag him away from here, dessert or not. Nathan, with his surprise literary bent, would find this line of thinking laugh-too-loud worthy and would probably support my keeping his brother out of trouble.

Thankfully, Everett doesn't go full Shakespeare.

"Why don't you surprise me?" he says. Which, honestly, is not much better.

One of the guys behind Kayla pops his head out and nods. "Got it. Two deluxes then." He nudges Kayla with his forearm. "Come on, there's a line, Kayla. Keep it moving."

I hand my cash to Kayla and toss the change in the tip jar, then I practically have to push Everett away from the window so other people can order and stop shooting us death glares. Our deluxe halo halos are in our hands moments later, and we seat ourselves on a nearby row of hay bales that conveniently has a view of Kayla at the Hello Hello Halo Halo ordering window.

It's not until two scoops of creamy ube ice cream and a spoonful of sweet beans and coconut later that I'm feeling energized enough to speak. My mood has improved exponentially in the past few minutes. Dessert does that to me. It's why Maddy's and my emergency care packages for each other always include some sort of sweet treat. I dragged her out for a chocolate sundae the size of her head, complete with multicolor sprinkles, when she thought she bombed her cheer tryout a couple of years ago. She was already feeling low after her mom threw out a "It's not like they would've let you on the squad anyway, not at your weight," so I even splurged for the lit-up sparklers they stick into the top of the sundae. Talking it out and sharing that massive amount of chocolate with me lifted her out of the worst of it because Maddy's unhealthy relationship isn't with food: it's with her mom. A whole childhood of cutting remarks about her appearance led Maddy to struggle with her body image, to fixate on calorie counts and exercise in a way that made nearly everything unenjoyable. She embraces her curves and her dessert now, thanks in part to some wonderful teachers and body-positive celebrities. It's been a while since we've had crisis management dessert together, though it's not for lack of crises.

I pause my inhalation of my halo halo to check on Everett. "You know we're searching for your keys and not your soulmate, right?" I joke.

"We can do both."

"Well, keys first. I'm still miffed that that muscle-tank guy was so rude about those keys I picked up. How was I supposed to know?" I scoop up another bite of halo halo. "I don't know what to do next. If the others don't find the keys, then what? Uber home? Because calling my parents isn't an option."

"Our parents aren't even home. They went to a wedding in Santa Barbara. That's why they were okay with me coming with Nathan to the Orchards," Everett says. "And the festival doesn't allow rideshare apps, part of their protest against their wages or something, according to my brother."

I nearly drag a palm down my face until I remember it'd smear glitter and probably ube ice cream everywhere. "Do you think anyone in our group's got a couple hundred dollars on them for a two-hour, multi-stop cab ride home?"

"You'll have to ask the others. You're the one who paid for my seven-dollar sundae thing."

I peer down at his dessert. He hasn't touched most of it. "Do you not like it?"

He shrugs. "It's good, just not my thing, you know? I'm more of a chocolate guy."

I start to feel a little guilty that I was the one who pushed us to this truck. "We might have time to order something else if you're hungry."

"Nah, I'll finish off the ice cream part and be fine. Plus I've already got a couple clips of me chowing down on this. Gotta stay genuine for my Clippity followers, you know?" He angles his phone to show me at least a dozen saved videos of him grinning before taking exaggerated chomps of his dessert.

I smile. I, personally, would not have such a sparkly attitude after a dessert that doesn't fulfill every one of my expectations. It's why I naturally gravitated toward the halo halo truck: tried and true. Again, I find myself admiring him for how easygoing he is, and to be honest, I'm a little jealous. It's like watching a young child riding on a carousel for the first time. It's warming to see their sheer joy, but sometimes you can't help but wonder just when the world lost that radiance for you and if you'll ever recapture that same thrill.

I stir at my halo halo. "Does this have anything to do with that girl watching you from the truck?"

"Wait, she's looking over here?" The slightest hint of pink

stains his cheeks again. For all the suaveness he's trying to portray, there's still an endearing nervousness in there somewhere. "She isn't. Quit messing with me. Kayla doesn't seem like just 'some girl.' There's something special about her, you can tell right away."

I don't see what he sees, but then again, I'm more focused on downing this halo halo than finding love.

"So go get her number or username or whatever it is people do," I say.

My lack of dating experience is showing, despite my having a few years on him, but I truly do not want to stand in the way of someone pairing up with the soulmate they've been searching so earnestly for. I just hope it all doesn't prevent me from meeting my curfew tonight. "But then we keep searching, okay? Maybe check closer to the stage too and any other spots we might've missed."

"All right. I'll do it." He sets his halo halo down next to me, then unzips his fanny pack to pull out his medicated lip balm. One pungent, eucalyptus-scented swipe later, he rises. "Wish me luck," he says before heading back to the truck.

I would, but I don't really have any luck to give.

SEVEN

SATURDAY, APRIL 23
9:34 pm

Everett tosses away our compostable bowls while I rub my coconut-scented hand sanitizer around my fingers. It feels somewhat futile, but I do it anyway because I don't even want to think about the level of grime and non-handwashing happening here, especially with all these bright blue portable bathrooms. I don't want to bring home any germs. Mom's health as she physically recovered took enough scary turns that I've been ultra-aware of coughs, sneezes, and other possibilities for illness transfer ever since.

"Ready when you are," Everett says. He shakes out his limbs like he's about to run onto a game field instead of plunge into a festival crowd.

I glance down at my phone. "We've got less than half an hour before we have to meet everyone at the Lost and Found tent."

Everett shrugs off my guilt at being late. "It's fine. We were hungry. They can wait. They'll let us know if something comes up."

Nathan was right not to let Everett go off on his own: with that attitude, we'd never see him again.

"I've still only got one bar of reception though, and no texts. No one else must've found the keys yet. So maybe we take a route closer to the stage where—" My voice withers.

The next set at the Avocado Stage is starting. The dance-pop headliner in rhinestone-studded thigh-high leather boots struts onto the stage to raucous applause, her thick natural hair bouncing and shimmering in the spotlights. A crowd apparently had begun gathering while Everett and I were refilling our stomachs. Tyler had said there was another performance after CoGo. That detail had gotten swallowed up in my hunger-induced fog.

I grimace. "Oh no. This is going to make it much harder to search."

"Maybe we should split up," Everett says. "Cover more ground?"

Nathan's earlier vetoing of his brother's antics floats into my head. Combined with the utter lack of phone reception and the heart eyes I just saw him flash at Kayla, I'd lose him completely if we splinter off now. And if we're not leaving here without the minivan keys, no way we're leaving without the driver's little brother.

"No, we should stick together. Come on, let's tail this group in."

We shadow a handful of already-singing people into the Avocado crowd, letting them do all the pushing so we don't have to. I gather from their excited chatter that the name of the artist is Larissa—one name, like Prince or Rihanna—and that the Orchards is her first big festival in the United States.

Onstage, Larissa is chatting with her keyboardist in a rapid-fire mix of English and Spanish, and the way she throws her head back and laughs already oozes professional showmanship and the promise of a stellar time. Any other day, I'd be thrilled to catch a set by an artist flashing such charisma and killer footwear. But the fact that she's drawing an immense crowd makes finding our keys somewhere in this dirt more challenging by the second.

"It's getting really crowded. I don't like this," I say. It doesn't help that I can barely see over anyone's shoulders. It feels like I'm surrounded.

Everett lifts up on his toes for a second to glance around over our heads. "It might work out in our favor. One of these Larissa fans might find our keys and turn them in."

"You think anyone's going to leave in the middle of the set to do a good deed like that?" Muscle Tank immediately floats to mind. He probably didn't even leave to use a porta-potty and just peed right where he stood.

Everett frowns. "But that's fine, right? We're in no hurry."

"You're not, but I am. Midnight," I say.

It occurs to me then that I may be the only one with a real time crunch. Nathan knows I need to get home by midnight, but his and Everett's parents are out at the wedding and won't be around to witness their sons raid the fridge and plop face-first into bed. And who knows what Maddy and Tyler told their parents. Maddy probably claimed that she's staying at my house, even if the reality is that we haven't been on speaking terms.

Lovely. Not only do I seem to be the most responsible one in this group, but I'm the only one with actual consequences riding on our finding a way home immediately.

Everett shifts the fanny pack at his hip. "Well, most sets are an hour or an hour and a half. Would that be enough time for us to dump you at your door at midnight?"

"I don't know. You have to tack on the unknowns of whether someone will actually find the keys and how long it will take them to make their way to the lost and found. Assuming we don't get the keys back until after this set, this puts me way past getting home by midnight."

I grimace. I'd been holding out hope—maybe foolishly—that we'd have the keys in hand by ten, then speed home in time for that midnight deadline. But breaking down the courses of action for Everett shatters any vague illusions I have about this night working out the way I wanted it to. I need to start preparing myself for a much-dreaded phone call to my dad. He's not going to like the lateness—of the call or of my picking him up at the resort—but I'm not that eager to have that conversation so early in the night. I'm already borderline panicking, and that's without any actual tirades from my parents.

"Sucks, dude."

That seems to be a genuine expression of sympathy from Everett.

"Thanks."

The group in front of us stops, and we've come as close as we can to the stage by coasting. A mob of people presses up behind us, penning us in. From here on out, we're going to have to shove our way through to get any closer to the stage.

"Excuse me, I dropped something," I say a dozen times as we inch forward. People shift aside, reluctantly, but some definitely try to hold their ground against what they think is someone trying to steal their view of the stage.

A few feet away, I notice a hint of purple on the ground next to an empty Cheetos bag. Could that be the Lakers key chain? I nudge Everett and he reaches for it, but it's a discarded vape pen.

I've made it about ten more feet forward before I hit a wall, or more specifically, a wall-size back clad in a black leather vest with a silver skull stitched into it.

"Excuse me," I say with a firm tap on the Wall's shoulder. "Looking for my friend's keys!" I have to shout this part because Larissa launches into a reggaeton dance hit I recognize from a few viral videos.

The Wall turns around, and it's a bearded guy in his fifties, with the look of someone who would be an extra in a biker gang television series. Larissa's musical appeal is universal.

He takes one annoyed look at me and doesn't even bother to answer. He turns back around to face the stage.

My jaw sets.

I tap his shoulder again. "Excuse me!"

He angles his head over his shoulder and booms, "Whatever it is, no."

My frustrated grunt is drowned out by one of Larissa's flawless high notes. I peer to the left and right of the Wall, but he's here with a few more of his biker friends and it's impossible to get past them with how tight the crowd is packed in now. The only options are staying put or going up and over—which I'm not about to do, after Nathan's knee-tweaking crowd-surfing experience.

The despair rises in my throat. It's not the halo halo, I'm sure of it. It's the fact that this is the last place I want to be right now, wedged in the middle of an immovable crowd, my nose dangerously at armpit level with this biker wall.

A tap on my own shoulder cuts my despair spiral short. I look over to Everett, who is bouncing to the beat. "She's good, right?"

I swallow back the lump in my throat and nod. Larissa is good. Her music is contagiously fun, like you can't help but smile along. I force myself to breathe—away from that biker armpit level—to really take in the music, because I don't have any other options. I don't have the keys, I can't pass the Wall to make it closer to the stage, and if I dwell on this miserable situation any longer, I might just scream at the top of my lungs and incur the wrath of the Larissa fans around me.

Before I know it, my own head is bobbing up and down. Each movement chips away some of the stress that's built up on my shoulders, little by little. Music can be therapy. I should've known this, for how much CoGo affects the ebb and flow of my moods like the moon.

The song ends and Larissa reaches for a bottle of water as the drumbeat for the next song begins. Everett takes the relative quiet to speak.

"I think we're stuck here," he says. He motions behind his shoulder, and I look back at the throngs behind us. It's confirmation that even if I wanted to leave, I couldn't. I'd be a salmon all over again, but this time ruining people's good times and likely making more enemies along the way.

He's right, of course, but I can't help the surging guilt at how I should be doing more: impossibility doesn't seem like an excuse, even if it's the truth. "But the keys," I argue weakly.

Everett shakes his head. "If they're in here somewhere, they're stuck too."

"So we stay till there's a break between songs and we can squeeze out? And text the others we'll be late?"

"Yup. Till there's a break. Or till the end."

I sigh, trying to push out all the frustration at how my halo halo detour and this Larissa trap puts us off course. I do feel a little lighter afterward. It could be this new song that Larissa's belting out about dancing at the beach, but it could be that I didn't realize how heavily this night was pressing on me, the weight of needing to fix this, fix everything. And weirdly, I got permission from Everett and this whole crowd to let go, for just a while. To imagine I'm on a hot, white-sand beach, sipping an icy fruit smoothie, eyeing a gorgeous stranger in the water.

I wiggle out my phone and try to shoot out a text.

Me to Nathan, Tyler, and Maddy:

stuck in the Larissa set, near the stage. Will try to make it to lost and found by 10. Keep us updated on keys

Three minutes later, I feel a buzz that my text finally went through—thanks, crappy reception—and two minutes after that, I get something back.

nothing yet. But the doc gave me some meds and an ice pack

Tyler to the group:

Wait, we were going to leave without seeing Larissa?! And she's at the CoGo stage? Losing those keys was fate! #LariStan

I smile at Tyler's text. I would've never pegged Maddy's boyfriend as an unabashed pop-diva fan. Then again, I guess I don't know much about him, other than what I learned through Maddy.

When she first mentioned the cute photographer in our English class, I, the good best friend, giggled along. I helped her search for him on all the different social media networks, dissect his texts, accidentally run into him at various school functions. I don't even like tennis, and I somehow went to a ton of home matches because Tyler does their photos for the paper. But I do like being there for my best friend, and Maddy threw in an extra bribe of post-game cheese fries now and then.

Then as she and Tyler got closer, I realized belatedly that it meant she and I would grow further apart. This hadn't been a problem with her other crushes. Most hadn't gone to Samuels with us, so they didn't lay as big of a claim on our time together. I don't know if Maddy even noticed how abruptly our hangouts dwindled. It must be hard to juggle everything if your hands are always stuck to your boyfriend.

While she and I are supposed to go to Santa Clarita in the fall together, complete with that matching bunk bedding and pajama sets, I don't know where Tyler is headed. I haven't asked, but maybe I should have. Maybe I would've learned by now that he's a LariStan. That's the kind of thing that Maddy would've definitely found hilarious but endearing. Does she know that tidbit about him? I wonder why she hasn't mentioned it.

I shove my phone into my pocket, brushing aside that unwelcome pang of sadness. This latest fight is her fault, not mine, I remind myself. She's the one who made it clear that our friendship isn't a priority. I don't forgive her for the awful things she said, the way she's ignored me even when I've tried to reach out and be a good friend. And yet Emotional Support Jana kept showing up, time and time again, when she needed me.

I can't let her continue thinking she can take our friendship for granted like this. I need an apology from her. She's the one whose lack of consideration took all the plans we have together, threw them in a blender, and pressed "pulse" first.

I blow out a breath, the last thoughts of Maddy and Tyler floating away from me into the fake fog coming from the stage. When I inhale, I soak in the energy: the pink and purple lights sweeping across the fog, the sweet crooning of the background singers, the unreal vocal tricks Larissa is pulling. And is the Wall in front of me mamboing?

A flash of black and white to my left catches my eye. Everett is peeling the backing off one of his stickers. I raise an eyebrow: there's nothing around here he can stick that on.

He seems to read my confusion because he grins, then puts a "shh" finger up to his lips. Then with all the care of someone trying to ace a chemistry lab without blowing the whole experiment up, he applies the sticker to the back of the Wall's leather vest.

This kid can't help but get himself in trouble.

And even though I know I should yell at him, a laugh bubbles out before I slap a hand over my mouth to shut it. That's what the Wall gets for being a jerk to me. I'd even said excuse me, twice!

I offer Everett a low-five like we'd just pulled off a diamond heist, and we bounce our heads together like we've been LariStans all our lives.

A MONTH AGO
Wednesday, March 23

Jana:

Mom said you're in meetings today but she wanted me to tell you about this latest round of admissions

Jana:

[Four images, screenshots of online admissions portals]
UC Riverside: Accepted
UC Santa Clarita: Accepted
ASU: Accepted
Chalmers Design: Accepted

Dad (two hours later):

Heading home early! What kind of ice cream cake do you want, college girl? Pistachio?

Maddy nudges her paper take-out box toward me on the curb. "You want my pickle?"

Our celebratory hoagie place is tiny, with only enough room to put in your order at the plexiglass window and use the condiments at the red counter beneath the sticky, framed posters of old mafia movies. Every time we come in here, the gears in my mind whir with the possibilities of creating more space and seating—moving the soda machine, adding a bar and some tall stools along the window—but the owner is only interested in hearing our order and whether we're paying cash or credit.

There are two round concrete tables and benches for customers outside, but both of those are taken up by a large party juggling sandwiches, strollers, and screaming toddlers. Normally, the noise would get to me and I'd suggest we go eat in Maddy's car with the windows down. But the gentle spring sun is out, we have our Santa Clarita acceptances, and I've already torn the paper holding together my #3 roast beef and provolone. Sitting on the curb, our flip-flopped feet on the hot asphalt of the street, is perfect.

I pluck the pickle from her take-out container and angle my kettle chip bag toward her in exchange. In the one earbud I have—Maddy has the other one—CoGo's "Your Move" begins, the sweeping orchestral strings giving way to a killer drumbeat. I chase the salt of the pickle with a sip of my sweet strawberry milkshake, and can say, without a doubt, that life is good.

"You think they'll have hoagies this amazing in Santa Clarita?" Maddy asks. She grips her sandwich with both hands, trying to wrangle the soft bread and overflowing fillings.

"I hope so. Their website says they've got top-rated residence hall food, but I have no idea if that extends to their sandwich selection."

"Well, they'd better, if you and I are going to be happy there for the next four years."

I chuckle at her seriousness on the matter. "It's only an hour or so away from here. We can always drive back down if we're hit with a craving. Or I guess you can drive down and I'll tag along. I don't think I'll have a car."

"Psh, what makes you think I'll be driving back here? I can't wait to get out of the house."

Maddy has made no secret of wanting to escape the Parsons homestead. She and her mom constantly butt heads over even the most insignificant things—their latest fight was over her mom saying Maddy doesn't have the figure for a crop top—and her dad has been flying so often that he's never around to mediate.

I steer around the mention of her family. "But if Santa Clarita is hoagie-less, you'll have to get your fix somehow."

"We can sneak a hot plate into our dorm room!"

I laugh again, this time at her easy disregard of the rules despite the fact that we're not even enrolled students yet. "I'm pretty sure they won't want us burning down the dorms by trying to make our own hoagies."

"We won't burn anything down; we'll be super safe. We'll cover up the smoke detector somehow. But I think re-creating this epic number three is going to be a challenge. We'll have to do a lot of test hoagies." She carefully picks a piece of roast beef out of her sandwich and pops it in her mouth. "We should get our rooming request in early, right?"

I nod, my mouth full from my latest bite. I'm the one who laid out all the deadlines for applications, answers, and tuition and housing deposits in a shared spreadsheet. We have until May to cement our place in Santa Clarita.

But as shiny and certain as our future gleams, something tugs at the back of my mind: my Chalmers Design acceptance, into the product design program I'd considered a long shot. It's an ultra-specific interest, something that just clicked in my head after I realized that my whole being is about fixing things, finding the best way to make them work. I didn't actually think I'd get in, but along with my Santa Clarita acceptance today, the Chalmers admissions portal showed me that "admitted" language too. And though Santa Clarita has a good design program, Chalmers is excellent.

The biggest hurdle to a cross-country move sits next to me: my best friend, who is already making plans for us to put each other's name on our residence hall rooming requests. I want to tell her about Chalmers, about all the what-ifs and if-onlys swirling around in my head, but do I want to ruin this moment? We're in a rare, luminous slice of our busy lives, where it's just us two best friends planning out our college careers, away from the intrusions of high school boyfriends and hovering family. It seems like we haven't hung out one-on-one like this in ages.

And bringing up "Hey, I'm thinking of going to a school nearly three thousand miles away from you" doesn't seem an appropriate addition to our joint celebration. Especially when she's fresh off a blowup with her mom that needed the intervention of Emotional Support Jana and a long bubble tea run this past weekend. Maddy's nerves are already frayed; the unwelcome shock of me announcing I got into a different school could throw her off further.

So I push the doubts aside. This is a joyous hoagie meal, and I'm not going to be the one to ruin it.

I reach for an easy response to hide the extra seconds I've spent in silence, lost in my own thoughts. "Seat deposits and housing requests are due at the beginning of May."

"Whew, good thing I asked. I thought we had all summer to get them in."

I snort. "God, Maddy. Read the materials."

Maddy grins and bumps her shoulder against mine. "See, this is why we're rooming together. I need you. What would I do without my Support Jana?" Maddy picks up her milkshake then and holds it out toward me. "Cheers! To our imminent takeover of Santa Clarita!"

My bite of hoagie goes down dry, a little less delicious than the last bite. I blame it on the fact that I'm probably just getting full. The guys behind the counter did overdo it with their generosity on the sandwich fillings this time. I grab my cup off the curb and bump it against hers, the condensation from both our drinks dripping onto the concrete between us. "Cheers."

Somehow, the milkshake tastes a little less sweet too.

EIGHT

SATURDAY, APRIL 23
10:08 pm

Larissa takes an extended pause between songs to deal with a wardrobe malfunction, and though I don't wish busted bra straps on anyone, I'm thankful for the way the crowd eases up. Everett and I manage to inch toward the Lost and Found tent, curving as close as we can to the stage, but other than a few beer cans, food wrappers, and the occasional glowstick littering the ground, the Avocado is fruitless.

Maddy, and probably Nathan, would've gotten a kick out of that joke.

I check my phone: 10:08 pm, and no messages from the group.

"Where are those damn keys?" I growl out my frustration into the universe.

"If they were already at the lost and found, Nathan would've gotten them and texted us by now," Everett says. He sweeps a candy bar wrapper aside with his foot. "Or maybe he has them and it's a cell reception issue again."

I sigh and give one long, last look at the dirt around us. "I don't see anything. Do you?"

He shakes his head, and the slight movement is crushing.

"Let's head to the lost and found then. No use wasting more time here. Maybe the others will have some ideas on how we can get back home."

"Good thinking. Are you okay with your whole curfew thing?"

I nearly flinch at the mention. "Not at all. There's almost no chance of making it home by midnight, but the sooner I get back, the better. If I'm late picking up my dad, I can blame the car or road construction or say I was driving super slowly and carefully, as long as I get home early enough for any of that to be believable."

I'll just have to deal with Dad's anger and hope that all the worse things my sister's ever done can be used as leverage to get him to ease up on me. I'm not the one who almost left college entirely with a whole bunch of debt my parents would be on the hook for, but without a degree. That's got to count for something, right? I guess it hasn't, so far.

Near the Lost and Found tent, we find Maddy and Tyler standing next to Nathan, his legs propped up on a hay bale. He's icing his knee, and he shoots a weak smile at Everett and me as we approach.

Before I can ask Nathan how he's doing, Tyler bounds over like an overexcited golden retriever.

"How close to the front were you?" he bubbles. "We caught a couple of songs from way at the back. Larissa's so amazing, right?"

Everett starts to launch into his favorite moments from the set, but I get straight to the point. "Any word on the keys?"

The disappointment plain on Nathan's and Maddy's faces is my answer.

Nathan adjusts his position on the hay bale, and I don't miss the clenching of his jaw as he moves. "Nothing. I've even been waiting here and watching people turn in stuff they've found too. A cell phone here or there, an ID. Some keys, but not ours."

"Jana almost stole a guy's keys," Everett cuts in.

"I did not! I thought they might be ours!"

My phone pings with a text then and my stomach flips.

Correction, not a text: an alarm that I'd set for myself to get my butt home.

> Directions to HOME? Based on current conditions, it will take you 2 hours 14 minutes to reach your destination.

Great. So even my phone wants to remind me there's no way I can make it home in time at this point. If the keys mysteriously dropped from the heavens into the minivan, which was also magically parked right next to us and not a fifteen-minute walk—not counting Nathan's injury—I'd still be late. Which means I'd be late picking up Dad from the conference resort unless I drove at an unwise and sure-to-be-illegal speed.

I tuck my phone away. I'll text my parents later when I'm not so frazzled. Sounding this stressed and having no plan for getting home is a recipe for an instant never-again type lecturing.

Ahead, a girl breaks off from her friend group to stroll toward the Lost and Found tent. Something purple and yellow glints in her hand.

"Hey." I nudge Nathan. "Is that the bottle opener? Could those be your keys?"

Nathan's eyes widen, and he in turn elbows his brother. "Ev, go check!"

Everett darts over. He chats with the girl, and he's far enough away that we can't hear him over the din of the next band warming up on the main stage. I can't read his expression either—worry? Relief?

"Oh god, he'd better not be hitting on this girl too," I mumble.

"Too? Was there another?" Nathan asks.

"Yup. But only one, and she was nice and age-appropriate. Don't worry. I keep getting accused of killing people's vibe, so I think I'm doing my job right when it comes to him."

He laughs in his way that is too loud for how low-level funny my comment was, and I feel the blood warming my cheeks. I don't know why I'm so flattered. He laughs like this all the time, doesn't he? Still, there's something gratifying about being the one to draw it out of him. Maddy raises an eyebrow at us but gets distracted by Tyler trying to show her a grainy, zoomed-in Larissa video he took on his phone.

Eventually, Everett jogs back to us, something clutched tightly in his hand. "So, the good news is that this is half our key chain," Everett starts. He uncurls his fingers and, sure enough, there lies a fragment of a battered purple-and-yellow key chain, complete with childhood photo of the brothers, that looks like it's been run over by a semitruck. "The bad news is that our van keys aren't attached to it. More good news is that at least they're around here somewhere?"

I groan, and in frustration, my palms fly up to rub my face. I don't even care that I've smudged my glitter eye makeup so much I look like some disco raccoon.

Maddy scowls. "First, who does good news, bad news, good news? And second, that's not really good news at all. That puts us right back in the bad news bucket."

"Um, it's called the sandwich technique? You deliver good, bad, good so that people feel better because you've ended with good stuff. I read it in a book."

"Ev. Cut it out, not the time or place," Nathan says.

Everett's lips purse, and for a second, I see beneath the fun, free, attempting-to-be-flirty fifteen-year-old. There's someone whose brain and heart work differently than the rest of us and he's used to people not getting it. So all this searching for a soulmate could be him trying to find someone who understands him, who doesn't shut down his asides and wackiness.

Someone like who Maddy is—was—for me.

I know friendships like ours are rare. For a moment, I consider being the one to reach out first, not to apologize but to at least say something kind so that we can begin to move forward from this awful fight. Then I'm stopped by the fear that this is all part of the cycle—me continuing to ignore little slights or forgiving larger ones, just to put myself in that same position to get stepped on again. Kindred souls or not, Maddy will keep asking more and more of me, and I'll keep having to stretch and bend to meet what she needs, what my family needs. I have too much weighing on me right now to figure out how I can possibly continue to do any of that.

I blink, and that vulnerability in Everett's eyes is glossed over too like he's slapped a QR code sticker over it.

"Hey, I'm not the clown who lost the keys," he says to his brother, his voice dripping with a mockery bordering on cruel.

Nathan's face darkens, and I physically step in between him and Everett. If they punch each other when they're joking, who knows what they'll do when they're actually mad at each other? "Let's focus on finding them. We all need to get home. Not just because of me; we don't have a place to stay here. They start kicking everyone out of the stage areas at midnight, and then what? We just huddle around the minivan?"

Tyler plucks his orange sunglasses off the top of his head and starts polishing the lenses with his shirt. "Can't hang out in the parking lot. I heard some folks complaining that security's cracking down on unauthorized camping. You either need to have a permitted, paid-for camping spot, or you can't be on the premises after one in the morning."

At this, Maddy and I simultaneously cross our arms. I immediately uncross mine so it doesn't look like we choreographed it.

"I'm not going to lurk outside the fences in the forest," Maddy says to her boyfriend. "There are bears here."

"Don't worry, I'll protect you," he responds, one hundred percent seriously.

I bite my lip—come on, how is Tyler going to fight off a bear?—and Nathan catches the movement. But thankfully, he holds in his laugh too. I really don't want to extend the argument between Maddy and me to whether her boyfriend can take on a three-hundred-pound black bear. Or even a thirty-pound corgi.

"If we can't hide out in the van, what other choices do we have?" Nathan asks.

The frustration in the air thickens like the fake fog at the Larissa concert. Any residual good vibes from the upbeat music earlier disintegrate. Louder and louder, the group talks over each other, flinging out ideas, shooting each other's down.

"Break into the minivan and hot-wire it," Tyler suggests repeatedly.

I scrunch my nose. "Does anyone even know how to do that? How do we know the minivan will even hold together and not peter out in the middle of a deserted foothills road?"

"Yeah, it'd actually be safer to stay here," Maddy says. "Does anyone have parents or siblings who can pick us up? Our car is in the shop. It's why I couldn't drive today."

"Our parents are at that wedding," Nathan says. "And Tyler, you said your dad had his LASIK procedure today, right?"

I don't realize I've groaned aloud until everyone's staring at me.

"Jana, what about your sister?" Nathan asks. "Isn't Jackie back home?"

"No, she moved back on campus at the start of this spring semester: fresh start and all that. I can't call my parents either. My dad's stuck at that work conference I'm supposed to pick *him* up from, and my mom doesn't drive long distances anymore. Especially not at night on the new medications she's on." The image of the orange and green plastic bottles lined up on her nightstand flits through my mind and stokes my anger. "No way in hell I'm going to make her trek out here. This is your fault, Nathan. You need to fix this."

Turning the blame on him is a nasty move, I know. But I can't have everyone picking at my reasons for not calling my parents. Because to be honest, it's not just that my parents can't come: I am afraid.

Dad would look for every reason to take away what he considers privileges—phone, laptop, even my part-time job hours despite them helping relieve the financial stress at home. He'll see it as pushing me back on the correct course to some successful future, even though one off-night wouldn't derail that.

Worst of all, I did this to myself: I'm the one who convinced him that I should pick him up from his conference. I swore I could be relied on, that he could let loose for once and I would be there to drive him home. One missing set of keys is ruining both our nights, torching whatever stability and freedom I've fought hard for.

Yet I can't help feeling a pang of deserved guilt when Nathan's mouth dips at the corners after I snap at him.

"I'm really sorry, guys. We do need a place to stay here if we're hoping to claim the keys as soon as they're turned in," he says with a sigh. "If we pool our money together, maybe there's an empty campsite we can book last minute."

"Campsites sold out minutes after the Orchards tickets did," I say. I remember the checkout page on the website, with its magenta "Sold out!" banners all over. No more campsites, no more VIP spots, not even any deluxe all-festival passes by the time Maddy and I got past the virtual waiting room. Fortunately, we had only needed (and could afford) this one-day pass to see CoGo.

"Ahem," Everett cuts in. He doesn't even fake cough. He literally says the word *ahem*.

When we turn to face him, he's got that Cheshire cat grin plastered across his face again. This smile means trouble.

"I found us a place to stay. And it's even in the VIP section. Well, VIP-adjacent."

Maddy's eyes widen. "Wow, how'd you manage to get us a campsite this late in the game? That's amazing. That's—"

"Not exactly what I said. I said I found us a place to stay. But I don't want to spoil the surprise. So, before I text back and finalize this: You in? Or out?"

How I loathe surprises, especially after the mess tonight's unexpected turns had brought. But honestly, it can't get any worse than us getting escorted past the chain-link perimeter of the Orchards after the festival grounds shut down.

There are apparently bears in the San Bernardino foothills. Are there big cats too? Wolves? For sure there are snakes: Everett had slapped a sticker on a sign warning of them. I should've researched this all better.

I lock the irritation and fear away in the pit of my stomach, sealing it in with a deep inhale. I can't believe what I'm about to say.

"All right. I'm in."

FIVE MONTHS AGO
November 16

The yearbook adviser has an emergency root canal, which means that the yearbook classroom is locked up and off-limits for the entire day. Fine with me—I could use this suddenly free lunch period to relax and eat my burrito without worrying about getting carne asada all over the keyboard. Jackie's unceremonious return home this past weekend, along with all the chaos that came with it, has frayed every one of my nerves, so time away from any sort of work or obligation is welcome at this point.

Especially when there's a burrito involved.

Maddy and I lounge on a grassy hill shaded by an oak. Tyler is covering a big away game for the volleyball team, and Maddy, her binder perched on her thighs as a makeshift desk, finishes a Spanish worksheet that's due next period. Between us sits a basket of soggy but deliciously oversalted French fries.

"So Jackie's just moved back into your room?" Maddy asks. She flips a page on her Spanish textbook, searching for the verb conjugation key.

"*Our* room, as my mom won't stop correcting me." I kick at the grass beneath me with my heel. "Seventeen years sharing a room. I finally get to rejoice in having my own space while she's off at college, then bam, she suddenly reappears and it's all hers again."

"If you ever need to escape, you can always come over."

I smile at Maddy's offer, hiding a tinge of sadness. She's almost always with Tyler these days. As generous as her gesture was, she's not exactly home enough for me to take her up on it. "Thanks, I'll keep that in mind in case I'd ever prefer your little brother staring silently at me to Jackie snoring in the middle of the afternoon while I'm trying to finish my homework."

Maddy laughs. "Okay, Mark did that once. Once! He doesn't even have a crush on you anymore." She finds the page she was looking for, then positions her phone on top to hold it open. "Is it really that bad, having her home?"

I sigh. "To be honest, I wouldn't mind having her back that much—we clearly lived together without killing each other for seventeen years, so I can do it again—but my dad's suddenly decided that everything she's going through is a direct reflection of his parenting. So he's started micromanaging everything I do. He seriously asked to see my calculus homework last night so he could check it. I don't even think he remembers calculus! I hope this little phase of his passes."

She shakes her head in sympathy. Her phone buzzes then with a text. I spot Tyler's name. Maddy doesn't move to pick it up. She's still only halfway through her worksheet and needs to get this done to keep her grade afloat.

I pick at the fries between us, my appetite dwindling. There's a conversation I've been avoiding all week: the Sadie Hawkins dance we've both been looking forward to all month. I've known that I can't go to this Friday's dance since this past weekend, but I haven't told her yet. Because if I say it aloud, that makes it real, and I really wanted to live in a reality where I was still fun and unfettered and could go to a silly dance with my best friend, guilt-free.

"So that dance on Friday." I tear into a soggy French fry instead of looking at her. "I, um, can't go."

Maddy stops her writing and turns to me. "You serious?"

"I had this big fight with my parents over it. After all this Jackie stuff and my extra Callaway shifts this week, they want us all home for a bit."

"We have our matching T-shirts ready and everything!"

My shoulders tense. I wasn't happy about this, and I knew she wouldn't be either. "Hey, I was looking forward to it too! But Jackie's mess-up spilled over onto everything, and I hate it."

Her eyebrows knit together, her lips pursed into a puppy-dog pout. Our one hangout in a long time, and I've played a discordant note into it. "You can't let them do this to you, Jana. If you want to go, fight for it. You didn't do anything wrong. Or"—and there's that signature mischievous glint in Maddy's eye—"I can just swing by and pick you up on Friday, whether they like it or not."

I shake my head. That rebellious approach may fly with Maddy and her parents, but it won't with mine. "It doesn't work like that in our family. I really do want to go. It'll be one of our last corny high school dances together. But it's so complicated."

"If you want to go, then go: it sounds pretty simple to me."

Her response rankles me. Would I have put off this conversation with her if it was as simple as she says? I want to attend the dance as much as she does. I begrudgingly find myself having to defend my parents' position, one that I wasn't too thrilled with in the first place.

Maddy narrows her eyes slightly. "So when were you going to tell me? Because the deadline for refunds was literally yesterday."

"They just told me last night that I couldn't go." A lie, but I don't want to confess that I've been putting off this conversation, that I've been secretly hoping that either my parents or Maddy would forget the dance altogether and spare me their disappointment. And by the time I admitted defeat, the refund deadline had passed and I didn't have the heart to call Maddy and tell her. I wanted to break the news in person so I could soften the blow—or so I tell myself.

Maddy's shoulders droop. "This sucks. The dance was going to be so much fun."

"I know. You could always come over though. We could still wear our matching shirts and everything."

"It's senior year! We can't just stay in, streaming some crappy movie and eating awful, cheap pizza. We should be out living it up."

I freeze my smile to keep from betraying how much it stings that she shot down my idea. It's the kind of Friday night we've had dozens of in the past. Apparently, these hangouts aren't enough for her anymore.

"Hey, that doesn't mean *you* can't go to Sadie's," I say, forcing some lightness into my voice. The worst part of the conversation is over: she knows I can't go to the dance. But, of course, I still have the urge to find a way to fix it thanks to the guilt over potentially ruining her senior year. "If you want to go, maybe you can ask Tyler?"

Maddy's face relaxes then, and I can see her waver. This is when she'd usually pepper me with are-you-sures and maybes, trying to walk that delicate balancing act of having fun but making sure your best friend doesn't feel left out. Like when I sprained my ankle back in eighth grade and couldn't go to Ben Boswell's swim party, and she offered to come over to my house instead, with a make-your-own-sundae kit. It took me a whole afternoon to convince her that I'd be fine and she could go without me. She still made her dad stop by on the way home so she could bring me two half-melted ice cream sandwiches from the party.

So hiding my disappointment now, when she immediately spouts out an "Okay, if you say so," is near impossible. She doesn't even offer to drop by before or anything. Worse, she continues with "He can use your ticket, right? Since you can't get a refund anyway?"

I'm crushed that I can't go to this dance. After how much she just prodded me about it, shouldn't she be more upset too? Or upset at all?

This solution of bringing Tyler: This is what I do. I fix things, even if it works out for everyone but me. It would've been nice to have her try to fix something for me this time though. I swallow hard. "Um . . . yeah. That makes sense, I guess."

My failed attempt to hide how crummy I'm feeling doesn't matter: Maddy isn't paying attention to me anyway. Her phone is already back in her hand. She texts Tyler, her Spanish textbook pages flapping in the cool breeze coming off the concrete quad below and floating up our grassy hill.

If Maddy had been looking at me, she might've seen the loneliness that bled into my gaze, the kind that comes from reaching out a hand for help, only to find that the other person never extended theirs at all.

NINE

SATURDAY, APRIL 23
10:34 pm

We stroll down the long aisle nestled between rows of tents toward the place that Everett swears has space for us. I wouldn't have pegged him as a social butterfly who knows VIP-adjacent, tent-having people, and he hasn't been out of my sight for more than a minute, but he's been nothing but surprises today.

Everett ushers his brother forward, Nathan's arm braced across his shoulders. Tyler and Maddy walk hand in hand immediately behind them, and I trail a few feet at the back. Tyler whispers something to Maddy, and she breaks out into a full-throated laugh.

I shift my gaze away from them. I hate that I always feel like I'm interrupting something private. Between them and the brothers, there isn't anyone left to distract me from the misery descending as quickly as the temperature around us.

To say there was one big, friendship-combusting fight between Maddy and me would be a misstatement. It's been a slow crumbling, a weathering from everything that life has thrown at us.

I don't know if I can even fairly blame Tyler for being the

wedge that drove us apart. There may have been a space between us well before he showed up, one that we made ourselves. It was just easier to gloss over it then, to pretend that the ship would right itself somehow.

It began with a small missed text here or there, a call that she was supposed to return, plans she canceled last minute. And that's fine—friendship can withstand a little distance here and there.

When our UC Santa Clarita college admissions portals showed the same "Accepted" message, suddenly I, Jana Rae Rubio, was Maddy Parsons's best friend again. She made plans for us to room together, to road-trip up on move-in day, to sneak in that hot plate so we can perfect our roast beef and provolone hoagies. And I got caught up in the thrill and attention of her needing me again. Forms, processes, deadlines: she spent the first couple of days after receiving our acceptance letters peppering me with questions, excited to have a partner (or more accurately, a guide) in everything. I even got in trouble at work for having my phone out so often, responding to her texts.

This all meant going back to the kind of closeness we had in the days of sixth-grade science projects and sleepovers sneaking R-rated horror movies. Santa Clarita could actually solve this rift: we would be around each other so much that even her time away visiting Tyler, wherever he ended up going, wouldn't crack this renewed bond.

For the first time in what felt like ages, we had plans together.

But rewind to Sunday.

Maddy called me, crying. "Jana, I'm panicking. I forgot about the US government test tomorrow! My grade's already on the edge in this class. You think Santa Clarita would somehow un-admit me if I failed?"

My fix-it instinct rallied. "Don't worry about that. I can help you study."

"You'd do that? You're the best! Meet me at the coffee shop on Barcelona. First tea latte is on me."

I hastily packed up my backpack and tugged on socks as I mapped out the route to the coffee shop. I double-checked with Mom that she didn't need the car until seven, which gave me plenty of time to calm Maddy down, run through the past month's worth of classes with her, and collect on that tea latte promise.

As I drove, I couldn't help but wonder whether this was how things would be at Santa Clarita too: us continuing to be there for each other, through the good surprises and the panics. The uncertainty of high school over, we could turn the page to this new chapter in our friendship. I don't know what had broken between us the past few months, but our time at Santa Clarita together would mend it, and we were getting a head start.

Maddy was there for me when they kept Mom in the hospital for days after the accident. Maddy answered her texts, any time of day. She snuck me a cookie from the bake sale at school when I hadn't gotten a chance to get breakfast. She threw a couple answers my way on homework that I fell asleep doing, though I had to be careful that she wasn't saying something completely out-there, like "Francis Bacon was the father of modern meat-curing methods," to make sure I was paying attention.

That was the Maddy I'm proud to be best friends with: thoughtful, considerate, a mischievous sense of humor, and spontaneity that could sometimes border on felonious.

The Maddy here at the Orchards comes off like someone else entirely.

As if she can hear me thinking about her, she glances briefly over her freckle-dusted shoulder. We lock eyes for the tiniest of moments, then she faces forward again, pointing out a snow cone stand in the distance to Tyler, laughing at whatever he says to her after.

Her silence is a twist of a knife. I'm not sure she realizes how much it hurts that she keeps choosing him, not me, even in the smallest ways. But whether pain is inflicted on purpose or accidentally, it feels all the same to the one on the wrong end of the blade.

I'm so caught up in my head that I don't notice the knee-level crate that I bang into. As I begin to tumble, a hand latches on to my forearm and steadies me. It's ube-colored-hair Kayla from Hello Hello Halo Halo.

"Whoa, whoa. If you really hated that milk in the halo halo, you didn't have to try to destroy the whole supply," she says with a smile. One of her incisors is crooked, and that little bit of imperfection actually makes her seem friendlier.

I glance around, the group trudging ahead without me. "I don't see the truck. What brings you out here?"

In answer, she hoists up the crate of canned milk. "Bringing these back to our tent. My brother kept bumping into these in the truck and his wife convinced him to stow it back in the tent with her. Who even makes crates this trippable height?"

Ahead, I see Everett pull back the door flap to a massive orange camping tent structure that could fit twenty people easily. It's actually two roomy tents specially zipped together—I can tell by the fade that one side is probably a little older than the other. Maybe whoever's tent this is has been coming to the Orchards for years, their group expanding each time.

I make a note of the location of our home for the night before turning back to Kayla. "Do you need a hand with those?" I motion at the other trippable-height crate nearby.

"Yeah, but if you need to get back to your friends, I can—"

"No, I've got time, unfortunately," I say, already lifting the crate.

I don't want to explain to a stranger that I'd actually prefer a moment away from Nathan, Everett, Maddy, and Tyler. I need to let some of this anger cool off, and I know erupting in their direction is a bad idea. I may not have a solid best friend right now, but I for sure don't need to make enemies.

Kayla beams. "Great, follow me. We're right over there."

We move slowly—cans of milk are much heavier than I thought—and on the way Kayla tells me about her family and their truck.

"This is my first year pitching in," she says. "Business has gotten so big that they needed an extra hand. They couldn't leave their free-laboring little sister at home anymore."

"Makes sense. People seem to have had this big discovery

moment with Filipino food, like all of a sudden it was trendy to take a selfie with a sizzling plate of sisig. It's kind of weird to have all these folks 'discovering' something that's always been ours, and has always been amazing, though."

She nods knowingly. "Tell me about it. If I have to read one more review with the phrase 'hot new trend,' I'm going to scream." She pauses in front of a door. "Here we are. Tent, sweet tent."

"You've got to be kidding me," I say, my mouth drying out like the mountain air. We stopped in front of the orange two-tent complex. "You're who Everett asked for a place to stay? Someone we literally just met an hour ago because we bought food from you?"

She laughs. "Okay, so you think it's ridiculous too then, right? Well, he seemed really nice, like he wasn't going to murder us. And sometimes you just have to go with the flow. Helping seems like a good thing to flow with."

"That sounds like a very Everett thing to say."

I'm not going to argue my way out of a roof over my head, but it's entirely bizarre and unsafe that Everett would ask a stranger to shelter us. But then again, as I remember the way he stared at her as she explained the menu to new customers earlier, this could all be some master plan to get close to her.

This kid's search for a soulmate is going to kill me.

With a sigh, I follow her into the tent and deposit the crate. Someone has strung up battery-operated white lights inside, giv-ing the place a magical, twinkly feel. Rolled-up sleeping bags line one wall—no one's asleep yet—and Everett squats next to a large plastic cooler, swapping out the ice in Nathan's cold pack.

Nathan waves me over. "Hey, there you are. Thought we lost you!"

"She's not your keys, Nathan," Everett jokes, earning a punch in the arm from his brother.

Lovely they think we're at the point where we can joke about this. I, however, am still not entirely sure how I'm going to explain any of this to my parents.

"Speaking of the keys, what's the plan for getting them back?" I ask. I take the plastic baggie from Everett and hold it open while he scoops in chunks of ice. "We've at least got a place to stay for a while in case security bugs us for hanging around, but it's not even eleven o'clock. We still have a couple of hours to keep searching the festival grounds."

Tyler lowers to a seat on one of the plastic coolers. "Well, I'm starving. So maybe we eat something and head back out there?"

I frown. "Are Everett and I the only ones who thought about dinner?"

The blank looks from Maddy, Tyler, and Nathan confirm that. If being hangry impacts them as much as it does me, they're going to need sustenance, fast.

"I'll ask Kayla what the campsite food situation is like," I say. "Then maybe Nathan can ice his knee here while the rest of us keep looking." I zip up the full ice pack and hand it to him.

He shoots me a thankful smile, and I ignore the flutter in my stomach. I'm still too annoyed at him for losing the minivan keys in the first place. Or maybe that's what I tell myself when I pull my hand away after it makes contact with his when he reaches for the pack.

I seek out Kayla. She's sitting cross-legged on the floor watching her sister-in-law rearrange the crates we've just hauled in. According to her, there's a sandwich truck at the end of this row of tents, but she hasn't checked it out yet.

In the interest of getting everyone fueled up and jump-starting this search again, I head for the truck alone. It's plain white—too plain, compared to the gorgeousness of Hello Hello Halo Halo—and the ruddy-faced man taking orders reminds me of our third-grade cafeteria staff, right down to gruffness and grimace. I shell out sixty dollars for three sandwich combos, then juggle them all back to the tent.

Someone has laid out a thick blue blanket for our group to sit on, and Nathan's legs are stretched out in front of him. Next to him are Tyler and Maddy, Tyler showing them some more photos he snapped around the Orchards. Maddy scoots aside to let me set down the three Styrofoam boxes, three Cokes, and three generic-brand bags of chips.

"You're a hero, Jana," Tyler says, grabbing a box. He opens the lid, and his smile freezes in that way that kids do when they get a birthday gift they don't love. "Oh, this looks . . . delicious."

I raise an eyebrow, then open another box. There sit two unnaturally bright orange cheese slices between slices of plain white bread. It looks like someone tried to smear butter on the outside before toasting it, but the bread is cold and the cheese not anywhere near melted. "What the . . ."

"It's fine," Maddy says quickly. She takes a huge bite out of her disgusting-looking sandwich. "We need to get our energy up."

I slide the open box over to Nathan.

He smiles graciously, like I'm handing him a feast and not a pathetic excuse for a sandwich. He's smart enough not to complain either.

I open his bag of chips for him as he takes a tentative bite of bread and cheese. "I should've known from the quickness of the transaction and the lack of other customers that this place would be a bust."

"What do we owe you for the meal?"

"That's the worst part. It was sixty dollars for what is clearly four dollars' worth of food. That's like four and a half hours' worth of Callaway Drugstore time for something a kindergartner could've concocted for us."

Nathan laughs and the noise draws the attention of Kayla's sister-in-law, who mumbles something under her breath.

I take a chip. "I can't believe they billed the Orchards as having top cuisine, a foodie destination as much as a musical and cultural experience. The halo halo was a hit, but these sad sandwiches are a miss a mile away."

To my surprise, Tyler inhales the not-grilled cheese, his chips, and his soda in a matter of minutes.

"Wow, you really were hungry," I say.

Tyler stuffs a used napkin in the Styrofoam box and closes it. "Yup. Those weed gummies kicked in."

I blinked. "Wait, weed gummies?" Not that I have anything

against weed (it helped one of my uncles with his appetite during chemo), but when did this even happen? When I was out getting everyone food? How can someone be called a hero but still be excluded?

"Chill," Maddy warns. "It's not a big deal, Jana." Of course she'd come to Tyler's defense. From the second he came into her—our—lives, he could do no wrong. "One of Kayla's cousins offered."

"Did you eat any gummies too? What about all your cheer rules?"

"Of course I didn't have any. I had a beer. You know they can do random tests for anything harder."

My jaw drops. "This isn't happening. I can't seriously be the only one legally sober enough to get us home."

Nathan lifts a finger. "I didn't have anything. I can still drive. My right knee is fine."

"Yeah? Did they give you anything besides an ice pack at the medical tent?"

"Um, just some Tylenol or something."

Tyler giggles like a grade-schooler at a low-level prank on a substitute teacher, and I know something's up.

"Or something?" I ask slowly.

"I was complaining about my knee. That cousin with the gummies overheard and said he had something for the pain; it helps him with his back."

"And what exactly was that something?"

"Um, it was small and white and yellowish? And my knee doesn't hurt as much anymore, so that's good, right?"

"Seriously? Is that what being a guy is like? Just being able to casually ingest whatever a stranger hands you? It's like neither of you has ever seen a Lifetime movie."

The clueless glance Tyler and Nathan exchange is my answer. If they'd even watched a promo for a made-for-TV movie of a party girl gone wrong—a favorite theme of these kinds of prime-time cable watches—they'd know they'd made about a dozen key mistakes right now and should probably start double-knotting their shoelaces to race for their lives.

My shoulders droop. "Great. So we've got no ride home, a uselessly high friend, a driver who isn't sure what he—" I glance at him and my eyes widen. "Nathan, are you really falling asleep right now?"

"No," he says two seconds later, with a wide yawn, his eyes blinking at different speeds.

This sends Tyler into another giggling fit. I realize this would be hilarious in any other situation—a TV show, perhaps, or if it was happening to literally anyone else—but I can't find a single ounce of amusement in how much worse my situation has gotten in the span of fifteen minutes.

Before I can say another word, Maddy grabs my hand and pulls me up and toward the tent door. The shock of her even associating with me keeps me quiet until we're outside.

She whirls around, her eyebrows pinched. "You need to relax and stop being so mean to everyone, Jana. Nathan losing the keys was a mistake. But we don't need all five of us to keep pestering lost and found or staring at the same concert venue dirt. We can find the keys on our own and let those guys sleep it off. We still have time before the stages close, like you said."

The sourness spills out of me before I can stop it. "Oh, so now you're talking to me?"

Her glower deepens. "What did I just say about being mean?"

"And you don't think it's justified after how immature everyone's being?"

"Who cares if it's justified? It's not like it makes the keys easier to find. So stop being such a jerk."

I force myself to take a deep breath. I'm annoyed that she's right. This isn't helping. With a two-hour drive between me and home, I've already blown past the possibility of picking up Dad when I said I would. Every minute of delay makes it worse, like leaving something in the oven too long. Sure, a few minutes may leave you with a drier banana bread than you counted on. But that doesn't mean you leave it in there forever. At some point it'll harden and char and fill your house with so much smoke the smell will linger for days.

Maddy and I and the rest of the group have a common goal here: locate the keys so we can all get home safe and sound. We're more likely to do that if we're not digging at each other.

I drag a hand through my hair. "This night has just . . . not been what I expected."

She frowns. "Yup."

The silence sits between us after that one-word answer. There's no hint of apology, no more reaching out to me as a friend. She must be as angry at me as I am at her. We're not going to argue it out right now—like she said, it won't make the keys easier to find—but we're not going to forgive and forget so easily either.

"Let's grab Everett and start looking then," I say. I shove my hands in the pockets of my shorts to keep from fidgeting and giving away how anxious I am. "The sooner we get those keys, the sooner we get out of this place, the sooner you can go back to not speaking to me again."

I don't wait for her to answer. I stomp back inside and take a moment to let my eyes adjust to the change in light. Across the room, Kayla's brothers and two of their friends unroll their sleeping bags. Another pulls a couple beer cans out of a cooler and passes them around. Nathan's groggily nibbling his cheese sandwich. Tyler's asleep, slumped against Nathan's shoulder.

To most people, this would look like a well-earned, peaceful wrap-up to a chaotic night. But the wrongness of the scene immediately hits me.

"Where the hell is Everett?"

FIVE YEARS AGO
November 5

Jana:

Can I stay over at Maddy's tonight?

Mom:

You stayed over last Saturday

Jana:

Maddy's mom got that new musical on demand.
Please?

Mom:

Fine. I'll call Mrs. P for details. But we're picking you up early so we can make it to the 8 am mass.

Jana:

8 am! So early!

Mom:

Gotta get home to watch Dad's team, morning game.
Uncles coming over. See you bright and early!

Jana:

Thanks, I guess?

TEN

SATURDAY, APRIL 23
10:59 pm

Around us, Kayla's family and their friends sip cheap beer and laugh and drum their fingers against their legs like the music will never end. In the far corner, a few people huddle up in puffy sleeping bags, blankets pulled up over their heads to tune the rest of us out. A hastily ripped open box of foam earplugs lies next to a phone plugged into a portable battery.

"Everett!" I whisper harshly for what feels like the dozenth time.

For that dozenth time, no answer.

Nathan tries to call his brother on the phone, but from the flat line of his lips, he must still not be getting any signal. He yawns so wide that I can almost see his molars. Our group is dropping like flies. If flies took way too many weed gummies or ran off with their instalove soulmates.

I tiptoe over to the folks comfortable in their sleeping bags and peer into the cracks and open zippers as best I can. Some black hair here and there, a white-and-gold Larissa beanie over a bald head, but none of the familiar shade of brown hair shared by Nathan and Everett.

I rise and post up next to Maddy, who's surveying the rest of the space for any clue as to where Everett disappeared to.

"Maybe Kayla knows where he is," I wonder aloud. Something brushes the back of my hand: a stray pink thread from the cuff of my jacket. Even that is unraveling.

"Who?" Maddy asks.

"The Hello Hello Halo Halo girl who got us into this tent. Everett's in love with her, I think."

Maddy smiles at the thought. She has always been a romantic. Which is why, when Tyler first texted her about a date, I'd helped her dissect the message while she squealed and kicked her legs in the air like a toddler. "What's this Kayla girl look like?"

"Can't miss her. She's got purple hair and—" The words die in my mouth. My eyes sweep around the tent. I should've been able to spot someone with such a distinctive look immediately. "Unbelievable. She's gone too."

"Who's gone?" one of the stocky guys from the Hello Hello Halo Halo truck asks. He sets his can of beer on the ground next to three crushed empties, then pushes himself to his feet.

I recognize the guy from the truck; he was the one who told Kayla to stop socializing and get through the orders. He's still in that white, airbrushed Hello Hello Halo Halo shirt, but he's traded those cargo shorts for swishy black basketball ones. A red bean is stuck to his dark brown forearm, but now does not seem the moment to point that out.

"I'm Kevin," he says, eyeing us, "and this is my tent. Who the hell are you?"

I need to stay on the good side of someone who is gracious enough to share their expensive lodging and save us from getting evicted from the Orchards grounds altogether. We're in no position to run from squatter-seeking security with Nathan's injury and Tyler being blissfully unconscious. "We're, um, friends of Kayla's. She invited us."

Kevin lolls his head back in frustration. "Of course she did. She's like that. Friends wherever she goes."

"And now she's gone!" Maddy cuts in with her big mouth. "We think she's got our friend Everett with her."

Kevin's dark brown eyes narrow. "Wait. Who's Everett? Where'd he take her?"

I catch that familiar, protective glint in his eyes. It's the look my dad gets whenever he suspects my sister or me of sneaking out of the house and dating (for my sister) or working extra hours (for me). The idea that someone may be taking advantage of their wonderful girl (via romance or capitalism) sets off some weird animal instinct in some folks.

"Nowhere. I mean, I don't think he *took* her. They probably went together," I say, trying to reverse the stranger-danger damage that Maddy had instigated. I channel my annoyance at her into tugging at the thread on my jacket, but it doesn't come loose. "Is there anywhere she might have wanted to take Everett? Some cool thing to show him?"

Kevin doesn't buy my attempt at a redirection. He pulls out his phone and frowns. "The damn reception in this place." He sighs, then runs a hand through his short black strands. "I should've listened to Papa and not brought her." Then he gazes up at me, and there's a curious look of calculation in his eye. "So my sister's the one who let you horn in on our tent, right?"

Maddy and I nod. I'm not sure where he's going with this, so I decide against answering him with anything but the truth.

"Well, looks like your boyfriends there are fast asleep." He juts a thumb out at Tyler and Nathan, now both snoozing together, cozy as peas in a pod. "They're probably not going anywhere anytime soon. How about you go find my sister and this Everett kid and bring them back safe and sound? We'll watch your friends here while you look around."

I don't miss the barely veiled anger in his voice. He must be exhausted from a day of dealing with increasingly drunk festivalgoers demanding this and that in their halo halo and the constant explanation of "yes, there are beans in here. It says on the menu! No refunds." But he could've asked for our help rather than force it. I'm about to say so when Maddy makes it all worse, which honestly seems to be her specialty.

"Are you holding my boyfriend hostage?" she shrieks.

Across the tent, a couple people lower their beers and stare at us. Nathan and Tyler, however, barely rouse.

"Hostage? No, no." Kevin smirks, despite the seriousness of his tone. "I'm simply letting them stay here, in this very precious, expensive campground that I paid for and that my sister, who had no right to extend invitations to, let you all hang out in. So out of the goodness of my heart"—he splays a hand across his chest, as if silly girls have no idea where human hearts are—"I'm going to let your friends catch some shut-eye right there. And out of the goodness of your heart, you're—"

"Going to find Kayla and Everett, safe and sound. Got it," I say, trying to keep the tired resignation from my voice. We were going to do this anyway, but now we've got the extra incentive of a-stranger-has-our-friends further motivating us.

I wrap my fingers around Maddy's forearm, lean closer, and lower my voice so only she can hear me. "Let's go. The sooner we find those two, the sooner we can resume our hunt for the keys and get out of here."

Her black eyeliner is smudged, and she makes it worse with an absent-minded rub of her eye. "But Tyler is—"

"Asleep. Or passed out from those gummies. Whatever. The point is that he's safer here than roaming the Orchards in his state, right? Nathan too, with his knee."

Maddy nods, sending a purse-lipped look at her boyfriend. "I tried to stop him, but he popped the gummies in his mouth like they were, well, candy. It's literally street safety 101: don't take candy from strangers. The guy gets straight As, but I swear he must run at night with earbuds in or take bubble baths next to a toaster."

I chuckle. Maddy understands, and I'd forgotten how funny she can be when it's just us. She drops her forearm away from me then, as if she suddenly remembered she's angry at me. My laughter fizzles too. This lighter moment was a misstep, not a change in trajectory. It's also the most she's said to me all day, other than her telling me to stop nagging everyone.

Turning to Kayla's brother, I cross my arms. Between the ride, the keys, and now Everett, so much about this night has already slipped from my control, and it feels like I'm caught in a current, watching the shore tear farther and farther away. I need to regain my footing. "All right, we'll go find your sister. But don't let those two wander away, please?"

Kevin nods. "Kayla likes that neon Ferris wheel. You might try there."

Maddy is unzipping the flap of the tent before I know it. I peer back at Nathan and Tyler, hoping one of them is awake for me to reinforce that message to stay put. Kevin is already depositing two water bottles next to them. So he's not a terrible person: just worn out and probably weary of the antics of the youngest member of their group. Relatable. Meanwhile, the sister-in-law who reorganized the milk crates scrubs her face with a makeup remover wipe and glares at Kevin, mumbling something like "damn sister" and "not my problem."

It could be worse, I tell myself. Nathan and Tyler could be out in the dirt by the minivan, getting hassled by security. Or a bear.

I zip up my satiny bomber jacket tight to shield against the plummeting temperatures and rip off that stray thread on my sleeve. Then I exit the tent behind Maddy.

She angles away from me and squints at the artificially lit-up horizon. "There, the Forest Wheel," she says, gesturing in the distance. It's clear across the Orchards, a neon green circle blazing in the night sky. But where stars should be is a thick blanket of dark, gray clouds. As if driving home a point, the wind picks up, and I'm thankful then for the jacket I'd thought to bring from home.

"Let's go," I say, readjusting my collar to provide a little more shield from the wind. "I don't like the look of these clouds."

"Ugh. I wasn't expecting rain," Maddy says in her thin shirt that matches mine. She unknots the bottom and lets the long hem fall to her hip, as if those extra four inches of fabric will save her from the storm.

"You never do."

She looks at me then, the first bit of eye contact since we exited the tent. Her mouth pinches slightly, like she's trying to figure out if she wants to respond. She turns away again. It's as if I'm not even worth the attention, however negative, and though I shouldn't have made that baiting comment anyway, it still stings to be dismissed.

The grounds ahead of us are emptier, as people have headed into their tents or hotels for after-partying or sleep. I shove my hands in my jacket pockets, and we trek down the long aisle to the Forest Wheel together, in silence.

ELEVEN

SATURDAY, APRIL 23
11:09 pm

Maddy stays a few steps ahead of me, her pace quick and her fingers wrapped around her goose-bumped upper arms. She'd let down her fishtail braid at some point, and the harsh white from the stadium lights overhead reflects off her free blond strands. It reminds me of when my parents took us to Universal Studios for my birthday. Maddy and I splintered off from my family early in the day and stayed until the park closed, the neon lights from the rides and attractions keeping us wide awake. We dissolved overpriced cotton candy on our tongues and screamed so much our voices were hoarse for days.

We're in no danger of that now, when we're barely speaking.

But the memory drags me down, slowing my gait. Maddy has stayed distant tonight, the aftereffects of our fight lingering and keeping us separated. Again, I consider bridging the gap, if only to get us on better terms as we try to turn this night around.

Even if we laid everything out between us right now though, how would I be sure any apology from her is real? I know her:

Maddy might apologize because that's what people do to ease temporary strain, because it's a shortcut to peace. It's what she does when she's sick of fighting with her mom. She's learned to say whatever it takes to get her mom to back off, to throw on a loose sweater to appease her mom's absurd sense of appropriate curvy-girl fashion, then strip it off to reveal her cutout strapless top later.

A quick, possibly insincere apology won't mean Maddy understands what's at the root of this growing rift. Then I'll fall right back into being the best friend who drops everything when Maddy calls, only to be burned yet again.

My feet stop completely, and Maddy continues ahead.

The deadline for the Santa Clarita seat deposit is in a week.

And there's something big I've been keeping from Maddy. I swear I would've told her by now if we were actually on good terms.

I don't know how to tell my best friend that I haven't yet paid the seat deposit at the college she's made elaborate plans for us to attend together. I haven't turned in the housing request form that could bind us as roomies for the next year.

At first, it was a money issue. We needed some paychecks and insurance reimbursements to go through, then I had to pin my parents down to borrow their credit card for a moment.

But once I had that plastic in hand, I still didn't click through the website to finalize my enrollment. I froze. Then I returned the card to Mom and claimed that the website was down, that I'd take care of it later.

Why didn't I submit the seat deposit? It's everything we planned, everything I've come to expect for my future.

What am I afraid of?

And why am I afraid of even asking that question?

I suspect it's the tab lurking at the back of my browser: the one for Chalmers Design. Maddy and my family all assume I'm heading to Santa Clarita in the fall. I can't rail at my best friend for ditching me when I'm the one whose dreams threaten to pull me to a school on the other coast.

I wouldn't really blame her for being angry either. She thinks she can count on me, her Emotional Support Jana all these years. Every snide comment from her mother, every canceled plan with her father, every heartbreak from a crush: I've been there to pick her up, brush her off, and help her remember she's great as she is. Her confidence has taken some heavy blows, which begs the question she half-jokingly poses through her sniffly sobs: What would she do without me? I've been that support for so long that I'm scared what could happen if I suddenly step away and let her battle through her unsteadiness on her own. Angry as I am right now, I can't do that to her. Maddy does need me.

"This way is blocked off and— Where'd you go?" Maddy calls over her shoulder before whirling around to see me yards behind her. I didn't realize I'd stopped walking. "Catch up, Jana!"

My mouth is dry. "I'm coming. I'm just"—I make a show of scouring the floor, partially to hide the tears that somehow collected in my eyes when I was lost in thought—"being thorough.

In case the keys are here somehow."

"Well, I'm going to go ahead to the Forest Wheel. Take your time, I guess."

Without waiting for me to answer, she keeps walking.

Just like that, she's moved ahead, presuming I'm on board with a plan we'd vaguely come up with together, one that I realize now she only did the lightest of consulting with me for. The thought grates me.

"It's always what *you* want," I whisper into the air, merely to give voice to the anger and let it escape. Maddy's too far away to hear me.

I said the same exact words earlier this week, the day I drove to that coffee shop to help Maddy study. I'd left Mom alone at our yard sale, then took the car with the promise of coming right back once we got through the exam material.

When I got to the coffee shop, I spotted her at a small table by the front window. She was hunched over her textbook, her fingers worrying the edge of the page she was reading. I plopped my car keys and notebook down next to her coffee cups.

I reached for one of the cups. "You got me the sugar-free vanilla syrup, right?"

She raised her eyes then and practically snatched the drink out of my reach. "Oh, hey, Jana. That's, um, actually not yours."

My shoulders tensed then, because deep down, I knew the answer to what I was going to ask, and I didn't like it. "Why? Whose is it?"

The sound of a chair scraping the tile floor drew my attention. Tyler stood there, grinning. "Hi, Jana. Come to join our study group?"

The anger came on so quickly it felt like being pushed into a pool unaware. I wasn't ready for the water over my head and I floundered, with nothing and no one to grab on to to haul myself out.

I picked up my belongings again. I hadn't even sat down. "I— actually, I have to go." My voice wavered for a second, betraying more emotion than words alone let on.

I headed for the door before the anger forced tears out of my eyes or made me say something I'd regret. The coffee shop door clanged behind me, and I stomped back to the car, fumbling with the car keys.

A hand on my shoulder stopped me. "Hey, what the hell was that about?"

I whirled around to face Maddy. She looked angry. How dare *she* be angry. "You tell me. You're the one who begged me to come study with you, and I show up and Tyler's already here? Was I just an afterthought? A backup?"

Shame on me, the fool again. I had been so ready to hop back into the role of a good best friend to someone who'd kept treating me like I wasn't.

Maddy scoffed. "It's not like that. We can all study together."

"I don't need to study together! I'm supposed to be helping my mom at our yard sale, and I ditched her for this fake emergency."

She had the sense to look contrite. "Sorry, I—I didn't know. I'm just freaking out about this test, and I didn't know if you'd show up, and—"

"Of course I'd show up," I snapped. The fact that I even had to say that aloud was offensive. But part of me wondered why she questioned that at all. "It's always what *you* want. You could've told me Tyler was already on his way. I could've stayed home."

Maddy crossed her arms then. "Why do you hate him so much? You are so rude to him. I can't believe you just stormed off back there."

My grip around my keys tightened. "I don't hate him, Maddy. But if you've got him, you don't need me to drag myself out here too." I blew out a breath. This was going nowhere good. "I have to go."

I got into the car, drove home, and ignored her texts later that night. Immature, I know. But part of me wanted her to wonder about my radio silence, to let it eat at her and ponder whether I was avoiding her. Maybe it would finally make something click in her mind that she was being awful for putting everyone and everything else above our friendship and she needed to step up and address it. Sometimes doubt is the only weapon we have left.

Fast-forward to Monday morning. She strolled right up to me at my locker like nothing had happened, as if she didn't totally ruin my weekend. She went on about how nervous she was about the test.

I hugged my comp sci textbook closer to my chest, as if I could hold back the venom begging to spill out. It didn't work, of course.

And days later, as Maddy and I walk through the Orchards grounds near each other but not quite together, I'm still raw from that fight.

Even now, I have to push away the feeling that this fight is different: as far as she knows, we have our Santa Clarita roomie plans in place, and she hasn't mentioned that changing. It can't be any worse than that time in seventh grade when she told Joey Tam that I had a crush on him and kept the copy of a comic he drew in a secret pocket in my backpack. That had taken a whole two weeks to blow over.

I have to believe this is fixable. This friendship is worth holding on to. Since fifth grade, we've been such solid, stable forces in each other's life. That's why I'm fighting so hard to get past this. If only she'd realize that how she's acting is driving a wedge between us. We're stuck until that happens.

What if she doesn't apologize? some part of me asks.

I shake that thought away. This isn't like a fading crush or an oops-you're-a-terrible-person partner. Maddy is my best friend and we've been there for each other through thick and thin. This just happens to be the thin. The very thin.

I catch up to her as she's lifting up a line of caution tape and ducking under. She's never been one to think a rule or obstacle applied to her.

Maddy rises on the other side and holds the caution tape up for me. I squeeze under and join her in the narrow space between official white Orchards organizer tents. A few cargo vans are parked nearby, folded tables and chairs propped up next to them as staff pack and lock up for the night.

"You sure we're allowed to be here?" I ask.

Maddy rolls her eyes, more amused than annoyed at my question. "There's caution tape. Of course we're not supposed to be here. But it's faster than going around."

She points ahead and I follow her gaze to the Forest Wheel, on the other side of this row of tents. She's right: we can cut through here and weave through a few tents, cross a large walkway and a line of handwashing stations, and be at the base of the Forest Wheel. I walk toward the tiny sliver of dried grass between the First Aid and Donate to the Foothills Foundation tents, then pause when light glints off a stack of plastic to my right: cases of water bottles.

I eye them longingly. "I am so thirsty. I polished off my bottle before CoGo even went on."

"I don't think they'll mind if we take some," Maddy says, already reaching for a couple of waters.

"Um, I think they will. They're selling these for three dollars each at the trucks."

Mischief sparkles in Maddy's eyes the way it did when she used her brother's Clippity account to check out Concession Stand Dan's profile last year. "You're thirsty, aren't you? Hydration counts as first aid or something, right?"

We may be angry at each other, but Maddy's clearly not above setting those feelings aside to get into a little bit of trouble.

I must be severely dehydrated because she's making enough sense that I snatch the bottle from her hand. I consider this a small peace offering, the start of a cease-fire.

Together, we take long swigs from our flimsy plastic bottles, and I could cry at how welcome and delicious this water is. It douses some of my crankiness too. I can settle more into this weird, unspoken truce between Maddy and me, at least until we can get home. There's no use fighting each other when we've got so many other hurdles to overcome. And I know from so many group projects over the years that we can be a great team when we want to be. Like when she called me sobbing that her cupcakes for the cheer bake sale had sunk in the middle and I just filled them in with frosting and we pretended they were a new thing: bestselling item that year.

"Hey, what are you two doing here? This is off-limits!" a bass-heavy voice booms somewhere off to our left.

I nearly choke on my water at the sight of the Orchards first aid staff member in his dingy white polo shirt. Caught stealing, physically drinking the evidence. We're never going to find Everett or the keys if we get booted out of the Orchards. And with Nathan and Tyler out of commission as a search party? It'd be a miracle—or a mess—if I made it home before the three-day festival was over.

I brace myself for the yelling that's sure to follow, pulling together any possible defense for why we're standing here chugging three-dollar bottles of water we didn't pay for.

Maddy, on the other hand, has other ideas. She drops her bottle entirely. The precious water splashes in the dirt, the half-empty plastic landing with a thud.

"Run!" she shrieks, but without an ounce of fear: she thinks this is *funny*.

She takes off to the sound of the Orchards staffer bellowing "Stop!" but not before grabbing my hand and yanking me behind her. I may have been livid at her days ago for forgetting about me, but her remembering me this time may make up for that. I move as fast as my legs can take me, a laugh bubbling in my chest.

ONE YEAR AGO
April 19

My forehead rests on my crisscrossed arms. I stare at the black dashboard of Maddy's car, listening to the thousandth repeat of the hospital's bland on-hold music.

"It's been what, twenty minutes now?" I ask. I don't raise my head. Partially because no one needs a peek at my splotchy, tear-streaked face, but I also don't want to catch the look of worry on Maddy's.

That pinched look has been there since I turned on my phone after the movie and was bombarded by a dozen notifications. Dad and Jackie alternated in the blur of text messages and voice mails that I missed. According to Dad, Mom was driving on the freeway when a sports car merged out of nowhere, sending them overcorrecting into the concrete median. Good Samaritans made sure an ambulance showed up quickly to whisk them to the emergency room. According to Jackie—from her dorm room across the country but still with more information than me—Dad is up and walking around with some bumps and bruises, but

Mom's injuries are more serious. I don't know what "more serious" means, and that latest, damnably vague message was from almost an hour ago.

The recurring theme of their communications: *Where are you, Jana?*

I was sitting in an icy movie theater with Maddy, crunching on deliciously over-buttered popcorn courtesy of Maddy's latest crush, Concession Stand Dan. I was giggling at slapstick humor and licking salt off my fingers, all while my family needed me.

A fresh wave of guilt nearly starts my tears up again. Mom, Dad, and I were supposed to go to my uncle's house for lunch earlier when Maddy texted me about an impromptu movie and crush-scope-out as I was getting ready. I waffled over whether I should go with her. At this family party, my mom's elderly aunt would be making her last stateside appearance before going home to the Philippines. Selfishly, even without this special guest, my uncle is the king of barbecue, and I was starving in a way that Red Vines and popcorn wouldn't fix.

But then Maddy threw her ace on the table: *Come on, I can't do this without you!*

My parents were not happy with my last-minute proposed change of plans, and to be honest, I understood why. This gathering was important to them. But being there for Maddy was important to me too. Last weekend, she'd called me crying after a full-on screaming fight at home. Her mother, once again, had decided to put the entire household on a diet and had even gone so far as to suggest that Maddy would be more attractive, more worthy of love and attention, if she just shed a few pounds: this latest absurdity was likely a side effect of one of the dozen self-help and wellness books Mrs. Parsons collects each month.

So when Maddy asked me to come with her to check out a crush—one who would arguably like her just the way she is?—as much as I wanted to go to this family party, I had to help my best friend pick her confidence up off the floor.

So I'd pushed back on my parents' demand I join them, slightly altering the tale to morph "going to the movies so Maddy could flirt" to "holing up in the library to finish a research paper worth thirty percent of our grade." And though I could tell Mom and Dad weren't happy, they relented. I won.

But after the frantic helplessness in my dad's tone in his voice mail, I swear to myself that none of this stress and guilt is worth that momentary thrill of "winning" something as trivial as a stolen afternoon. Logically, I know it's better that I wasn't in the car with them, but I can't escape the crushing feeling that I should've been there, that maybe there was something, anything, I could've done to help.

My phone sits on the center console between Maddy and me, and she taps the screen to view the call duration. "According to your phone, it's only been about seventeen minutes," she says gently.

I could almost laugh aloud at that. Seventeen or twenty minutes, the difference is so minuscule in the grand scheme of things. But leave it to my best friend to try to spin it in a positive way.

"And no texts or anything? You think being on hold will stop the notifications from popping up?" I reach for any explanation for the radio silence from Dad and Jackie since Maddy and I screeched into the parking lot.

"No, I haven't seen anything, and I don't think it works like that. You should keep getting messages and calls." She shifts in her seat, and the black leather seats of her hand-me-down Civic squeak as she resettles. "You know, they're probably still running tests and everything. She hasn't been in there that long. I don't think they'd want to worry you."

I angle my head then and peer at her. I hate that she's making sense. The illogical part of me—the part that wishes I could rewind and make it all better somehow or simply *be there*—wants to dash back to the ER reception desk and demand to see my mother. It didn't work the first time though.

My slight move out of my facedown position must encourage Maddy, because she adds, "Or maybe there isn't even cell reception way in there. They might've been sending you updates this whole time."

I slouch back in the passenger seat, the grooves of the dashboard imprinted into my skin. "Maybe. It is a big building. And my dad's phone has been having trouble connecting to Wi-Fi anywhere."

The sharpest edges of my panic dulled, I flip down the sun visor to check my mess of a face in the mirror. Maddy's red duffel bag sits in the back seat.

My heart sinks, weighed down by another boulder of guilt.

"You have a cheer thing today." A statement, not a question, because Maddy doesn't carry around that duffel bag unless she needs it.

"Don't worry. It's an optional clinic. I can miss one." She gives a dismissive wave, but her smile seems forced in a way that tells me she's not giving me the whole picture.

"Oh no, I'm so sorry. I'm making you miss it right now, aren't I?" My hands fly up to my hair in a hurry, retying the ponytail and making myself somewhat presentable before I barrel out of Maddy's car. When she texted me this morning, she probably hadn't counted on a whole, full day dealing with my family crisis.

"No, no, I said it's fine, Jana. I already texted the coach."

"What time does the clinic start? Because if you leave now, you can—"

She places a firm hand on my arm. "Hey, stop. I said it's fine. This is more important, okay? I'm not going to leave you waiting outside the ER by yourself."

I know better than to fight her on this. When Maddy Parsons is determined to do something, virtually nothing can stop her. And I'm suddenly so grateful for that stubbornness of hers right now. I'm the one who fought and lied to my parents, and then they get hurt the one time I'm unreachable and not where I'm supposed to be. Being alone right now is a guaranteed guilt spiral.

"Thanks, Maddy."

"You don't have to thank me. You know I'd be here. You can't get rid of me that easily." She squeezes my arm.

My mouth curves with the first hint of a smile this afternoon. "I know."

"And stop beating yourself up. Don't pretend like you're not: I know you. But this? This isn't your fault."

I nod, mostly because I don't want to explain how I can't turn off guilt like a light switch. But her words stir up a darker thought. I would've been there to help them if Maddy hadn't dragged me out to the movies.

No, I tell myself. Maddy's here with me right now; this isn't her fault either. No one could've predicted the accident. I lock the horrible thought away, but its presence lingers like the bitter scent of a blown-out match.

From my phone comes a prerecorded message, a woman's voice designed to be the perfect mix of friendly and soothing: "Thank you for holding, a representative will be with you shortly. If this is a medical emergency, dial—"

"Now it's got to have been twenty full minutes on hold, right?" I ask, focusing back on the real issue.

Maddy nods, then something gleams in her eye. "Well, if we're going to be stuck here until a live person picks up the line again and gives you an update on your mom, we might as well listen to something better than this crappy elevator music."

"I don't know. I feel so bad being out here while my mom's . . ." The words stick in my throat.

"Look, Jana. They won't let us in: we've tried. And you're no good to anyone out here panicking. So let's calm you down so you can jump in when they need you, okay?"

I drag in a deep breath. The very least I can do is be strong when my family needs me again, considering I've failed at the other very basic responsibility of simply being there. They may want my help talking to doctors, picking up prescriptions, and filling in relatives on what's happened. I must stay calm, steady, reliable.

"What did you have in mind?" I ask.

Maddy plucks her own phone out of its air-conditioning-vent holder, then scrolls through her music app. "You in the mood for some CoGo?"

And this is why Maddy has been my best friend since fifth grade.

She gets me.

Even when I don't totally get myself.

TWELVE

The night air whips through my hair as I run. Maddy pulls me faster than I'm used to moving. My legs wobble at the forced speed and I feel like I could stumble at any moment, but Maddy holds me upright.

Irritated voices pursue us. Apparently, the Orchards staff are not so much about festivalgoer well-being as they are the bottom line. They'll patch you up only as long as they make a profit.

Maddy and I round corners too fast, squeeze between tents and unsuspecting groups. We don't stop. Not only because we might end up on the Orchards Most Wanted list for lifting six dollars' worth of water (it was probably only worth thirty cents, but the markup is a killer). But now the gray clouds that had served as the dark, picturesque backdrop for the Forest Wheel have ripped open, and I can see the wall of water approaching.

Ahead, people sprint toward shelter. Maddy and I dart by a couple of empty organizer tents that haven't been secured yet, and they're full of damp concertgoers, huddling together to escape the downpour. My hair begins to grow heavy with drops of rain.

I tug Maddy toward the overhang of one of the dozen short trees dotting this area. It's mostly been dirt, dried grass, and rocks, so this tree feels like a sign from the heavens that we need to pause and catch our breath. We're still not far enough from the pursuing Orchards first aid staff, but with so many folks scurrying around for cover, we at least have a moment to regroup.

We squat to fit into the relatively dry spot under the tree. Maddy finally releases my arm and plants her hands on her thighs. She laughs easily as she gulps in air, like the rain had started to wash away this tension between us. Wet strands of hair cling to her neck and upper arms. "Did you see that guy's face? You'd think we broke into a vault or something."

"Stealing water in California is a huge deal. Though I guess if I knew it was going to pour five minutes later, I would've just waited and opened my mouth." I lift my gaze to the skies and wipe a few drops of glitter-flecked rain off my face. My meticulous eye makeup job is now officially ruined.

She snorts out a laugh, and I suddenly wish we could stay here in this moment, in this tiny bit of peace that has descended between Maddy and me, away from my parents and Tyler and everything uncertain about the world beyond this tree. But the rain is going to end sometime, and our problems will be waiting for us the moment we step out from this dry patch. Nothing lasts, even if we desperately need it to.

I brush droplets of water off my sleeves. "All right. We need to find Everett. So maybe we—"

Maddy puts a hand out to stop me. "Before you finish that, I think we need to find somewhere to wait out this rain. Not all of us had the foresight to bring a jacket."

She eyes my water-resistant bomber jacket greedily. I'm almost too proud of my planning skills to be embarrassed that I'm probably the only one-day attendee who brought a jacket to a festival on a 70-something-degree evening. I should've thought to bring an extra sweater for her. Then I remember that I didn't even want to run into her at the Orchards. How quickly one good moment manages to erase days' worth of unhappiness.

"We should try to keep moving forward though. I have no interest in crossing that First Aid tent line to get back to Kayla's family's place again."

Maddy snickers. "Look at us, living sordid lives of crime. You think we can pull off a campsite infiltration like Everett did?"

"You mean beg total strangers to take us in?" Relying on anyone else right now could derail our night even more. It's cleaner if we find a way to solve this ourselves without dragging more people in and possibly ruining their time at the Orchards too. "No, no way. I'm surprised that even worked in the first place. And unfortunately, I don't think I met any tent-having soulmates here."

"Well, you got a canopy or beach umbrella in that mini-backpack of yours? Because unless you do, we're going to need to find somewhere to hunker down until the rain stops. This tree isn't cutting it."

I'm not totally heartless. I'm not going to keep dragging her through the cold rain in that already soaked tank top of hers. The wind picks up, sending the rain hitting us sideways.

Wiping a little more water and ruined makeup off, I squint toward the nearest signpost. My dry contacts stick to my eyelids and remind me they've been in too long. Mom had warned me about this before I left, and I'd shaken her off. Joke's on me. Repeatedly, lately.

"There's no harm in asking around for help," Maddy adds, "and I'll do the talking."

Maddy, with her bright eyes and cheerleader charm, can make it uncomfortably difficult to say no to her—I would know. So as much as I don't want to hassle some strangers for shelter, she does need it, and at least I won't be doing the begging.

"It looks like the VIP campers are set up over there," I say, following the arrow of the signpost to a field of hulking RVs parked in neat lines.

As if the universe wants to evict us from under this tree this second, lightning flashes and thunder cracks overhead.

I gather my wet hair and pull it over one shoulder, out of my eyes. "Ready to make a mad dash? I'm not about to die from a lightning strike at a music festival, a wanted water-bottle thief."

Maddy brushes her own sopping hair away from her face. "Yup. How about that big silver Airstream?"

Ahead, a long, rounded silver camper gleams in the lightning and festival lights. Warm orange light seeps out from the windows, a soggy pink banner dangles above the door, and all in all, it looks inviting. Well, more inviting than standing under a tree in the middle of a downpour.

I nod, and we take off toward the Airstream. The water and stray strands of hair slap against my face. Maddy is faster than me, always has been. She makes it to the Airstream first and is rapping on the door by the time I stagger over. Our feet are muddy messes, our hair wild and water-logged. If we were hoping to throw our pathetic, miserable selves on the mercy of some kind strangers, we at least look the part.

The door opens an inch and a Black woman in her twenties peers out. "Oh my god, are you okay?" She swings the door open wide, revealing three other women gathered around a cramped dining table or sitting on a bed amid piles of clothes.

"We got caught in the storm and don't have a place to wait it out," Maddy explains, amping up the frantic notes in her voice in a way that would tug nearly anyone's heartstrings. "Can we come in for a few, at least until the rain stops?"

The woman nods and moves aside. "Of course, of course. Come on in."

We kick off our disgusting shoes and tuck them under the steps before entering the warm, bright interior of the luxury camper. We shuffle in behind the woman, dripping all over their dry floor. On the wall over the bed is a bright pink banner with "Hallie's getting hitched!"

It's then that I register the pink sash on a brown woman with a pixie cut and a plastic tiara—Hallie, I presume—and the cloying scent of fruity body wash and moisturizing products. The diamond on Hallie's finger is so bright and big I would've thought it was fake if not for the seven-thousand-dollar Cartier watch she's sporting too. I only know because it's the same one Rihanna has, and Maddy had once spent a whole afternoon scrolling through affordable fakes on her phone while I was trying to do my biology homework. This rich girl has some guts showing up to a crowded, muddy outdoor festival with expensive designer jewelry like that. I didn't even want to wear the thirty-dollar music-note studs I got from a cheap accessory chain store at the mall.

Between Hallie and the other woman at the table is a half-eaten cake that must've at one point been shaped like a champagne bottle on its side, spilling blown-sugar bubbles all around it. The Airstream residents sport matching white T-shirts with #Hallies-gettinghitched in pink and gold sequins across their chests.

We've stumbled upon a bachelorette party.

"Chrissy, can you grab them a blanket?" the Black woman says.

The short, curvy white girl on the bed tosses a pink fleece throw to Maddy. "Right. Here, get warm."

I didn't even realize Maddy was shivering. I unzip my bomber jacket, to set it aside to dry.

The girl on the bed, Chrissy, laughs. "Oh my gosh, aren't you two the cutest with your matching tops!"

"It wasn't on purpose," Maddy says through the chatter of her teeth. She draws the blanket around her shoulders tight.

"Oh, no, don't worry," Hallie says. "Shannon and Chrissy here have been together for years. We're cool."

Chrissy smiles at us from the bed and the ultra-toned redhead at the table, Shannon, waves at us. From the quick peek of muscle in Shannon's arm, I bet she probably spends half her time at the gym embarrassing the amateur weight lifter bros who try to offer pointers on her already perfect form.

"We accept everyone here, no matter what the type of relationship. Love is love, right?" Shannon says.

I respond with a relieved smile that we at least landed among decent people. Our gamble in seeking shelter could've ended much worse: we could've been locked in a trailer packed with too-drunk folks like Muscle Tank from earlier. This baked-good-full, inclusive bachelorette party is a slice of heaven in comparison.

The woman who let us in closes the door. "I'm Pam, and welcome to the Bach' Bullet. You want cake?"

Accepting a total stranger's weed gummies like Tyler is one thing. But custom cake? And are those Funfetti sprinkles I see? "Yes, please."

Hallie jabs a plastic knife into the cake and saws me a slice.

THIRTEEN

SATURDAY, APRIL 23
11:34 pm

Maddy has a way of looking glamorous effortlessly. It's not the makeup she uses or the way she does her hair. She has attempted her cosmetic magic on me during multiple failed makeovers. It's definitely not how she styles her clothes, considering we're somehow matching today. I simply do not have that same signature glamour.

It's the way she's learned to hold herself despite the words of people, like her mom, who'd tear her down: straight back, squared shoulders, open heart. I've known her long enough that I've seen the few times she's temporarily lost her shine. Like when her dad flaked on their plans celebrating Maddy finally getting her driver's license (she drove over and we ordered weird-tasting pizza with a coupon instead), or when her sophomore crush broke her heart by gushing to her about the cute girl she met online (turns out the crush was getting catfished, but by then, Maddy's feelings had worn off). Part of my best friend duties is to restore that shine.

I don't know what's stealing her sparkle right now, considering we're in this unspoken truce. Sure, we both look like drowning rats from our impromptu race in the rain, but I've seen her in worse: she wore a glitter-covered poofy abomination to homecoming. And she's never looked that downtrodden when offered cake before. Did I do something to throw her this off-kilter all of a sudden? I should ask her what's wrong.

I almost have to pinch myself to stop this line of thinking.

Stop being the one always trying to fix the broken things in the world, I tell myself, particularly when Maddy has stopped doing that for you. Maddy doesn't even seem to consider what she smashes in her wake sometimes.

I fold my arms tight across my chest, as if the motion will quell those thoughts. A few drops trickle off my hair onto the muddy gray towel someone's laid at the Airstream door.

Hallie hands Maddy and me flimsy paper plates piled high with green-fondant-covered Funfetti cake. I dive in, almost immediately polishing off the whole serving.

"Oh wow. I'm the one who demanded Pam order from my specific, favorite bakery, and I didn't even dig in that enthusiastically," Hallie says with a laugh.

No use feeling embarrassed. I really did demolish that hunk of cake. Out of some weird sense of courtesy, I scrape at the bits of frosting on the rim of the plate to avoid gobbling up the last few bites. The seven-dollar halo halo and half a stolen water bottle weren't enough to fill me up. Or maybe my brain needs more calorie power to get us out of this mess that everyone else has gotten me into.

"Sorry, I guess I didn't realize how hungry I was. We were

supposed to be on our way home by now."

Shannon raises a thin eyebrow. "Supposed to be?"

Maddy readjusts the blanket slipping off her shoulders. "Driver lost the keys. And we lost his little brother. Need to find both," she says, still chewing.

"Yikes. I do not miss being a teenager," Chrissy says.

The other women laugh along, as if they each hold tales of nights as rough as ours. They probably do. They're sitting here casually digging into a fancy, custom cake and drinking expensive champagne out of lipstick-stained plastic cups: you don't get to this point without having a few things going wrong and right in your life.

Then Chrissy rummages through a pile of clothes and tugs out a white T-shirt. It's another custom bachelorette one, with #Halliesgettinghitched on the front. "Either of you want a change out of those wet shirts? We have an extra one of these. Our friend ditched us last minute."

Behind us, Pam snorts. "Said her boyfriend had an art show. Dude literally writes his name on a bar bathroom stall door and calls it an installation."

Shannon and Chrissy laugh, but Hallie's face goes a little pink. "You guys, be nice. It's cool that Muriel is really supportive of her boyfriend."

Something in my heart twinges at her tone. She sounds like she's trying to convince herself of the truth of her own words. It's almost like how I keep telling myself that my fight with Maddy is a one-off, an easy fix.

Pam squeezes by to plop down next to Chrissy. The Airstream bounces with the movement.

"Take it from me," Pam says to us, slinging her arm around her friend. "Always choose your friends. Partners will come and go and sometimes just be selfish pricks who pretend that drawing on a bathroom stall door is a personality. The right friends are worth their weight in cake."

As if she's somehow looked into my soul, I stop chewing. My mouth is dry as I swallow down the Funfetti. Out of the corner of my eye, I peer at Maddy. Does she feel that prickle of unease too that we're still fighting?

Maddy's gaze is on the ground. But whether it's because of what Pam said, I don't know, and I'm not going to ask in front of a bunch of strangers.

"Maddy can take the shirt," I say, to redirect from the awkward too-real knowledge drop. "My jacket shielded me from the worst of it. I'm pretty dry."

"Thanks. At least we won't match anymore." Maddy sets down her half-empty plate and takes the shirt from Chrissy.

Shannon points her to the camper's tiny bathroom to dry off and change, leaving me to fend for myself for a few minutes. Hallie and Shannon don a couple flimsy plastic Orchards ponchos and step outside to vape.

I check my phone for reception. Only one bar. I try to unlock my phone to read my messages, but the damp from the rain messes with the face recognition (this is what I tell myself to avoid facing the fact that my makeup has melted in a way that has made me unrecognizable to my own phone). My stomach gurgles with a mix of anxiety and too much cake during the extra second and a half it takes to punch in my passcode.

No messages from the rest of our group, and no messages from my parents either. It's a little after 11:30 pm; my parents must trust I'm already on my way home. It's nearly impossible to gulp down the guilt. I should've called earlier to tell Dad that I won't be there on time to pick him up from his conference, that he'll have to stay at the resort a little longer. But I kept hoping the keys would appear, and now it's far too late: I need to figure a way out of the Orchards before calling home and admitting to Mom and Dad that I've messed up.

"The rain sounds like it's getting lighter. You might be able to search for your friend again soon," Pam says. She holds up a gold compact mirror to watch herself dab on eye cream.

"Well, technically it's our friend's little brother. He's fifteen. He disappeared with some supposed soulmate he met a couple of hours ago. Considering he's already shown a startling lack of common sense when unsupervised, we need to find him before he somehow makes this all worse," I say as I scroll to find a selfie of us I'd snapped earlier in the day, before everything went wrong.

I'm smiling and flashing a peace sign. Everett grins goofily next to me. Or maybe that's just how he smiles. Behind us, Nathan's face is a blur of movement. I zoom in on Everett's image. "You haven't seen him, have you?"

Pam and Chrissy lean toward me to check out my phone.

Chrissy gasps, then her eyes narrow. "It's that little shit with the stickers!"

I'm torn between shock that she recognizes him and amusement. Here I was thinking those stickers were altogether useless. They got Everett exactly what he wants: attention.

"Yes! I mean, he's a pretty good kid. I tried to talk him out of those stickers but obviously he's got an issue with good judgment. Where did you see him? And how long ago?"

I peer back at the closed door of the bathroom. If we have a lead, we can get out of here the second Maddy finishes changing.

"It was right before the rain started," Pam says, tapping her lip in thought. "So maybe fifteen minutes ago? Twenty? It's honestly hard to tell. We weren't really paying attention to the clock when we caught him trying to plant one of those stickers on this camper."

Chrissy shakes her head. "The rental company would've slapped us with some ridiculous fees. I'm already paying extra because of Muriel flaking."

Before I could apologize on Everett's behalf, Pam smiles. "Don't worry, we stopped him. Chrissy can pull off a really menacing-mom voice. Kid took off running."

"Wait, 'kid'? Was he alone?" I ask. "He's supposed to be off with this girl Kayla. Purple hair. We need to find her too."

Chrissy shrugs. "I didn't see a girl with him."

"Me neither," Pam says.

At least we have a lead on Everett, but it's hard not to deflate a little. We have to get Kayla too, like we promised her brother who is not so subtly taking our friends hostage.

The bathroom door unlocks, and Maddy walks out in her dry #Halliesgettinghitched shirt. Her wrung-out tank top is in one hand, and she's towel-dried and finger-combed her hair into something slightly less wild looking. "What'd I miss?" she asks.

I fill her in, and she stomps her foot like Everett's a bug under her heel. "That damn kid. All right. Let's go find him. Did you see which direction he went?"

"Toward the festival grounds entrance, I think," Pam says.

"So we're heading in the right direction. That's promising," I say to Maddy. She nods. "He's probably heading to the Forest Wheel, so once the rain—"

The main door creaks open and Shannon and Hallie pop their dry, rain-poncho-hooded heads back in. "Good news! The rain stopped," Shannon announces.

A small blessing, hopefully one of the first in a long line of things actually going right for us. "Thanks so much for the shelter and the cake," I say.

Chrissy hands Maddy a grocery bag for her discarded shirt, and we move toward the door.

Shannon lightly shakes the poncho she's just taken off. "Rain wasn't in the forecast, and we totally got suckered into spending twenty bucks on each of these things."

"Better than shelling out the fifty dollars for Orchards brand umbrellas," Hallie says with a sigh. "This place is so damn expensive."

As someone who spent sixty dollars on the world's saddest cheese sandwiches, I nod in agreement. I zip up my still-damp jacket and peer outside. The clouds look a little thinner, but the dirt floor has turned into the kind of mud that squishes at each step, like it's protesting your every move.

"Good luck finding your friend's little brother," Pam says.

"When you find him, tell him to quit that vandalism shit. It's not cool. Deposits for these things are enormous, especially on a festival weekend," Chrissy adds. She really can pull off a menacing-mom voice spectacularly.

I descend the Airstream steps first and tie on my wet, muddy shoes. The feeling of squeezing back into these blistermakers makes me cringe, but I'm not about to wander these wet festival grounds barefoot or in only my socks. Judging by the likes of Muscle Tank and the people we saw shotgunning beers, there are probably hot tubs' worth of vomit and other bodily fluids now sloshing around in this mud along with the rain.

Maddy angles toward the Forest Wheel. "Hopefully he's still in that area somewhere. Once we find him and drag him back to—"

A series of text notification chimes ring out from both our phones, and we tug them out of our pockets just in time to see a rare cell phone service bar flatten again.

Maddy frowns down at the group text we read at the same time. "Nathan's awake, but his knee's still giving him trouble. Kevin told him where we are. They want to know how the search is going."

"We'll update them when we find Everett. I'm not about being micromanaged by someone who lost the keys when so many of us had perfectly good purses and non-crowd-surfing pockets."

"Cut him some slack, Jana. I think he likes you. You saw how sorry he was for the key thing."

Does everyone know something about Nathan that I don't? But even if, in some alternate universe, I did want to prod into whether my friendship with him could be something more, we literally have a ticking clock working against us. So I respond with a curt "Well, he should be sorry. I should be home in my corgi-print pajamas, not wading around in festival filth."

Maddy shakes her head and puts her phone away.

Why did I hear more text notifications than she did? It's then that I see it.

Mom:

Call me.

FOURTEEN

SATURDAY, APRIL 23
11:41 pm

Worst-case scenarios tornado through my mind like a scene from the *Wizard of Oz* movie. A fractured plank of wood here, a cow, a rocking chair. Is Mom feeling well? Does Dad somehow sense I'm not on my way home? What fresh hell did Jackie bring upon us this time?

I force myself to draw a deep breath before dialing. I could be panicking for no reason.

But there's always that worry whenever you've gotten unexpected bad news by phone before. It might be nothing. Or it could be *something*.

And the last time it was *something*, I wasn't around.

"What's wrong?" Maddy asks, drawing me out of my head.

"I— My mom texted."

"Everything okay?"

"She just said to call her." The flitting one bar of reception taunts me. I raise my arm up toward the clouds and for a moment, I see a rare second reception bar before that too dances away. "But

I'm barely able to text. I haven't had reliable service since we got here. If only we were on our way back home, I could—"

"Maybe we'll stumble on a couple bars of reception as we walk?" Maddy says.

She doesn't seem to recognize the urgency in me reaching my mom. She's probably even side-eyeing me for trying to respond immediately, as if this is some function of the leash my parents have on me. Sure, Maddy doesn't share the same kind of tight-knit relationship with her own family, but she should know better about us, after our afternoon in the hospital parking lot. I don't *have* to call my mom back immediately; I *want* to. I want to be there for them. And I'm not going to waste time wandering the Orchards hoping for passable phone reception.

"I need to get somewhere higher up or maybe even away from these mountains altogether. But we're still without a car, and even if we had a ride, we can't just ditch the guys." As much as they may deserve it.

She scans our surroundings. "Maybe we don't need to get away from the mountain. Like you said, if we just get high enough, then . . ."

Her words fade as our eyes both land on the highest point in the Orchards.

"No, no way," I say, stumbling a step away from the Forest Wheel. "It's not even running. I think they closed it when the rain started."

"It wouldn't hurt to check. And it's where we think Everett's headed too, so we can kill two birds with one Ferris wheel."

"First of all, that is definitely not how the saying goes. Second, wouldn't that huge metal wheel be the worst place to hang out with these storm clouds around?"

She plants her hands on her hips. "Please. It's not that bad of an idea. Face it: we're not getting out of the Orchards until we get Everett and those keys, and we have no clue where either of them are."

I sigh, all my possible protests escaping with my breath. The biggest mental block is getting around the this-should-have-happeneds. They haunt me, the visions of the magical night I could have been having if everything had gone right—or at least not horribly wrong. There's no way to rewind. I can't hit the stop button and track back to grab Nathan's keys or try a different tack with Maddy hours, days, weeks ago. This record only plays forward, and I have to see it through to the end.

A CoGo lyric comes to mind, from a song I'd blasted through my headphones the many autumn nights I'd been kept up by Jackie's snoring: *Bet on me, honey. We won't always win, but we'll always have fun.*

I always say CoGo is the soundtrack of my life, and they've got at least one thing right: we won't always win.

Scaling a rain-slick, closed Ferris wheel on a stormy night: this for sure won't be fun. But my options are as waterlogged and defeated as Maddy's formerly-matching-me tank top.

The mud sloshes and sucks at my shoes with every step toward the wheel, as if even the earth is begging me to reconsider.

* * *

The five-story-high Ferris wheel towers above us. A strong wind blows, sending a few of the open-top cabins swinging and spilling gathered water right onto Maddy and me. The chain and sign at the top of the entrance ramp proclaim the ride a firm "Closed," as I'd assumed it was, but the sheer fact that Maddy and I are standing here means that we aren't going to let that stop us from checking.

"Where are the controls for this thing?" Maddy asks, glancing around.

I almost choke. "No way. We're not starting this up. Once it moves, security is going to surround us in a second, shutting it down and dragging us away. I . . . I'm going to climb."

Her eyebrow rises. "That doesn't really sound like a Jana thing to do. Are you sure that's a good idea?"

"It's not a good idea at all. You're the one who does all the acrobatics in cheer. The most athletic thing I've done lately is stand up on a swivel chair to get a book on the top shelf at the library. But I'm desperate, and the metal looks dry . . . um, dry enough."

"And remember, you don't need to get to the top. Just high enough to get a signal."

Of course I could count on Maddy to encourage this reckless, likely illegal course of action.

I gulp and shake out my limbs like I'm getting ready for a track meet. I purposely disregard the smile Maddy's trying to hide. She finds this hilarious, the turning of the tables rendering me the one who has to perform wild physical stunts. That day I stretched for the top-shelf book at the library, I thought I pulled something in my side. Not about to disclose that to Maddy right now though.

"Here." I slide off my backpack and hand it to her. "I don't need this throwing off my balance while I climb."

I glance down at my outfit through my sandpapery contact lenses, frowning at the cute but functionally useless shorts I'd chosen today. Why women's clothing has pockets barely big enough to hold two jelly beans is beyond me. I shimmy the phone into the next best place—my bra—then stroll up to the vertical-barred fence.

On the Ferris wheel, there's a mast with crisscrossing bars, almost like a ladder. This will be my best bet for climbing. I'm not fit enough to execute superhero-style leaps from spoke to spoke.

"Need help getting over this fence?" Maddy offers.

"Yeah. Would you mind?"

"When have I ever said no to helping you?"

Her comment lands on a sore spot, and I can't help the sarcasm that hits back. "Oh, I don't know, maybe when you were supposed to drive us to this festival."

I try to throw some playfulness into it at the last second, but the same way her attempt at a lighthearted response fell flat, my tone is off. It's more snark than silliness, and by the droop of her smile, she hears it too.

"You're kidding, right? Never mind my car isn't even working. You're the one who told me you were getting another ride."

And back then she was supposed to say, *No, no, I'll drive. Don't worry about it.*

But she didn't.

She instantly made plans with Tyler instead, just like how she roped him into the studying that she begged me to help her with. It doesn't matter that her Orchards drive plans fell through too and we ended up in the same predicament.

I know better than to piss off someone whose shoulders I'm going to leap off of, over a slightly rusty metal fence.

"Forget it. Lean down a little. How do you cheerleaders do this?"

Maddy bites her lip, as if she wants to say more, then stoops down and clasps her hands. "Put your foot here, and use it to push yourself up and over. You want to practice?"

My phone practically burns a hole in my bra with how many minutes have passed since Mom's text. "No, I'll be fine. I need to hurry up and make this call."

I scuff the mud off my shoes onto the makeshift metal ramp beneath us before planting my only-mildly-less-muddy foot in Maddy's hands as she instructed. Ill feelings or not, some sort of muscle memory takes over for her. Her hands are steady, her voice confident as she talks me through it. The bars of the fence are cool from the night air, and the top bar is damp with rain. Up, over, and I land with an unceremonious grunt and a whole lot of pride that I was able to accomplish this one act without cracking anything.

I begin to scale the Forest Wheel mast.

"When you're up there, keep an eye out for Everett," Maddy calls from below. She has her hands cupped around her mouth, like a bullhorn.

I reach for the next rung and force my legs to follow. About twenty feet up, I pause. My cell phone reception is still too spotty. I need to keep climbing.

"You're not scared, are you?" Maddy says. She must've noticed my pause but assumed it was fear, not function. "Just don't look down."

"I don't need a pep talk. I just need cell phone reception," I call back. I push myself to climb faster, the guilt as potent a motivator as adrenaline. "And how am I supposed to look for Everett if I can't look at the ground?"

Her answering snort is loud enough that I hear it from up where I am. "Channel that sassiness into getting your ass higher!"

Rather than respond, I focus on the ascent. It occurs to me that she really is a good cheerleader if she can motivate me like this even as we're sour at each other.

I don't know how long I'm climbing until I stop and check my phone again. And there they are: three glorious, steady bars. It's the best I'm willing to do. I can't bear another second with the lump of dread growing in my throat and threatening to choke me.

I wrap one arm tight against the ladder, securing the rung in the crook of my elbow. Then I tug out my phone and dial. I hold my breath as it rings, the fear of what Mom's calling for making it impossible to relax.

She picks up after three rings. "Hi, honey, you—"

"Hi, Mom. What's up? Is something wrong?"

My franticness is at odds with Mom's sweet greeting. "No, no. Just checking to see how you're doing. You almost home?"

A breath finally comes as I realize this is normal Mom stuff, not emergency your-world-is-falling-apart stuff. Too bad there aren't two types of ringtones based on the urgency of the message. "Oh, okay. Um, funny story: No, I'm not. Not yet."

"Jana . . ."

"Nathan misplaced his keys, but we should be heading back real soon. We're getting a hold of them any minute now. It's fine."

I fudge the truth because it's easier to hope for a miracle than admit defeat. In my mind, it's still possible that we collect Everett and the keys and speed out of the Orchards soon: that would be the fastest way out of this mess. I just need to get off the phone, down this Ferris wheel, and back to searching.

"What about your dad?" Mom says, panic in her voice. "How is he going to get home? You were supposed to—"

"I swear I'll be home as soon as I can! Then I can zip over and pick him up a little late." A promise I clearly can't keep because somewhere, in the expanse far below me, is a tiny set of lost keys.

"Have you told him this?"

"No, not yet, but—"

"It's nearly midnight! We let you go to the Orchards on the condition that—"

"I know, I heard you." The frustration bubbles up and an "I'm not Jackie" slips past my lips.

Mom pauses at my sister's name. "What's that supposed to mean?"

"It means I'm trying. I know I was supposed to be on my way home now, but things didn't really go to plan."

"This has nothing to do with your sister," Mom says.

How Mom is reacting to my very reasonable assurances right now has everything to do with Jackie and how she tornadoed back home and out again months ago. But this moment, clutching this ladder high above the festival grounds, is not the time to delve into that.

Mom continues. "We were relying on you tonight, Jana. I'm so disappointed."

The word crushes me: disappointment cuts differently than anger. "I'm really trying to fix this and get home as soon as I can. You know how far this place is."

Mom sighs then, and there's a heaviness to it that twists my heart. "So I—I guess I'll have to pick him up."

Plummeting from this Ferris wheel would hurt less than the realization of what I've done to my mom. I've put her in a nearly impossible bind. "No, Mom, you don't have to. If he can wait, I can still—"

"It's fine," she snaps in a way that makes it abundantly clear that it's not fine at all. "I have to. Your dad can't stay there. How embarrassing would that be if his boss found him sleeping in the lobby? Or if he got kicked off the premises?"

Tears gather behind my eyes, blurring the faraway lights. Mom is right, of course: Dad can't stay there. But it hadn't occurred to me that tonight's mess-ups would force Mom to face a feat that's been nothing short of terrifying for her since the accident. I didn't see any solution to this complex problem of rides to and from home, so I'd put off that dreaded call to her and Dad. Now it's too late for any of us to easily solve this mess. Mom has to do this because *I* failed. I didn't even give them the chance to avoid my failure.

I grasp for solutions. "Don't. He can get a rideshare. It'll be what, two hundred bucks? If I work extra at Callaway for a couple weeks and—"

"Jana, no. Enough." She pauses, and I imagine her staring at the kitchen ceiling, her shoulders drooping, her eyes on the brown spot that bloomed the last time it rained. "I have to go get Dad, and you have to get home."

"But—"

"Stay safe, honey. See you soon."

When I hang up, I feel like I flung my heart from the top of the Forest Wheel. The guilt is as strong as if my parents were here in front of me, calling me irresponsible and threatening to take away phones, cars, computers, everything. I'd give all those up willingly if it meant sparing Mom the task ahead of her, if it meant taking back everything I did to disappoint her so soundly. Something warm lands on my cheek—a tear. It's a good thing I'm so far up. No one can see how one short conversation caused so much damage.

"Everything all right up there?"

Maddy's voice rings out clear.

I peer down at her. How could she have possibly known something was wrong? "Yeah. She was just checking in."

"Okay." The word is loaded. There's more she wants to ask, and yet she doesn't. But maybe it's because I'm four stories up and yelling out a whole conversation would be a great way to attract security. "Anything from Everett?"

Wiping away a tear with my sleeve, I check my texts: nothing new. Of course I couldn't have expected that kid to check in with us. But then it dawns on me where he is checking in: Clippity. Everett's whole life goal, aside from finding love, is going viral. I pull up the app, eyeing the flickering service bars. I just need this to hold for another minute until I can see if he's posted. The sooner we get him and the keys, the sooner I can be home, minimizing the destruction I've wrought.

"Aha!" I scream when his face and that inane sticker of his fills my screen. "We might've just missed him. You see a sticker down there? By the 'this tall to ride' sign?"

Maddy lopes over to where the front of the line would be, and her fingers graze the sign. "Yup. There it is. Did that jerk say where he's off to next?"

On his video, he slaps his clown sticker onto the metal sign then flips the camera to grin and throw a thumb-and-pinkie-out shaka sign. Great, so he's a vandal and embarrassingly awkward, if not culturally appropriative. Thankfully, he's also attention seeking enough that he hints at his next sticker drop.

"To a bonfire!" I shout. As quickly as I can without jeopardizing my hold on this ladder, I twist around and spot the glow of a fire in the distance. "There!" I point in that direction.

From my perch, I can see the beginning flames of a bonfire in a small clearing where the parking lot meets the Orchards fence. Trucks and vans have begun parking in a circle, like old-timey covered wagons in the Wild West, creating a makeshift arena for what's sure to be the huge Saturday Orchards after-party.

It's then that the view of the Orchards festival grounds, in its neon and laser light glory, hits me. At this last set before the official festivities shut down for the night, crowds sway in unison in front of the outdoor stages, and people dance in and out of tents. The dark mountains loom behind it all, making us and even this giant Forest Wheel seem minuscule in comparison.

Surveying it from the peacefulness of where I cling to this mast, I have to admit that the frustration, pain, and unnecessary risk earlier might've been worth it, if not for what my coming to the Orchards forced Mom to do. Today's chaos put me at my most desperate. It drove me to attempt things I would've never done, like scaling an off-limits Ferris wheel just for cell phone reception. But I'd be lying if I said it wasn't damn beautiful up here.

I tuck my phone securely away in my bra again and descend. I spy a podium tucked in the corner and use that to launch myself back over the fence to join Maddy.

"The bonfire's just over there, in that corner of the parking lot," I say, wiping off the rain and nervous sweat from my palms onto my shorts.

"Ready to catch this kid and get home?" Maddy asks.

"More than ready." We head in the direction of the blaze.

SEVEN YEARS AGO
May 2

School Staff Incident Report

Student names: Madeline Parsons and Jana Rae Rubio, sixth grade

Date and time of incident: Tuesday, 11:50 am

Description of incident:

A sixth-grade student complained to a staff lunch monitor, Mrs. Gutierrez, that Maddy had pushed his lunch tray onto the floor on purpose. Accompanied by the student, Mrs. Gutierrez asked Maddy for an explanation.

According to Maddy, "[Student] started it. He kept asking if Jana was eating dog for lunch." Maddy considered this "super racist."

Jana confirmed Maddy's account and added that the complaining student had told Jana to "go back to wherever the *expletive* [she came] from" and accused her of spreading "Asian germs" at school. The complaining student did not deny saying this. Student actually repeated the statements in front of the staff lunch monitor.

Action taken:

Verbal reprimand of Maddy, Jana, and the complaining student

Allowed complaining student a replacement lunch free of charge from the cafeteria and directed him to avoid Maddy and Jana

Parents contacted?

Complaining student will receive a call home from lunch monitor explaining the unacceptable nature of his comments to Jana; recommend possible detention or further action if he repeats this behavior

No further action needed for Maddy or Jana

FIFTEEN

SATURDAY, APRIL 23
11:47 pm

On the ground, I can barely see the bonfire, but it's impossible not to move in the direction of the crowd. Maddy and I shuffle along, swept up in the current of people. We keep our eyes peeled for Everett. I'm warm from my climb, so I peel off my bomber jacket and shove it and my phone into my mini-backpack.

Maddy keeps her phone out and continually glances at it in between steps and dodges around stopped groups.

"Anything new from the group?" I ask. I don't know why I don't say *Nathan and Tyler*. As if simply speaking her boyfriend's name would somehow invite him to psychically invade our space.

Maddy shakes her head. "Not enough bars in this place. I'm trying to check on Tyler, but I don't think any of my messages are going through. Let's just grab Nathan's brother and get out of here. This isn't fun anymore."

I cast a skeptical glance at her and narrowly avoid stumbling over someone stooped to tie their rainbow combat boots. "Wow, now is the point of the night where you stopped having fun? I stopped having fun the second Nathan said the word 'keys.'"

Weaving through a group of girls fixing their makeup—at one am, but who am I to question their timing—I keep my eyes roving around the crowd. Someone has set up speakers in their red pickup truck and is blasting rap music, the heavy bass reverberating through the ground. People dance in place, plastic bottles and shiny aluminum cans in hand. Some have their eyes closed as if it'd help soak up the music more. Others laugh with their friends, slinging their arms around each other or sharing their drinks or smokes. On the darker edges of the crowd, where the light of the bonfire flames doesn't intrude, a few couples get handsy in a way that makes me extremely uncomfortable staring to make sure none of them are Everett.

The fashion here is across the spectrum. I catch more than a few hints of red plaid flannel, only to be disappointed that the wearer isn't Everett. A handful of folks are in string bikini tops, despite the night chill. Someone paired a puffy ski vest and a Speedo. I can't decide if that person's wardrobe choices are nonsensical or somehow ultra-prepared for whatever the weather may throw at them.

Maddy taps me on the shoulder. "Jana, is that him?"

I follow her outstretched finger to the other side of the bonfire, where Everett is having an arm-wavingly emotional conversation with Kayla. The mixture of relief and rage is overwhelming.

"Yes! And they're together! Now we can kill two birds with one stone. Or I mean return two people back to the tent. Alive. You know what I mean."

"Honestly, you had it right with that first instinct to 'kill,'" Maddy says with a frown. She forges ahead in the direction of Everett, jostling her way through the crowd.

I trail behind her and slip into the narrow path she leaves in her wake. But making our way through this mass is difficult. The music has changed to a high-tempo, grungy hit on the top-ten chart, and the dancing becomes chaotic. People shove and jump around, and I do my best to avoid getting trampled.

"Hey, wait up!" I scream to Maddy. Ahead, she's managed to squeeze past two people in matching green band T-shirts and is almost out of sight.

I brace myself and plow through, right behind her. People grumble and glare, but I don't have time to apologize. No way I'm losing another person tonight.

I've had my fill of trying to pick up every piece this group misplaces. All I came to the Orchards for was a good time watching my favorite band: I did not sign up for whatever rodeo this is.

Someone halts my already frustratingly slow progress with a hard yank of my mini-backpack, and I almost choke at the impact.

I whirl around. "What the hell?"

But there's no one behind me to confess to the offense, and all I've done is turned to face the people angry at me for shoving them on my way through. I turn my glare on the first person who makes eye contact.

"Did you see who pulled my backpack?" I ask the tall Indian guy with a goatee so precise he might've had it cut by laser.

He lowers the silver flask from his lips, and the glow from the stadium lights across the bonfire make the flask sparkle as he moves. "Did what?"

Around him, three friends snicker in a way that isn't malicious, but isn't purely kind either. So even if Goatee's friends aren't the ones who executed a sneak assault by mini-backpack, they did see something but are choosing not to share.

My jaw tightens. "My backpack!"

"Oh, for real? What happened to it?" Goatee asks, a very poor simulation of shock spreading across his features.

His friends laugh louder this time, emboldened by whatever they're sharing in their silver flasks, also matching. It's like everyone at this godforsaken festival is in a bachelor or bachelorette party or a roaming gang of partiers with a strict, matchy dress code.

"I don't have time for this. You could've just said no. Whatever. Screw you guys."

I move to catch up with Maddy again when an arm on my shoulder stops me. It's Goatee, and he's not as amused as he was a moment earlier.

"What'd you say to us?"

I shrug off his hand so violently I almost stumble over. "Back off. I was just asking you a question. You didn't need to be rude."

"I'm the rude one?" He raises an eyebrow, and somehow his

friends take that as a cue to murmur their agreement. "You know, your boyfriend needs to put you in your place."

My fists clench in reaction. Not that I know how to use them, but I need to channel that anger somewhere: now is not the time or place to try to make a point on behalf of feminism, especially when the intended audience is this drunk and I'm wholly without backup. I can't even begin to correct him on everything wrong with what he just said. Even if I had a boyfriend, the very idea that said boyfriend would put me in "my place" is laughable. I may tend to be a rule follower, but that doesn't mean I'm a card-carrying patriarchy supporter. And in the seconds that tick by as I'm tamping down my rage, Goatee and his friends have only begun to laugh harder, like they've won some argument on merit rather than my good judgment and, to be honest, sheer exhaustion.

Then I actually feel, rather than hear, Maddy's presence next to me. "Way to show off how tough you are, picking on someone alone in a crowd."

Goatee's face crumples in disgust. "Psh, she started it, accusing us of messing with her."

"Doesn't change the facts, jerk," Maddy says, wrapping her arm protectively around mine. "Let's get out of here, Jana. The company's better on the other side of the bonfire."

To the sound of Goatee's jeers, Maddy and I wind our way through the crowd. I'm thankful Maddy keeps our arms linked long after we've put some distance and people between us and Goatee.

"Thanks," I say, hopefully loud enough for her to hear me through the bumping beat of the new song. We may still be fighting, but that doesn't mean I shouldn't acknowledge the kindness she did.

"For what?"

"For coming back for me."

She smirks then, but not without a weariness about it. "God, Jana, haven't I told you? You can't get rid of me that easily."

The gloom around my heart starts to dissipate as this hint of the friendship I remember—the one I'm used to and have been trying so hard to get back to—beams through. Her words are a reminder that, at its root, our friendship is the same as it always was. We just need to do the work to scrub and peel away this mess that's been mucked on top of it.

As we near the other side of the bonfire, I try to squint through the flames. The familiar patch of red flannel is not where I'd spotted it earlier.

"Hey, do you still have eyes on Everett?" I ask, my heartbeat already speeding up in anticipation of the answer.

"No, I—I don't think so. Do you? He was right there, near that trash can!"

I look for Kayla's purple hair too, and nothing. "Damn it, they're gone. That obnoxious Goatee distracted us while they got away."

"They can't have gotten too far, right? Look how long it took us to get over here." She tugs her phone out of her jeans pocket then.

"Hey, I have two bars somehow! Maybe Everett does too. Let me see if I can text on the group chain to tell him to get his scrawny little butt back here."

She rapid-fire types and shoots out her text. I wait for the "received" chime to ring out on my end, to confirm that her text went through. But there's nothing but the bass and *yeah baby*s of the song.

"You sure it sent?" I ask Maddy after a moment.

She angles her phone to me. "Yup, no error messages. Says it was delivered. Oh, and there goes those two bars, back to one and . . . now they're all gone. Wonderful."

"Huh, it did go through. Then why didn't I get it?"

I swing my backpack around, and that's when I notice the top flap is unclasped. My heart thuds against my chest as I dig around through the main pocket. "My phone! I can't find it!"

I wad my bomber jacket up under my arm and comb the backpack pockets again. I pat everywhere on my clothes I could've stowed the phone, even my bra from when I was climbing and these useless jean pockets that barely hold a tube of lip balm. Nothing.

I choke back the tears. My one, very expensive lifeline to our group, to my family, is gone. If I thought my parents were going to be mad before, they will be livid when I've stopped responding to them altogether because I lost my phone. After everything that's happened tonight, I might claim Jackie's throne of "the bad daughter."

I can't think of any way this gets worse.

And then it does.

Maddy gasps as a text rings out, and she swings her screen back at me.

A message from *my* number on the group text, my own profile image grinning at me:

How much do you want this phone back?

SIXTEEN

SATURDAY, APRIL 23
Midnight

I blink hard before I reread the text on Maddy's screen, as if the words would somehow rearrange themselves into something easier to understand. My contacts may have shriveled to Death Valley–dry levels, but I doubt they'd mess with my vision this much as to form a whole fake text.

"I—I don't get it. Someone has my phone and they . . . don't want to give it back?"

There goes my trust in humanity, yet again. Though to be honest, this whole day has been humanity screaming a big "gotcha, Jana!" right in my face. I shouldn't have expected everyone around me to be nice, honest, or reliable. That's just asking for a heartbreak.

In a matter of taps, Maddy dials my phone and places the call on speaker. "We have one flickery bar of service. No way we're letting this go to waste." The second the line picks up, Maddy practically growls, "Who is this?"

To her vinegar approach, I add a sweeter, more civil "I'd really like my phone back. Please."

There's some muffled discussion on the other end, as if someone has stuffed my phone under a sweater to distort the sound.

"Hello?" I try again.

Another beat of muffled noise, then a deep, gruff voice says, "Text only" before the call drops completely.

I drag my palm over my face, and it comes off with smears of glitter and eyeliner again. I have no clue how I keep finding more makeup on my face after that much time in the rain, but I realize now that those girls who were touching up their looks at the bonfire had the right idea. They're going to gleam fresh and rested while I haunt these grounds looking like a damp raccoon.

The service bar jumps around again, and a minute later, a direct text is sent from my phone to Maddy's:

> Want the phone back? $300. Date Tent, second porta-potty from the left.

I'm as dizzy as I was when I looked down from my high-up perch on the Forest Wheel. "They're ransoming my phone?"

Then something between a gasp and a sob escapes me.

Maddy's eyebrows knit together as she considers the text and me. "How much you got?"

Defeat heavy on my shoulders, I lower my mini-backpack and fish out my wallet, which had thankfully escaped the thief's claws. A rock forms in my throat as I count and recount the small stack of bills. My and Everett's halo halo earlier left me with sixty-three dollars.

I glance up at Maddy then. I cringe at the idea of asking her for money—I don't want anything from her right now. We're not even in a good enough place for me to ask her to keep trailing me around the Orchards, solving problem after problem.

And of course she wouldn't just offer. Maddy's brain doesn't work like that, like mine: she isn't always looking for ways to fix things and lift us back into a sense of normalcy.

I clutch the bills tight. "Maybe the guys can lend me some cash."

At the mention of Tyler, Maddy whips her own wallet out. Interesting. She's all about smoothing the road when it comes to him, but not necessarily when it comes to me. I didn't think it possible, but my mood sours further.

"We don't need to walk all the way back and bother them," she says, plucking the cash from her wallet. "Okay, and I've got a hundred here. That leaves . . ."

As always, I do the math. "A hundred thirty-seven dollars short. I don't even have that much in my bank account, after buying this overpriced Orchards ticket."

I kick at the dirt on the ground, unreasonably enraged that the rain has caked it into a hard, cement-like floor. It would've been nice to at least stir up a cloud of dust or send a pebble flying, some physical destruction to match what I'm feeling.

Maddy coughs, and I finally take a good look at her. The rain has frizzed the little hairs around her face, and her makeup has all but wiped off too, probably while she was changing into that ridiculous bachelorette party shirt of hers. Without the thick black cat eyes and paint-by-numbers-meticulous bronzer and blush, she looks younger. And she looks tired.

Some of my anger at her melts away. Yes, I'm in an awful situation, but technically, so is she. She may not be causing actual harm to her family with every second she's out late at the Orchards like I am, but even her more hands-off parents are going to wonder where she is, especially if she's out with Tyler. And she just offered to help pay the ransom for my phone.

"I—" The beginnings of an apology start to form but then I can't remember what I'd be apologizing for. I'm not the one who keeps dropping their best friend for a boyfriend. Her helping me is really her helping *him*. And even if she is offering the cash because of our friendship, she still owes me after how she so unceremoniously ditched me, causing me to have to rely on key-losing Nathan. So I swallow the word *sorry* and instead say, "Thanks. I appreciate every cent toward getting my phone back."

She shrugs, like she's more than willing to ignore all the emotional undercurrents roiling beneath the fact that I just borrowed money from her. We're alike in that way at least—saving the fight between us for later, focusing on the other immediate battles at hand. "I know how much you need that phone. Your mom and all."

A memory flits back to me then, of when I begged out of that family party so we could go to the movie theater and I'd silenced my phone. Fast-forward through the missed texts and calls, the blur of a drive to the hospital, and the sounds of CoGo as we waited in the parking lot, in Maddy's car, for an update on Mom.

You bet I never had my phone more than arm's distance away from me since then.

Up until today.

I drag in a ragged breath. "I'm still short a hundred thirty-seven dollars. I don't know how—" A red plastic card in her wallet snags my attention. "You have your dad's ATM card?"

Her fingers graze the card. "Yeah, for emergencies."

I wait to see if she'll notice how desperate I am. Maddy uses her dad's card for the silliest things sometimes—it's her dad's way of being there when he isn't, I guess. If she can spend a hundred dollars on a gourmet chicken and waffles pop-up "emergency," she can take out a couple bills to help her best friend, can't she?

But just like earlier, her sense of heroism seems to stop just short of me. Maybe it's because I'm the one always repairing everything that she never thought I might need a hand here and there.

I hate that I need help paying off this ransom. When it comes to big expenses like the Orchards ticket itself, I don't mind working extra hours and somehow paring back expenses even more. This isn't a problem I can immediately solve myself though.

And as much as I dislike having to ask for extra cash, I loathe that I have to spell it out for my best friend. The words creak out, rusty from lack of use. "This is kind of an emergency, so do you, um, think we can use the card for the rest of it? You know I'll pay it back when I get my next paycheck . . . or two."

Maddy doesn't seem angry at my request, but she doesn't seem to notice how much it pains me to ask her for any sort of help either. "I guess I can. My dad will understand, if he even notices. If we can find an ATM, I can withdraw the rest of the money for your phone."

"That at least solves one of a thousand problems right now. The keys and Everett—"

"Can wait. Let's get your phone back first."

It's a relief knowing she's at least willing to stick with me on this side journey to get my phone. She could've easily shrugged this off as my problem, not hers, then went off to find Everett alone or, more likely, headed back to the tent to hang out with Tyler. This gesture isn't enough to snap us back into being the usual Maddy-and-Jana, but it's a start. I smile at her, and it seems to dispel the tension enough for her to joke.

"Besides," she says, a gleam in her eye, "we can just charge this hundred and thirty-seven dollars to Everett for making us hunt for him like this. Plus interest, however interest works."

My laughter is sad and thin, but it's real. "All right. Sounds like a plan." And plans are my version of a comfort blanket. I reclasp my mini-backpack closure and slip the straps onto my shoulders. "I think there was an ATM by the food trucks."

Maddy looks even younger when she smiles. "Thank God. I'm starving. I didn't want to say it in front of the guys but those cheese sandwiches you got us were disgusting, Jana. Seriously? Processed cheese?"

"If only I could get that sixty dollars back," I say, shaking my head. "That would put us closer to this three-hundred-dollar ransom goal."

"Well, let's charge that cheese sandwich dinner to Everett too. Plus a second dinner, because the kid owes us. Now, big questions: Which way is the ATM, and do you think people are still grilling this time of night?"

SEVENTEEN

SUNDAY, APRIL 24
12:12 am

The way the ATM spits out the ten twenty-dollar bills is the stuff dreams are made of. If I could make that lovely, mechanical sound my ringtone, I would. When I get my phone back.

Maddy hands me a hundred and forty to bring me to my ransom goal.

I hold the three hundred dollars so tightly my knuckles go white. I calculate the number of hours I'd have to work at the drugstore for this. I'd already put in extra time to pay for the Orchards and the end-of-the-year Disneyland trip our whole yearbook staff is taking. They say to spend your money on experiences, not things, but whew, experiences are expensive.

Then one bad decision after another led to me butting my way through a thieving crowd to an ungrateful, evasive fifteen-year-old. I still don't have that fifteen-year-old, I'm out three hundred dollars, and I'm indebted to a friend who I was barely on speaking terms with a day ago.

Financially, socially, familially: everything about my life feels wrecked.

Maddy doesn't seem to notice my quiet. She's focused on assessing the food truck options around us.

"I'm going to grab some garlic fries. You can text the phone thief while we're waiting so we can make the exchange." She unlocks her phone and hands it to me. There's a dinosaur charm dangling off it, from our Universal Studios trip ages ago.

If I already owe her money, one little extra request won't hurt. "Can you grab me a drink? A zero-sugar Dr Pepper?"

She rolls her eyes, amused. "That's oddly specific for an outdoor music festival that sold you processed cheese slices on white bread."

"Fine, fine. Just something with caffeine."

Maddy saunters over to the fry truck, and I navigate to the text thread between her phone and mine. I reply to the ransom message.

Have the cash. Will drop off in ten minutes.

Every character I type feels like a slap in the face. I pause, considering a follow-up text. I don't really know how this ransom thing works.

Where can we find the phone?

I wait for it to send, but the lack of cell phone service is thwarting us, yet again. Maddy is still ordering at the food truck, so I take a few steps away, holding her phone high above my head, hoping for just enough signal to send the message.

Finally, on my third circle around the makeshift food truck plaza—as if I'm some forlorn Jane Austen character taking turns about the room—I hear the tone of a successful message sent. Then I hear two receiving chimes. That can't be the ransomer answering that quickly, can it?

I lower the phone to eye level and check the texts, immediately realizing they're not for my eyes.

Tyler:

you all right? Still woozy but I can come help.

Tyler:

Everything okay with Jana?

I lock her screen. Is everything okay with *me*? What did he mean by that? What is Maddy telling him about me? The idea of them having some whispered conversations at my expense riles me.

It's bad enough that I've somehow been shelved second despite being Maddy's friend all these years. But to have her gossiping about me to the one who replaced me? What right does she have to relay anything about my life to him? It's a stomp on a heart that was barely beginning to mend.

I must be scowling when Maddy returns, garlic fries in hand, because her face twists in confusion. She hands me a room-temperature can of Coke.

"Fry?" She holds out the basket of fries topped with so much garlic I'm hit with a cloud of the scent a second after.

As delicious as those smell, I shake my head. I don't want anything more from her. She might turn around and blab to Tyler about how I ate all her fries or that I chew funny or something. I just want to get my phone and go home and erase this night from memory. "I texted the ransomers, waiting for a response."

I raise her phone overhead again, wishing for both a cell phone signal and Maddy to not realize she'd missed two texts while she was grabbing food.

She devours her fries in silence—that cheese sandwich really must have been awful and unfulfilling—and I sip at my warm Coke. My energy and my mood are waning, and I need every bit of caffeine this soda can offer. Three minutes later, the buzz of the phone vibrates down my arm. I hand Maddy her phone so she can unlock it. We read the text from the ransomers together.

> Leave the cash in the second porta-potty closest to the Date Tent. Will text you the location of your phone when you exit

I clench my jaw as I type.

> How do I know you'll actually give it to me and not just steal my cash?

> You can't just trust me?

FaceTime this phone and we'll leave the camera on so you can make sure it's staying put

"Seems like whoever took your phone is a pro," Maddy says through a mouthful of fries. "They thought this whole thing out."

My shoulders are so tense they could snap. The same thought had crossed my mind about the ransomers. They would've had to unlock my phone in order to text, so it's likely we're dealing with some tech-savvy, professional thieves. Or, more unnerving, someone may have been watching me unlock my phone the many times I checked my messages in the past few hours. Amateur or not, it doesn't matter who has my phone: it only matters that it's not in my hand.

"I just need it back. I hope they don't make this even more complicated than it is. I really don't have any choice but to trust them though. What if my mom's trying to reach me?"

Maddy wipes fry grease onto the hem of her bachelorette shirt. "Well, hopefully the ransomers won't answer."

I cast a glare at her. Unhelpful, yet again. "You mind if I text her from your phone? So they know they can reach me through you if something really important comes up." The only way this night could get even worse is if Mom's car somehow breaks down on the way to pick up Dad. I shut off that thought immediately, as if even dreaming it up might make it come true.

Maddy chomps on a fry and nods, so I shoot off a text to Mom, complete with another profuse apology for running so late. The sheer fact that Mom is likely in the car right now, fingers cemented on the steering wheel, means that she and Dad are going to be livid about my lateness no matter what I do. It's really my own sense of guilt that compels me to text them that apology: it makes me feel like I'm doing something good, even if they won't accept it. I toss Maddy's phone back to her once I've confirmed the message had been sent.

One problem temporarily fixed: a communication line to my parents has been somewhat reestablished. They wouldn't send me angry texts or yell at me over Maddy's phone at least. No, they'll wait until I get my phone back or I'm face-to-face with them, whatever time I end up dragging myself through the front door.

It buzzes, then she raises her gaze to mine. "Your mom texted back. You want to see it?"

I wince. While she was driving? No way this was anything positive. "Um . . . maybe later."

"You want me to just read it aloud for you?"

I can guess what the text says. I don't need visual confirmation of just how much trouble I'm in. But if I went through the effort of borrowing Maddy's phone to open that line of communication with my parents, it wouldn't make any sense to not use it. I nod.

"She says she's on her way to get your dad and that there's a spare key under the light-up snail statue in the garden."

It may sound like a simple status update to anyone else, but the guilt crashes into me hard. Even when I mess up, they're thinking of me, making sure I get into the house okay whenever I get home. Why can't I be there for my family the way they're there for me? It's a reminder of how royally I've screwed up tonight.

Dad is going to call me the second he realizes Mom is the one driving him, and he will not be happy. It's why I wasn't overeager about calling either of them to spill the news that I wouldn't be home as promised.

The next problem to solve: getting my phone back. As I double-count the cash, Maddy polishes off her garlic fries and searches for a nearby trash can.

"You done with that paper bag? I think I can put the cash inside that. I can't leave a bunch of bills out in the open in some porta-potty."

Maddy pulls out a handful of used napkins from the bag then gives it to me. It reeks of garlic. With a wistful sigh—that is so much cash for minimum-wage me—I stuff the ransom money into the paper bag and roll up the end to seal it.

We're silent as we head to the drop-off point. Yes, Maddy's helping me, but there's still a tension there that's hard to crack through. I wonder if she's doing this so she can get back to Tyler more quickly. The thought bubbles the warm Coke in my stomach.

At the Date Tent, I count off the second porta-potty. It's thankfully unoccupied.

"I'll stay over here and keep an eye out," Maddy says.

"For what?"

"I don't know. What if they're watching to see if you put the money in there, or what if they try to mess with you or something? Like lock you in there?"

"Why would they lock me in the porta-potty *with* the money?"

Maddy rolls her eyes. "I don't know. I'm trying to be helpful."

Something prickly in me responds to the irritation in her voice. She's not having a great night either, I get it. And not that I want to weigh who's having a worse time right now, but I'm clearly winning gold in the Misery Olympics. I'm about to enter the poorly lit disgustingness that is a music festival porta-potty. How I wish I'd borrowed the bachelorette party's flimsy, overpriced Orchards ponchos, as an extra level of protection against the filth.

"Um, thanks, I guess."

Maddy then proceeds to pull out her phone and check for reception, probably so she can check on Tyler. Some lookout she is.

Before I reach for the porta-potty door handle, I pause to fish out my bottle of hand sanitizer from my backpack first, to keep it in easy reach. I don't need to taint my belongings with whatever plagues are incubating in this corner of the festival. Then I hold my breath, pull my jacket sleeve over my fingers as a physical germ barrier, and open the creaky door.

Inside the porta-potty, the light from the overhead spotlights outside streams faintly in through the air vents above. Probably for the better—I have no interest in seeing every spot and stain around me. I try not to think about why it feels more humid in here than outside. Squinting, I do a quick survey of the small space for the most nondescript place to put this bag of cash. I settle on the tiny gap between the sink and the toilet bench.

The space appears a bit damp, and I tell myself it's water

splashed from the sink. Please let that be true. I give the ransomers the completely undeserved courtesy of putting down a paper
towel before setting the cash bag in place.

I don't inhale again until I've exited and taken a good couple
steps away, as if the germs and smells would've followed me out.

I drag in a breath as Maddy approaches.

"So what's next?" she asks.

"Does your phone have service? They're supposed to text or
FaceTime us once we've dropped off the money," I say as I douse
my arms in coconut-scented hand sanitizer. I don't care that
I smell like a cheap, tropical car freshener. I'd jump in a vat of
this stuff right now if it meant wiping away how disgusting I feel,
inside and out.

As I tuck the now-half-empty bottle into my backpack, a chime
rings out from Maddy's phone. She angles the screen to me.

> **Driver's side tire well of the blue tour bus parked at the
> service entrance to the Avocado Stage. Pleasure doing
> business with you** ☺

How dare they further taint this awful situation with an emoji.
"Where's the Avocado Stage from here?"

"It's at the far end, I think. They must not want any chance of
you running back and catching them getting the money," Maddy
says.

This added confirmation that it wasn't some punk kid trying
their hand at pickpocketing makes me angrier. This was some sort

of organized attempt to get money from me, to the point where they'd even planned out drop-off and pick-up areas like this.

"Coming to the Orchards was hands down the worst idea ever." I kick at the dirt beneath me. "Let's go get my damn phone."

Maddy FaceTimes my phone and the call connects, but with the phone's camera facing the shadowy inside of the tire well.

It's not until we've been walking for a couple minutes that I realize that Maddy not only hasn't said anything, but she's also trailing behind me a step or two. I don't stop, but I peek over my shoulder and ask, "What? What's wrong?"

She finger-combs back a tangled strand of hair from her face. "You've been cranky pretty much the entire time we've been here, but the Orchards hasn't been all bad, right? We got to see CoGo!"

"So that's what, one hour compared to the full night of just one terrible thing after another?"

"You're making it sound like this is literally the most terrible thing in the world to ever happen to you."

"It's kind of up there."

"You're so dead set on being unhappy, Jana."

Her words are a punch to the chest. "Excuse me?"

"We finally made it to one of the coolest music festivals in the country and all you can do is whine and complain about everything. Honestly, it's—" She catches herself then, and she shakes her head a tiny bit as if banishing the thought. "Forget it. Let's just get your phone."

I stop and whirl to face her. "No, no, we can talk now. Say what you wanted to say."

She crosses her arms and considers me. "It's like you always want to choose the harder way, like you're resigned to just never being happy."

"You think I don't want things to be easy?" Her words scrape a raw spot, and my first instinct is to lash right back. "That's ridiculous. Especially since I'm always the one fixing everything, taking care of everyone. It's damn exhausting."

"So why don't you just do stuff for you?"

"Because then what would happen to everyone if I did?"

Maddy doesn't quite comprehend how me prioritizing myself could backfire on her. She could lose out on her Emotional Support Jana, on her college roommate, but all she's thinking about is how I always seem to have a thousand responsibilities to my family.

"They'll be fine," she responds, reaffirming my suspicion that she doesn't see herself as one of the people I'm always saving. "But tonight, for example. You could stand to loosen up a little and take this for what it is: yeah, we're stuck, but look where we are!"

As if my body is physically opposed to what she's saying, my eyes stay glued on the path ahead. "Orchards or not, I still let my family down. You just don't get it. It's complicated."

"Complicated how? Your family seems to have all these requirements. I don't know anyone with parents as intense as yours. You need to push back on them once in a while, remind them you're your own person."

I could almost scream in response. I feel like we've run ragged over this line of thinking, and neither of us has budged. Maddy always says she understands, but I don't think she truly does. Maybe this time, when so much is broken, there's enough space between us for my words to leak through.

"It's not that simple, and honestly, you make it harder. Every time you invite me out and I even mention my parents, you either say straight-out 'just tell them no!' or you make this face, like you're doing right now," I say, pointing to the straight line of her lips, the wrinkle between her brows. "But I don't spend all this time and energy on family stuff because they're forcing me to: my family genuinely needs my help organizing our lives, and it's hard to ditch that for frivolous stuff."

"Frivolous stuff, like hanging out with me," she says slowly, filling in the blanks on her own.

"That's not what I meant." Not totally. "Look, I know my family comes off intense, but I *get* it even if I don't agree with it."

She scoffs then, and I wait for an explanation. I'm met with silence. That's apparently how far she's willing to go in smoothing over the cracks in the foundation tonight.

Still, I push. "What was that about? That little noise you made?"

Another pause, and I find myself disappointed and a little sad that our conversation has stalled. Sure, it's not a fun one, but it's a step toward getting back to our normal.

"It's nothing," Maddy says finally. "I'm just tired, and those fries I inhaled didn't sit well. We have a lot of other stuff we need to sort out tonight, so let's focus on getting your phone and dragging Everett and his little girlfriend back."

There's more there, simmering under the surface. But you can't pry words from someone's mouth, just like I can't shed the bad mood that's taken root so far into my bones it's coded in my DNA now.

For this past Valentine's Day, Maddy snagged some free tickets to an afternoon rom-com movie fest at a theater downtown. This is an event that, years ago, I would've jumped at the chance for. Six hours of coy banter and guaranteed happily ever afters? Who wouldn't love that?

But a quick look at the family calendar revealed a morning appointment that I'd committed to accompanying my mom to because Dad had to work that day. This would make the third straight weekend I'd had to bow out of an offer of something fun in order to help at home.

So when Maddy texted me a photo of the rom-com tickets, I didn't even want to bring up Mom's appointment. Instead, I sent a slew of texts explaining that I didn't really want to sit through six hours of rom-coms—a couple honestly looked awful, and the critic reviews agreed with me on those. I told her she could take someone else, i.e., her boyfriend, with my ticket. She eventually got the picture that I didn't want to go, or maybe she figured out the real reason and kept it to herself. Either way, I managed to dodge yet another Maddy lecture on how I need to stand up for myself more and do what I want. As if I don't want to make life at home easier for everyone.

It took a whole week for me pestering a more-silent-than-usual Maddy to learn that she'd been upset I didn't go with her, but she hadn't wanted to push it.

I get that same sense now, that she wants to push and is holding back for some reason. It's almost laughable, the restraint coming from someone who keeps telling *me* to fight for myself when she won't fight for us by talking through this with me. But I don't have the time for her to build up the courage to say something, nor do I have the patience to deal with someone who showed more enthusiasm about garlic fries than her best friend tonight.

"All right. Let's go," I say, letting the conversation drop like she asked.

We continue on to the Avocado Stage. The last of the music acts have played their encores and left the stages, and Orchards security have long since stopped anyone from entering the festival area. The din of crews moving heavy equipment and people plotting out the rest of their nights helps to disguise the silence between us, and we stick to the fenced perimeter of the Orchards grounds to avoid the more crowded walkways. This isn't the easy quiet that falls between friends who are comfortable together in a way that doesn't need words. It's the quiet that feels congested with suppressed outbursts and unexplained moods.

I don't know how to break out of it, so I stay silent and concentrate on making our way to the Avocado Stage. Each step brings us closer to my phone, home, and forgetting this night ever happened.

TWO MONTHS AGO
February 22

Maddy floats on her back, her face to the sun. Her hair fans underneath her and moves in slow motion with the water. That neon yellow one-piece would look ridiculous on most anyone else, but of course, not on Maddy.

"Come on in, Jana. The pool's heated and it's glorious." She draws out the word *glorious* like it's a satisfying back scratch, and for a moment, I consider jumping in too.

I stir the water around with my toes instead. A leaf gets caught in the current I create and submerges for a moment. "I bet, but the temperature isn't the problem. I've got a shift in an hour, and my hair isn't going to dry in time."

Maddy's cheer friend Serena invited a few folks over for an impromptu pool party at her place after school. I tagged along because I owe Maddy a hangout after bowing out of the rom-com fest last week, and because honestly, I was so curious about Serena's new house, courtesy of her mother's natural hair care start-up booming. I wasn't counting on being so tempted to join them in the water though.

"Can't you just skip today? That does sound like a nasty cough you have there," Maddy says, that mischievous glint in her eye. Maddy has perfected the art of faking a sick day.

I force a laugh. I told her I'm heading to work right after this and that's why I've got such a strict time limit. But in reality, I just didn't want to explain, yet again, about how I have to be home with Mom. Not for any tasks in particular—Mom's back to her teaching, cooking, cleaning, book-clubbing self—but she complained of a migraine this morning and I want to be available if she needs anything. She once missed a doctor's appointment because she didn't feel comfortable driving. Mom isn't one to call me and demand a ride, but if I'd been home and not hanging out in the yearbook classroom after school that day, I could've easily chauffeured her to her appointment. Plus I have a ton of homework to catch up on, thanks to my real, newly rearranged Callaway Drug shifts.

"Nice try," I say. "But that Orchards ticket isn't going to pay for itself."

She exaggerates an exhale and dips her head underwater.

I take a gulp of the cold root beer I grabbed from Serena's fridge. The condensation drips off the bottle and onto my rolled-up pants on this unseasonably warm February afternoon. Across the pool, Serena and three other cheerleaders slather on another layer of sunscreen as Serena's girlfriend tries to sync her phone with a speaker camouflaged as a rock. A few more people have trickled in since I claimed this corner spot, and they're in the kitchen scoping out the beverage selection.

A backpack drops next to me, and I glance up to see who's joined. Against the backdrop of the afternoon sun is Tyler. He's in the black polo shirt and khaki cargo shorts he calls his unofficial uniform as school photographer.

"Hey, Jana."

"Hey."

"You going in?" he says, with a nod at the pool. He's already in the process of kicking off his shoes.

I shake my head. "Nope, not today."

"Cool."

"Yup."

I tuck a strand of hair behind my ear and peer across at the pool, squinting as if I'm looking for someone. Serena's girlfriend has successfully paired her phone with the speaker, and a sugary pop anthem from last summer rings out.

Tyler takes the hint from my fake-distracted body language and spends the next minute in silence as he hurries off his socks and tucks them into his discarded shoes.

And thus go nearly all my conversations with Tyler. Despite being in a few of the same classes over the years, we just haven't found anything to connect on other than Maddy and the occasional chitchat on what cool new movie might be streaming this weekend. Unfortunately, our tastes diverge on what we consider "cool." For example, he apparently had a horrible time at that Valentine's Day rom-com movie fest he attended with Maddy last week. I would've loved every second of it, if I'd been able to go.

Maddy saves us from our awkwardness by coming to the surface. A wide smile spreads across her face.

"Tyler, you made it!"

She swims over to the edge and grabs onto the concrete. Tyler squats down to plant a kiss on her forehead.

I take this as my cue to pack up. I exaggerate a show of looking for my car keys. "Well, I'd better get going. You know how my new supervisor is."

Maddy casts me a sympathetic gaze. I've complained enough about Callaway Drug's newest, rule-enforcing addition to the managerial team that Maddy doesn't question my excuse this time. "You have to leave right now? You sure you can't stay at least a little while?"

Her question is so sincere that I actually feel guilty making excuses to head home. It's been a while since Maddy and I have spent time together after school like this, and it might be a good chance to get to know Tyler in a setting where we're not rushed around campus by school bells.

Tyler unloads his pockets, depositing his wallet and keys on his backpack, underneath his folded-up polo shirt. "Yeah, I think I saw the pizza delivery guy pull into the driveway right behind me, if you're hungry."

For a moment, they both look at me like they expect me to stay. And to be honest, I want to. I'm exhausted from juggling academics, work, and home responsibilities this semester, and I'm due for a nice afternoon off. I reach for my phone to check the time—maybe I can squeeze in a slice or two of pizza before jetting off—and notice a text message.

"You okay?" Maddy asks.

I didn't realize I was frowning. "Oh, yeah. It's Jackie. Something about forgetting something at home and needing it shipped to her."

And just like that, reality comes seeping in again. Outside of this welcome, sunny bubble I've been inhabiting for the past few minutes, there's a world of schedules and obligations I can't dodge without having to answer to my parents, bosses, or teachers. Jackie caught hell for her momentary detour from the successful collegiate life she was supposed to be living, and no way was I going to follow her example and incur the same wrath.

I sigh and let the dream of an idyllic afternoon in the pool slip through my fingers.

I take my feet out of the water to let them air-dry before pulling on my socks. Tyler joins Maddy in the pool. Apparently, his cargo shorts are swim shorts too? Again, I am in awe of how multipurpose men's clothing apparently is, in comparison to anything they have in the juniors' section of the department store. Someone brings a pizza over to the side of the pool, and Maddy and I exchange quick text-you-laters before she doggy-paddles away for a slice.

As I tie my shoes on tight, watching my best friend and her boyfriend playfully debate over whether pineapple on pizza is a good idea, I can't help but feel like there's more than just a few yards of water between her and me these days. It feels like an ocean, and we're drifting farther apart because of some thrashing, immutable force of nature.

The thought follows me to my car, like a shadow I can't escape. I turn up CoGo as loud as my eardrums can handle on my way home. I keep thinking I hear waves in those quiet moments in between songs.

EIGHTEEN

SUNDAY, APRIL 24
12:42 am

Slinking around a dark tour bus at one in the morning feels
so wrong. It's relatively quiet here, on the opposite side of
the Orchards from the campground and the bonfire. Too quiet,
perhaps. The calm doesn't necessarily mean the bus's inhabitants
are asleep. If they're anything like the rest of the festivalgoers, they
have plans to party until dawn, and I have no interest in alerting
them to my presence as I search for my phone.

Fireworks boom and crackle high above, and gold sparkles
shimmer against the dark storm cloud on its way out. The sound
makes both Maddy and me jump. I practically pancake myself
against the side of the tour bus.

"Relax, Jana, it's just fireworks," she says.

Tell that to my racing heart that assumed there was some sort
of anti-theft cannon mounted to the bus.

"Great, so the Orchards is hell for both me and local dogs." I
peel myself away from the cold metal of the bus. The driver's side
is straight ahead, and I creep over to the wheel well. I squint to

see in the shadows. Another round of fireworks booms, and in the faint pink light I see a glint against a glass screen: my phone.

I reach around the tire and grab it, and I'm so relieved I could cry. I don't even care that my arm is smeared with grime from the wheel well and that my phone is only at 46 percent battery—I'm the kind of person who reaches for a charger the second it dips below 60. I'm just overjoyed to have one fewer problem tonight. A tear starts to roll down my cheek, and I wipe it away with my forearm before I rise from the dirt.

I immediately end the FaceTime the thieves had used as assurance that they were the honorable sort—well, honorable for thieves. I'm out three hundred dollars and whatever my exorbitant cellular data bill will be after that extended video call.

Then it hits me that the FaceTime never once petered out, despite the communications black-hole nature of this place. As if the universe knows it owes me, I magically have two shaky bars of cell phone reception. At least tonight's runaround led me to the one, ground-level area that isn't a dead zone.

"No calls from my parents," I tell Maddy, "and look who finally responded to my Clippity DMs!"

She bumps her shoulder against mine in a rushed attempt to get close. The harsh way she whispers "Everett!" reminds me of a movie supervillain with a vendetta against the hero for foiling their plans, yet again. "He says he's heading back to the bonfire. Not even an apology or anything. I hate that kid."

"I'll hate him less when he pays for my phone ransom. In cash, not those gross stickers he has."

Maddy draws back. "So to the bonfire then?"

"Yeah. Though it's hard to leave this precious two-bars reception area. I should probably call my parents first."

"Why? They know you're here."

I run my hand through my hair, and though I know we come from vastly different worlds in terms of parental expectations, I let her convince me this time. "I guess I don't have anything new to report, since we're nowhere closer to getting the keys back and heading home. Okay, to the bonfire then. If we get there early, it might be easier to spot him approaching rather than picking him out of a crowd, Where's-Waldo style."

I don't pocket my phone this time. I grip it hard, so someone would have to physically knock me out and pry it away from me if they wanted it. I don't have another three hundred dollars, or hand sanitizer, for a porta-potty drop-off.

"You know, if we wanted to get there even faster, we passed by a golf cart on the way here. And there wasn't anyone around," she says, an amused glint in her eye. This lightheartedness may be her olive branch.

I keep my voice serious. "We are not stealing a golf cart."

"But—"

"Do you not remember how intensely we were hunted for two water bottles? They'd Mad-Max-chase us for a stolen golf cart. No thanks."

"For what it's worth, you would look great with a shaved head like Furiosa. You've got the skull structure for it. I don't."

I sigh, though the corner of my lip ticks up. "You are missing the point. Get walking, Parsons."

I poke her in the back, and she trudges forward as dramatically as if she were walking the plank. Now that I have my phone again and a lead on Everett, the gloom over me is finally dissipating. Contrary to what Maddy thinks, I don't *want* to have a bad time here, and these are steps in the right direction.

By the time we get to the bonfire, the blaze has grown. The rap and top-ten music has been replaced by some early 2000s rock, and the couples who were getting hot and heavy at the fringes of the crowd seem to have taken their romantic overtures somewhere more private. It's easier to weave through the crowd now, though I still keep my claw-grip on my phone. I turn my mini-backpack in front of me so it sits on my chest, another anti-theft measure in case someone tries to root around in it again and steal my empty wallet or precious hand sanitizer this time. After seeing the inside of that porta-potty up close, that hand sanitizer is worth its weight in gold.

Maddy and I find a relatively empty spot next to a stadium light that's been switched off. It's uphill from the bonfire, giving us the slightest higher-ground advantage in our search for Everett.

"Why would they even have this light here but not have it on?" Maddy asks, tapping at the rubber wheel with her shoe.

"Maybe someone turned it off on purpose. It would probably kill the vibe, right? Having industrial lights just glaring down on everyone."

A small smile flits across her lips. "Wow, who would've thought you'd care about vibe? I thought you'd launch into some lecture about safety first."

"Oh please, I may have intense parents, like you said, but I'm not that boring, am I?"

The look she gives me tells me she wants to say yes but is being nice. Maybe it's the win of the recovered phone and the resurging hope for a not-terrible rest of the night, but instead of staying angry, I laugh. "Well, it is nicer without the lights. You can kind of see a few stars in between the clouds. But yes, it's still a safety hazard. Someone could trip on a rock or passed-out partygoer. And that light probably would've driven away my phone thieves, saved us three hundred dollars."

"Probably would've driven away Everett too, if he was trying to sneak off to some dark corner of the Orchards grounds with his little girlfriend."

"You know, that's a good point."

She smirks. "You say that like you're surprised. We have already established that I can make some very good points, Jana."

"Sometimes I forget. You did try to get us to steal a golf cart like fifteen minutes ago."

"Um, you can make pretty bad decisions too. You're the one who made us volunteer for that beach cleanup the day after that international volleyball tournament."

"How was I supposed to know about those mountains of discarded protein bar wrappers and sunblock samples? I thought we'd be picking up an empty bottle or two or cutting up soda can rings to save seagulls."

"We saved seagulls from getting bulked up off protein bars."

The laugh bubbles up in my core and cuts through the thick

layer of anger. It feels like a turning point in our fight, finding that we can joke with each other again.

Maddy chuckles at her own joke too and sits on a small, low platform next to the stadium light generator. She scoots over so I can join her.

It's nice to relax my legs after trekking across these festival grounds and scaling a Ferris wheel. A hint of soreness spreads through them, and for a second, I actually regret not stealing that golf cart. You know it's bad when I regret not following Maddy's definitely illegal lead.

Since getting my phone back, it's started to feel like Maddy and I are on the road back to lunches together and swinging by each other's house unannounced like normal. And that leads right to us carpooling up to our shared dorm room at Santa Clarita, graduating together, getting apartments in the same high-rise then cookie-cutter houses in the same suburb, and being the old ladies at the nursing home who sneak gin and speak entirely in inside jokes.

Across the way, someone throws a glass bottle into the bonfire, and from the immediate flare, we can all tell it was alcohol. Luckily, the guy's friends drag him back before it ruins anything more than his newly singed eyebrows, but the sound of shattering glass seemed to jar people. A few folks back up from the bonfire, ready to leave altogether.

Next to me, Maddy pulls out her phone to check the time.

"Nothing from Everett yet?" I ask. We're back in the black hole of cell phone reception, but I trust him to show. Which probably goes to show how tired or foolish I am, because he really hasn't done much to prove his trustworthiness so far.

"Nope. Where is this damn kid?"

"He said he'd be here. I'll try to DM him again and let him know we're at this stadium light. Hopefully I'll get enough service for the message to send."

I yawn as I type out a message. It takes three whole minutes before the tiniest reception bar flits onto my screen and a whole other minute to confirm that the DM sent. I stretch back, hoping to infuse some energy into myself. The late night is catching up with me.

Maddy glances at me. "Why don't you close your eyes for a couple minutes? Leave your phone out in case he responds, but I'll watch out for him."

I was raised to be gracious even though I might really, really want something. "You sure?"

"Yeah. Red plaid shirt and a fanny pack, right? I'll wake you up in fifteen minutes."

At this point, I wouldn't even have the energy to argue with her if I wanted to. Running around the festival grounds and basically holding everyone and everything together has drained me completely. I hand her my phone, use my mini-backpack as a pillow, and let my eyes drift closed.

The pulsing bass of the music and the radiating warmth of the bonfire lulls me to sleep.

NINETEEN

I dream of our Monday morning break before third period, when folks were taking the extra minutes to lounge by their lockers, copy their friends' homework, or scarf down sugary granola bars purchased from price-gouging vending machines.

Maddy's locker is a few down from mine, so running into each other was unavoidable. After she traded a couple books out of her backpack, she sauntered over, either determined to smooth things over or willing to sweep away how broken we'd all left it the day before.

I kept my face buried in my locker, hoping she'd take the body language hint and keep walking.

She didn't. "So you think I can swing a B minus?" Along with a nervous smile, she wore a powder-blue T-shirt from cheer camp over the summer. She'd cut off the sleeves and tied the bottom hem so it sat at her hip. More of that effortless Maddy Parsons glamour. People would've thought I'd had a throwdown with a paper shredder if I tried that look.

Dream-me found a hair tie at the bottom of my locker and was trying to wrangle my hair up in a ponytail. The tie snapped and I remember the sting of it against my wrist. And I remember exactly how I responded to Maddy then because I didn't want to be around her yet. I didn't want to relive the way she completely second-placed me at the coffee shop. I'd tried to come to her rescue, and she didn't need saving at all. She didn't need *me*.

"I don't know, Maddy. I wasn't there studying with you."

Looking back, it's easy to notice the impatience of my response and the tight line of my lips, the way I didn't return her smile and how it made hers fade.

Sometimes, in that deep, uncontrollable space in dreams, there's a moment when things suddenly twist and morph into a nightmare, and you're powerless to stop it.

This was that moment.

What I'm reliving doesn't seem to be a dream, but a memory, replaying in my mind so vividly I can almost smell the new fertilizer they'd laid down on the grass by the gym.

Maddy angled her head. "What's up? You all right?"

I almost scoffed at how thoughtless that question was. "Um, no? Not after you called Tyler to horn in on the study session you swore you needed me for."

"I did need you! We could've all studied together. Oh, and you still haven't said sorry for so rudely ditching us like that."

"Me? You're the one who *rudely* dragged me away from everything on Sunday just to watch you and Tyler make kissy faces at each other. No thanks."

Maddy hiked her backpack up higher on her shoulder. "I was panicking, and I didn't know if you'd actually show."

I slammed my locker shut and tried to head to class early to end yet another repeat of that conversation, but steps pitter-pattered near me. Maddy's hand clamped around my upper arm. I tried to tug it away but she's stronger than I am: anyone who tells you cheerleaders aren't real athletes is dead wrong.

"Jana, what the hell? I'm trying to talk to you, and you just walk away. God, you've been such a bitch lately."

"I'm surprised you even noticed me being anything. It's not like we hang out one-on-one all that much anymore."

Her shoulders tightened and rode up an inch. "You know that's not fair. I've had a lot going on with cheer and ASB."

"Funny. You had cheer and ASB before and still had time to be friends. I wonder what changed and if it rhymes with soyfriend."

Nearby, a locker clanged shut. We stayed silent.

We keep fighting about this, and we can't seem to break out of this cycle. Her not responding to my texts, forgetting plans, or maybe just pretending to forget them. But she always apologized eventually, and we would make plans again, rinse, repeat. But one Friday movie or smoothie run can't mend everything, and at this point, we were running out of thread.

"What about you, hm?" she asked. "Between all those hours at work and you running home anytime your parents beckon, you're not easy to pin down either."

"That's different! Honestly, it's like you're so ready to drop me anytime Tyler looks your way."

She shifted her weight. "Not true. We're literally going to the same college together, Jana. We'll even be roomies! I'm making college plans with you, not him."

"But it's like we barely even talk right now. What will rooming together fix? Hanging out with empty space in Santa Clarita is the same as hanging out with empty space here."

She crossed her arms, covering the white decal on her DIY-modified shirt. "Everything's so busy right now and I thought you, of all people, would cut me some slack."

A little bit of guilt sliced through me then. Maybe she really was having a hard time and in my stubbornness, I hadn't noticed the signs. But I was already so angry that it was easy to steamroll over the guilt. "Well, lucky you, you've got Tyler now. He can help you with all of"—I waved my hand in the air because I sincerely didn't know what busy stuff she was referring to and my snarkiness didn't leave room for me to ask—"whatever."

Her jaw tightened. "I don't know why you hate Tyler so much."

"I don't hate him! But who you've become ever since you started going out? It's like you're a different person sometimes, not the same Maddy you were when we first became friends."

"It's not a bad thing to be different than when you were in middle school. If there's a problem here, it's you, Jana." She took a step back, nearly running into a freshman strolling by, and angled to turn away from me. "You're all hard edges and straight lines. It makes you so tough to talk to, like I can't tell you anything without you pointing out everything that's wrong with it, with me. I swear, ever since your mom's accident, it's like you don't even know how to have fun anymore, and you can't be bothered to learn."

Her words blindsided me. She'd nudged me in the past about loosening up and putting my own happiness first, especially when it came to how seriously I took my responsibilities to my family. But this wasn't like before: this attack felt personal and long held.

My reaction to pain was to inflict it right back, even if it hurt me too. "Since my mom's accident? The one I missed all those phone calls about because you dragged me to stalk some crush? I could've been there to help her if you hadn't been so damn selfish, just like you're being right now. Seriously, how long have you resented me for focusing on someone other than you?"

She blanched. "That's not what I meant. I don't resent you or your mom or—"

I didn't want to hear her explanation. Bringing up Mom's accident in such a petty way like that was a low, devastating blow. I wasn't going to stand there while she tried to convince me that it was my problem for not understanding her. "You know what? Have fun with Tyler at the Orchards. I'll get my own ride. I have zero interest in getting stuck in a car with the two of you."

She paused mid-turn, her face crumpling for a moment before she wiped away any sign of emotion. "Fine. Suit yourself. More room for me and him."

I lifted my chin in response. It was supposed to be a move to show strength, confidence. But it occurs to me now that it just left my neck exposed, ready for the blade I didn't see coming.

Maddy stared at me, the intensity of her gaze unnerving. We've had our fights before, but this felt different. This felt like something had fallen and we were just watching it tumble down to shatter against the earth. We expected each other to catch it but neither did. "Fine."

"Fine," she repeated.

Years' worth of friendship cracked and broken down to one-word responses.

The bell rang, and she turned toward her third-period class, art, and I to comp sci.

We avoided each other all week, which wasn't hard, given that we barely met outside of class these days anyway, but I still felt the absence.

The weekend and the promise of the Orchards loomed ahead. It had been rash of me to opt out of riding with her and Tyler, but I wasn't about to beg her to let me back into her car. She needed to apologize for how inconsiderate and downright mean she'd been. I'd told her exactly why I was angry, and she responded by calling me hard to talk to and not fun.

How do you stay friends with someone who thinks of you like that?

My anger simmered for days, but it dulled when Nathan said I could ride with him. I thought time away from her would let us cool off enough to eventually talk to each other and patch everything up.

But even in the uncertain, fluid space of a dream, I get the feeling that nothing is fixed, that ignoring what's broken for too long can render it irreparable.

FOUR MONTHS AGO
December 3

Maddy's whole car rattles as the door shuts behind Jackie. From the front passenger seat, I wave at Jackie's friend Cody, who reeks of whatever sugary alcoholic beverage they both overindulged in tonight.

"Thanks for picking her up," Cody says. "I would've let her stay, but my bed is covered in a mountain of jackets."

Cody's blue eyes are bloodshot and a little distant, and I'm glad neither they nor Jackie considered getting behind the wheel tonight. And that's even considering how livid I am that Jackie called, sloppily demanding a ride, while Maddy and I were in the middle of our Friday night bubble tea date.

Jackie answers for me as she clicks her seat belt closed. "See, I told you she'd come. Jana is so reliable!" She gropes forward then, trying to pinch my cheek like I'm a toddler. But between her drink-induced clumsiness and the fact that she actually can't see my face, she ends up just smacking me on the nose. Her hands are sticky and I don't want to think about what's caked on there.

In the driver's seat, Maddy suppresses a laugh but wisely decides not to comment.

"Hey, drink some water," I call after Cody.

They're already on their way back into their apartment, where, judging by the music and the laughter flooding out the front door, the party is still going strong. They don't turn around but they clumsily lift up their arm, the universal sign for "I hear you, but I really need to keep my eyes forward or I'm going to throw up."

Maddy puts the car into drive. "Where to?" she asks.

"Straight home," I answer, just as Jackie blurts out, "Anywhere but home!"

I whirl around to glare at her. She's in her full face of party makeup, which she learned how to do through Clippity tutorials. It makes her look years older, which only highlights how ridiculous it is that she's asking her little, high-schooler sister and her friend for a ride.

"Maddy's being real nice about playing designated driver here," I say. "We're not a rideshare. We're not taking you to another party."

Jackie brushes a sweat-dampened strand of long black hair back from her face. "I don't want to go to another party. But Mom and Dad can't see me like this. They'll get so mad."

I lower my head. She's right. It's still early in the evening, so our parents will likely be awake, plopped on the couch, catching up on whatever latest HBO show they're marathoning. They'd be livid if Jackie stumbled through the door in this state, and I won't get an ounce of sleep once they start arguing about her leaving school and not making anything of herself.

"How about the hoagie place? They're open till midnight," Maddy offers.

To the horror of my eardrums, Jackie screams, "Yes! Hoagies!"

I cast a sideways glance at Maddy and mumble an apology. A wide grin on her face, she's already selecting the hoagie place address—it's one of her "Favorites"—in her phone's map app.

"I'm glad you find this amusing," I say in a low voice.

"You kidding? It's a nice change of pace from our usual Fridays. And you know I'm always finding excuses to get hoagies."

In the back seat, Jackie rummages through her purse and yanks out her wallet. "Dinner's on me!"

Maddy laughs. "Free hoagies? I'm glad you're back, Jackie."

That makes one of us. I don't voice that sentiment aloud.

"With a strawberry milkshake," I say. "One each. You owe us, Jackie."

My crankiness must ring loud and clear because Jackie leans forward and drapes her long, bare arms across my and Maddy's seats. "Gotcha. Though it'd be supercute to have you two sharing one big milkshake with two straws, right?"

"Oh god, Jackie, stop!" As if I wasn't already mortified enough from asking Maddy to drive across town to pick up my drunk sister, Jackie has to ratchet up the embarrassment.

"Come on. You know how lucky you are to have each other? Making friends is, like, really, really hard."

My eyes roll at my sister's attempt at eloquence. "Thanks. But can you lean back a little? I don't need you throwing up on me. Or anywhere in Maddy's car."

Jackie giggles as if I hadn't just made a completely sincere request. "Just saying, whatever you have here"—she thumps her arms on our seats in emphasis—"you need to hold on to. Everyone in my engineering program was a big, pretentious jerk, waiting to tear you down the second your guard wasn't all the way up."

There's a sadness in her voice that lessens my crankiness. Jackie doesn't talk much about what brought her home from college mid-semester, but if this is even a hint of what she went through, supersocial Jackie must've been in her version of hell.

She slumps back against her seat and yawns. "Hold on to it, okay?"

"Fine, okay, we will," I say, mostly to shut her up. I already know how lucky I am to have a friend like Maddy, and I don't need my sister too-loudly proclaiming it and making this whole situation even more awkward than it is. Then I notice Jackie blink a little too slowly, her bright white eyeliner illuminated by the headlights of oncoming cars. "Hey, don't fall asleep, you owe us hoagies!"

"Put on some music then!"

Without even taking her eyes off the road, Maddy hands me a cable linked to the dashboard. I plug my phone into Maddy's car—I'm in here so often that Maddy programmed a whole profile for me—and find a playlist we all can agree on. Or that at least Maddy and I can agree on. Jackie doesn't get a say, not until she coughs up those free hoagies.

I press play, turn up the volume, and Maddy and I sing along to *Maddy and Jana's Intro to Newcomers and Goers Playlist* like no one else is in the car. Then we guzzle down our large strawberry milkshakes, one each, courtesy of Jackie, who falls asleep with her forehead down on the round concrete table outside the hoagie place.

TWENTY

SUNDAY, APRIL 24
3:14 am

The sense of something crawling across my cheek wakes me. A bug? I hope so. I am incapable of dealing with a rodent getting up close and personal with my face. I shoo whatever it is away and yawn, my lungs fill with enough cold, fresh air to draw me out of this much-needed rest. As my surroundings creep back in through my senses, I'm immediately struck by the relative quiet, the chill of everything. I'd fallen asleep to a roaring fire, bustling crowd, and bone-thumping music.

I force my eyes open, my dry contact lenses resisting me yet again, like they too want to punish me for missing curfew. Sleeping in these is a huge don't, but then again, so is falling asleep at an outdoor music festival you've accidentally gotten stranded at, long after you swore to your parents you'd be home. I fight the urge to rub them, because I really don't need a rotten cherry of "scratched cornea" on top of this mayhem sundae.

Too slowly, everything comes into focus, and my stomach plummets. The once raging bonfire flickers at a fraction of its size.

More than half of the earlier crowd is gone, likely having moved their parties into tents and campers much more comfortable than this cold metal platform. I'm certain I was asleep much longer than the fifteen minutes Maddy had allotted me.

Maddy.

This is all her fault.

This is what I get for relying on someone who, yet again, doesn't comprehend how serious the situations around her are.

I expect her to have accidentally fallen asleep, but when I glance next to me, she's wide awake, her eyes faraway on the dying bonfire.

I push myself up to sit. "What the hell, Maddy? You were supposed to wake me up!"

She looks over at me and slowly blinks her glazed-over eyes. "Yeah, but you looked so tired. I figured I'd let you sleep."

My pulse spikes. "But it wasn't time to sleep! It was time for us to grab Everett and get out of here. Now we've missed him and we're right back where we started."

She rubs the back of her hand against her eye. "I've been looking but I haven't seen him. Have you checked your phone? He might have messaged us or something. I tried to check for you but you changed your passcode from what I remember."

I changed it because I didn't exactly trust her around all my private info anymore. She clearly talks to Tyler about me, like how he texted Maddy earlier about how she and I were doing. And I can't have Maddy accidentally spotting my work schedule or texts with my parents. She might realize that I sometimes give her fake scheduling conflicts to avoid fighting about going out together or with Tyler.

My jaw tight, I reach for my phone. A couple new texts from Mom and Dad, but I leave those unread. Cowardly, I know, but I already know what they must say, and my overextended heart will snap if it gets pulled in yet another direction right now.

Then I open up Clippity and check my messages. Sure enough, there's a "Donde esta?" and "Hello?" from Everett.

"He reached out to us twice, Maddy," I growl. "If I'd been awake, I would've seen these and we might've been back in the minivan by now. Why didn't you wake me up like I asked? How could you be so irresponsible?"

Maddy's eyebrows furrow. "Irresponsible? I just let you sleep, which you clearly needed. You should be thanking me."

"I can take care of myself." I drag a hand through my hair. "I should've stayed awake. I never should have listened to you."

"Like you ever do anyway."

There's a hard edge in her voice, a rarity. For better or for worse, she's the most easygoing person I know. It takes a lot to rile her up, but something's tipped her over the edge. She doesn't get to be angry when this is her fault though.

I straighten. "What's that supposed to mean?"

"Exactly what it's supposed to. You don't ever listen to me. It's like you think I'm so beneath your intelligence."

"I—I don't think that," I stammer. I don't shrug off her advice or doubt her that much, do I? But I can't think of any examples on the spot like this, so I take the thornier way out. "Look how great your latest idea turned out. We're still missing the keys, still missing a whole damn fifteen-year-old."

Red starts to crawl up past the collar of Maddy's bachelorette shirt. "You're not seriously pinning the minivan key thing on me, are you? Nathan's the one who lost them."

"And I wouldn't even have had to ride with Nathan if you hadn't been such a terrible friend to me."

She actually tenses at the label like it was a physical slap. "What are you talking about?"

"You dropped me once you started dating Tyler! We don't talk like we used to, hang out like we used to. You go days without responding to my texts even though I know your phone is practically glued to your hand."

"What about you? You're never around either!" She shakes her head. "We literally just talked about this."

"We're *always* literally talking about this," I say, emotion starting to crack through the evenness in my voice.

She scoffs. "Come on, Jana. You're blowing this up out of nothing. I thought you needed rest, so I let you. I had it handled. You're not the only responsible one on this planet. But how was I supposed to know he'd message only you on Clippity? Or that you changed your passcode? You've had Keaton's birthday as your passcode forever. And so what if we missed Everett this time? We'll find him. He's not leaving the Orchards, and neither are we. You need to stop taking everything so seriously."

"But things are serious!" I practically scream. "You're always telling me to relax, but there are things in my life that are serious.

And your solution is to just brush over them."

Her eyes narrow. "How?"

I feel the anger avalanching. Normally, I'd have the energy to check these thoughts or at least pick one or two to focus on. But I'm tired. I can only hold things back for so long before they come crashing down with an energy that threatens to level everything in its wake.

"Like how you try to make me feel guilty for not doing whatever the hell you think teenagers are supposed to do. Go to parties or ditch class or yell at their parents or something. You know I'm not like that. I never have been, even before everything went sideways when Jackie came home, and yet you pick at me every time I won't go somewhere with you."

"Because you never go anywhere with me anymore, Jana. You always have an excuse and at some point, it just got easier to hang out with Tyler, who actually wants to spend time with me, than trying to pry you out of your rut."

She's pinning this distance on me? This, along with her absurd comment earlier this week that made it sound like my mom's accident resulted in me being less *fun*, is a smack in the face.

I know she'd backtracked and claimed I'd misunderstood what she said, but that does nothing to calm me now. Anger doesn't have to be logical. It's a fire, bright and uncontrollable, destroying everything in its path, no matter the value.

I lower my head. I'd rather stare at the dirt than at her. There was a time when this friendship was so solid we could stand on it. We could climb up and reach the highest stars together and not once worry about the foundation faltering. Maybe it's because we were younger then and our biggest problems were field trip rides and family events we didn't want to go to.

Life is different now, and there's more change ahead, with graduation and college hurtling toward us at breakneck speed. I can't step out of its way, but I don't know how to meet it either.

"This shouldn't be so hard." The words come out a harsh whisper, as if they have enough sense to emerge quietly because they know how loaded they are.

"What? What shouldn't be?" Maddy says after a moment.

"Us. This friendship."

The words form of their own volition. I could've said a fun night out, a much-anticipated concert, life, something. But the deep, raw truth has a way of surfacing despite how much you try to bury it.

Maddy scrambles off the platform and onto her feet. "If it's so hard for you to be friends with me, why do you do it?"

"We've been friends forever, Maddy. We're even rooming together in the fall."

She folds her arms across her chest, glaring down her nose at me. Her eyes are red, like she's battling back tears. "Inertia's not really a good reason."

"I didn't say anything about inertia. You're putting words in my mouth. You're the one saying none of this is that serious. No need to get dramatic."

Her eyebrows knit. "I'm not being dramatic!"

"You are. How are you the one to be mad right now? I'm

simply stating the truth. What you did tonight—this week, this month!—has been so much more damaging. You've really been making it tough to be your friend lately."

"Me? I've been making it tough? You need to take a good look at yourself. You're playing the wounded victim here because you don't think I talk to you as much? You shoot down all of my attempts to hang out with you, to draw you out of this mental jail cell you've put yourself in. You're the one who doesn't want to spend time with *me*, and that sucks. Also, you ever think another big reason we don't talk is because you're judgmental as hell? Like you're constantly focusing on what's wrong with everything and everyone."

I don't have a response to that. My mouth opens, empty, then shuts.

She uncrosses her arms, and her fists ball. "You put down Tyler, you make me feel like I'm always wrong, always messy, even when I'm trying my best. Everything has to meet your exact expectations, and if they don't, you look for someone else to blame instead of taking responsibility yourself or, God forbid, just rolling with it. Not everything needs to be perfectly under control all the time." She flares out her fingers like she wants to strangle something, but her hands remain at her sides. "I'm sick of constantly saying sorry to you just to keep the peace."

I don't do all that to her, do I? I may like things a certain way, but she's definitely being unfair painting this picture that I make life hell for everyone every time there's a slight deviation from what I want. And I don't shoot down every invitation of hers.

We're at the Orchards together. Disaster or not, that counts for something.

If she'd experienced the instability I've struggled with the past year with Mom's health, Jackie's whirlwind return home, and Dad's ever-increasing workload to make ends meet, she'd understand how vital it is to keep everything comfortably the same. If she had to fight her family for every inch of her social life, she'd learn to choose her battles like I have.

What Maddy seems incapable of understanding is that I don't do all this necessarily because I want to: It's a way to cope. It's survival.

I hop to my feet too, inches away from her. "Well, maybe sorry doesn't cut it anymore."

Her lip trembles the tiniest bit. "And maybe peace—or whatever this is—isn't worth it." Then she turns on the red Chucks we bought on a shopping trip back in August before school started and walks away, the dark of the night swallowing her up.

"Good riddance," I spit out into the frigid air, even though no one's around to hear me.

FRESHMAN YEAR YEARBOOK
SIGNATURE PAGES

IN MADDY'S YEARBOOK:

Freshman year done! Now just another three years.
I was going to try to draw a throw-up emoji face but
when I practiced it, it did not look pretty. Even for a
throw-up emoji. So just imagine it. 🖤, JR

IN JANA'S YEARBOOK,
INSIDE OF FRONT COVER:

We're going to be friends for as long as this yearbook message.
Turn to the back for the rest of it!—Mads

JANA'S YEARBOOK,
INSIDE OF BACK COVER:

We're going to be friends for as long as this yearbook message.
Turn to the front for the rest of it!—Mads

TWENTY-ONE

SUNDAY, APRIL 24
3:23 am

The Orchards grounds are harder to navigate with fewer lights and visible landmarks. Almost every food place has long since shut down: truck windows locked, windshields dark, a lone sleepy security guard pacing around them. The muffled sounds of partiers in expensive campers or crowded tents mix with the natural foothills music of crickets and rustling grass. The few people who wander around wield flashlights or phone lights just to get to the porta-potties and back.

I don't see Maddy anywhere.

Not that I'm looking for her.

Using the darkened Forest Wheel as a guide, I backtrack to Kayla's family's tent as best I can. It's possible that Everett and Kayla returned there after the bonfire when they couldn't find Maddy and me. At least I'm hoping that's the case because I'm out of ideas and sick of chasing him around.

For once, I'd like something to be easy tonight. The best time of my teenage life shouldn't have been anywhere near this catastrophic.

I should've been able to let loose with smiling, singing-off-key friends and continued the karaoke on the on-time ride home. My face carves itself into a grimace at the thought of what I should've had, and I don't even have the energy to wipe it off.

As wrong as they were, Maddy's words still sting too.

I can't believe she blames me for the breakdown in communication when she's the one who has trouble with "no"s and hearing the truth. I do admit, however, that on the accusation that I only focus on how everything's wrong, there might be some room for improvement. I could word things in a nicer way, like maybe Tyler has a unique rather than superannoying chipmunky laugh. Or maybe her idea of stealing the golf cart on an already trouble-filled night wasn't the most awful thing ever but perhaps a valid option to table for another time (i.e., never).

But I thought we were at the point in our friendship that she'd understand my good intentions. It's not like I don't want to hang out with her, but having competing priorities is a big part of our lives now. And if she can't handle the kind of truth I'm dishing out, that's on her. Right?

The problem with being alone with my thoughts is that there's no one to answer me back.

"Where you heading, pretty thing?" An unfamiliar voice sails at me from off to my right somewhere. My whole body buzzes like it's a struck alarm bell.

In a split second, I weigh my options. I could dart in between tents to lose whoever's trying to speak to me, but I don't recognize this part of the campground. I don't trust myself to make it back to Kayla's family's tent with how distracted I was earlier when we left it, especially with our fleeing from the Orchards staff and the sudden downpour. So I stick to the wide, well-trodden path between aisles of tents and force my gait faster.

To my horror, footsteps thud closer, like someone's jogging to catch up with me. Catcalls are annoying enough to deal with. Catcalls and physical follow-up immediately make me look for the nearest group of friendly-looking people, the nearest well-lit open establishment I can rush into. But the time of night is against me too, like even the clock is faulting me for being alone.

"Why don't you stop and talk with me a little?" the voice says. The words slur together: not a good sign. A couple drinks may make people friendly—like when my uncles come over to watch basketball over cheap beers at our house—but they can also make some folks volatile, easy to anger.

When Jackie first came home, I'd let her in at three in the morning after a friend dropped her off from a night at the clubs downtown. Turns out she is an emotional drunk, which I learned when I found her crying on the floor of our bathroom, mascara running down her face, as she cursed a few unknown names of former engineering classmates who'd made her brief university stint hell.

I hadn't realized how much being one of the only brown Asian females in her major made her a target, made her feel so isolated. At Samuels High, she was always smart, popular Jackie. But moving to a college across the country, away from the support network that wrapped you up cozy like a blanket for eighteen years, is a huge change: one that sent Jackie packing up and coming home when it became too much. Which was why part of me was so relieved that at least I'd have Maddy at my side at Santa Clarita. And I knew she needed me, her Emotional Support Jana, just as much, if not more. But I'm not so sure about that anymore.

I'd helped Jackie wash her face, and she thanked me no less than a dozen times, calling me the best sister ever. At least she was an affectionate emotional drunk and not a drama-starting emotional drunk. She occasionally texts me when she's back in that post-party state, and I'm thankful we live far enough that I won't be the one who cleans her up.

Right this second, I have no interest in finding out what kind of drunk my follower is.

I keep my gaze frozen forward and stay silent. Any turn of my head, any smile or softening could send the wrong hint to a guy who's already got the bad judgment of assuming girls speed-walking alone at night clearly want his company.

Honestly, do people just watch crime shows like *Law & Order* and think, *That seems like a solid way to win over the love of my life*?

My legs move just a little faster on their own.

Then it comes, the disbelieving snicker like this guy can't possibly fathom why anyone wouldn't want to be graced by his attention. "What, you don't speak English or something? Konnichiwa!"

So he's a stereotyping asshole too. At least he didn't try to make up his own Asian-sounding language, which, surprise surprise, also doesn't result in people falling at one's feet, hopelessly in love.

I realize then that my path on this main thoroughfare back to Kayla's tent has brought me near the VIP camper area. I catch a hint of a tattered pink banner dangling to the side of the door of a silver Airstream ahead. It's the Bach' Bullet where Maddy and I hid from the downpour earlier.

The bachelorette party folks were already kind enough to let us in out of the storm after Maddy asked. I hesitate to go to them again, despite how uneasy this creepy new follower is making me feel. If I keep walking, maybe I'll stumble upon a food truck or even a porta-potty line I can blend into.

"Hey, aren't you going to konnichiwa back?" The voice slurs too close behind me.

My resolve to continue on my way falters. I know that at least some of the bachelorette partygoers will be inside that Airstream: they wouldn't have slathered on that much nighttime renewal skin product if they were planning on leaving the camper.

With this creep on my tail, I need to get somewhere safe, and the Bach' Bullet is the best solution at hand. I'm not about to get lost at the Orchards by myself, or with unwanted chatty company, and with a spotty cell phone signal.

I do my best to suppress that hyperindependent part of me that insists I can solve this on my own. I'm so used to handling everything myself that I'm reluctant to ask anyone for help. But that side—or any side of me, really—might not even exist if this catcaller catches up with me and goes murderous. Angling in the direction of the Airstream, I break into a jog.

"Where you going? Can I come? Hey!" the voice calls,

increasingly angry, as if I would seriously choose to answer this of the many questions he's peppered me with. "Whatever. Your loss!"

Two figures lean against the side of the Airstream, the glow of cigarettes near their faces and a thin cloud rising with each exhale. They've moved on from the vape pens they had earlier. It's Chrissy and Hallie, the bachelorette herself, and the cigarette falls out of Hallie's mouth when she sees me.

"Um, hey," I say, fighting back that familiar awkward feeling that I've interrupted something but it's too late to back out now. "Sorry. Some guy was following me. You don't see him behind me anywhere, do you?"

Chrissy's lips purse and she scans the area. "Nope, you're safe. I swear, this place brings out the biggest pigs."

She's not wrong. Between Muscle Tank the key snatcher, the immovable Wall at the Larissa set, bonfire Goatee's lecturing about my need of a boyfriend, and now this late-night follower, the Orchards hasn't really put forth its best representations of maleness.

I reach for a reason to continue standing here, to put enough distance between me and the catcaller that I'd feel safe scurrying back to Kayla's tent alone. "So, um, you haven't seen Everett again, have you? He hasn't come back around this way?"

Chrissy and Hallie exchange glances. As Hallie finally rouses herself to stoop and pick up her dropped cigarette, Chrissy speaks up. "No, we haven't seen him. You still haven't found him, hm?"

I shake my head. "The night's been a mess. Even before that creepy guy following me. We— I keep missing Everett."

"Well, he's not here. Good luck," Hallie says with all the finality of a slammed door, so at odds with how welcoming and cake-pushing she was when we first met.

There's a clear strain in her voice that wasn't there earlier. My eyebrow rises, betraying my curiosity, and even in the dark, I see Hallie shrink into herself.

"She's just tired. And, you know, wedding jitters," Chrissy explains with a forced laugh.

It's one explanation, but I get the distinct sense it's not the entire picture.

"But you haven't seen him come by at all, right?" I say, shoving a proverbial shoe in the door Hallie's trying to close.

I'm not letting her get away with answering a question I didn't ask. I've done enough dodging of my parents' questions to know when someone's withholding information, and something is fishy about this bachelorette and her friend.

"I thought I just said that," Hallie says, inching toward the door of the Airstream. The muddy cigarette smolders in her hand.

The door to the Bach' Bullet swings open then to reveal Pam, the friend who had invited us in earlier. She's wrapped in a plush purple robe, with a matching silk bonnet. "Can you two keep it down? We're trying to sleep and you—" Her mouth snaps shut when she sees me. Then her hands go up to massage her temples. "For God's sake, give the girl her money back. I'm exhausted and really don't have the energy for this bullshit bingo you guys are playing."

"Money? What are you talking about?" I ask Pam as both Chrissy and Hallie try in vain to shush their friend.

Pam throws an argument-shriveling glare in their direction. "It's part of some messed-up party game, like Truth or Dare or something. Take a topless selfie, kiss a stranger, steal a phone . . ." I didn't know it was possible but her glare turns even more heated. "You two had your fun, okay? Now give the kid back her money. You are two grown-ass women with full-time jobs and your own health care."

"Relax, Pam, it was just a game," Chrissy says, trudging up the stairs into the Airstream. She returns a moment later with that paper garlic fries bag I'd hidden in the porta-potty and tosses it to me. I'm so floored by the simultaneous good and bad luck of this night that I don't even care that this bag is one hundred percent covered in germs. I slightly care about the yellow-brown smudge on the side, but not enough to give it back.

"I—um." A thanks is not appropriate, I know that much. They stole my phone as a prank. They ransomed it back, and I would've never seen this money again if I hadn't fled back here. "Seriously, what the hell? Do you know how much worse you made my night?"

Hallie has the good conscience to look guilty. "Sorry, Jane." I guess not a good enough conscience to remember my name after weaseling three hundred dollars out of me.

Chrissy, on the other hand, rolls her eyes. "I'm not. You ate all our cake, your little friend nearly cost us our security deposit with that damn sticker, and that shirt we gave your girlfriend was expensive. We had to get them custom-made! Consider us even."

My grip tightens around the bag. "Nowhere close to even." I wasted so much time chasing this phone when I could've been finding Everett and the keys and not getting into a friendship-ruining fight with Maddy.

The longer I stand here, the more likely I'll scream at them too, but these women aren't worth my time. This was a party game to them. And yet, somehow teenagers get the bad rap for being immature. I've overstayed my time here at the Bach' Bullet and at the Orchards. I turn on my heel and move to walk away.

"Sorry again, Jana," Pam calls after me. At least one of them is mature. The rest are brats with boobs and designer jewelry.

And because I feel the need to have the last laugh but aggressive or witty comebacks have never been my thing—those are Maddy's territory—I whirl back one more time to shout, "I hope it rains on your wedding day, Hallie!"

I know by her gasp that my curse landed exactly how I wanted it to. I don't need Maddy after all. I've got my phone, my cash, and I'm on my way.

SEVEN MONTHS AGO
September 24

Dad:

Where are you? Isn't the football game over? It's almost 11

Jana:

Maddy's car won't start. Waiting for AAA

Dad:

You could've called me to pick you up

Jana:

Can't leave Maddy here by herself

Dad:

I'm coming. Will wait with you. Send me the address

Jana:

**at the Clearview Charter field. At the side near the Jack
in the Box**

Dad:

Google Maps says twenty minutes. Stay where you are

Jana:

thanks

Dad:

**don't thank me yet. You should've called. We'll talk when
we get home**

Dad ended up jumping the battery in Maddy's car, and we canceled the AAA request. It would've taken them another hour anyway. Apparently Friday nights are a popular time for car batteries to peter out and strand motorists.

"Thanks, Mr. Rubio," Maddy calls from the driver's seat of her car.

The lights in the Clearview Charter High School football stadium are beginning to dim, but streetlamps scattered throughout the parking lot provide enough orange-tinted light for us to see each other clearly from our cars. There are three other cars, empty, still in the lot. At almost midnight, we're the last ones here.

Dad nods. "Anytime, Maddy. Text Jana when you get home so we know you arrived okay."

Maddy puts her car into drive and checks her mirror. "Will do."

I wave at her from the passenger seat, then Dad and I wait in silence until she is out of the parking lot and past the next two stoplights. Then he turns on our car and heads for the exit too.

"I really wish you would've called me earlier," he says. He has changed out of his workweek attire. No contact lenses, tie, or button-down shirt. Instead, he has on an old 10K race T-shirt from before his knee started giving him trouble and one of the cheap pairs of glasses he ordered online. I'm not fooled: Weekend Dad often isn't any more relaxed.

"We had it handled. Maddy has that auto club membership. They just took a lot longer than we thought."

"The game ended almost two hours ago, Jana. They covered it on the local news, the two-point conversion that Katz kid made. Your mom was worried when you weren't home when you said you'd be. She wanted to check on you but . . ."

She wouldn't have driven out here by herself, not this late at night. I flinch at the mere thought of her worrying about me. That's how I gauge the level of seriousness of my offense: how quickly Dad mentions Mom being worried. And he played that card pretty early in tonight's conversation.

I immediately shift into damage control. "Sorry. We didn't know it was just a battery thing. I honestly thought I'd be home earlier."

He shakes his head at that. "Jana, what you thought would happen and what *did* happen weren't the same thing." He pauses as he rounds the corner into the Jack in the Box drive-through.

"You're going to be in college next year, and you need to be mature enough to speak up when you need help."

Why does this sound like it's not really about me? Jackie's been calling home more often lately—I've walked in on a couple hushed, grim-faced FaceTimes between her and my parents. But she and I aren't the same person. I shouldn't be punished for what she is or isn't doing. My parents should recognize that.

"I am mature enough. I really did think we had it handled."

"You were in trouble, and you didn't even let your mom and me know. That doesn't sound like you had it handled at all."

I cross my arms. "Seriously? It was just a small car problem. It wasn't the end of the world."

"But how were we supposed to know that if you didn't tell us?" he snaps back. The anger in his voice matches mine, which makes sense: I get my temperament from him, according to Mom. "Do you know what crosses our minds when it gets late and you're not home yet? We don't just put these rules in place to be mean, Jana. It can be scary out there, especially for a girl."

What in the misogyny is he talking about? I can't stop my eyes from rolling. "You need to watch less local news."

"And maybe you need to watch more." Dad's lips purse for a moment before he speaks again. "There are going to be times when you'll be stuck in a situation that isn't as easy a fix as me coming to pick you up. You should at least tell us when something's wrong. And there'll be times we need you too."

Whether he was referring to how I was unavailable during Mom's accident or not, my mind goes there anyway. But that was never going to happen again: I wasn't going to let them down. And it's insulting that I keep having to tell him that and that he assumes I can't fix my problems myself. They don't know half of what I go through with juggling work and school and schedules to make their own paths smoother.

Dad pulls the car forward to shout his order into the drive-through intercom. He peers at me over his shoulder. "You want anything?"

"Aside from you getting off my back? No, thanks."

He sighs, and I pull the hood of my sweater up, pretending to fall asleep in the passenger seat. I have no interest in reviving this conversation. How are they mad at me? I was just trying to be a good friend by waiting with Maddy. Once her car was up and running, she would've dropped me off at home too. And wouldn't that have been better, not needlessly dragging them out of the house on easily fixable crises?

If I keep quiet, maybe Dad's Oreo shake and tacos will put him in enough of a good mood that he'll let this misunderstanding blow over.

It doesn't, in fact, save me from a weeklong grounding after all.

TWENTY-TWO

SUNDAY, APRIL 24
3:30 am

Having my phone ransom back invigorates me like a quadruple-shot latte. The world may be finally falling asleep around me, but I'm wide awake as I march down the main thoroughfare. My phone buzzes, and I'm so shocked that I have service that I immediately fish my phone out of my backpack.

It's Dad.

And it's not a text. It's a phone call.

This is probably the dozenth time he's tried to call me and was met with a voice mail thanks to the horrible reception. Experience has taught me that Dad only gets more upset with each failed attempt to reach me, so it's simultaneously a good and awful thing that we're managing to connect right now. I plant myself exactly where this one bar of cell service appeared, then answer.

I force some lightness into my voice, as if it's a delight to hear from him and not an absolute terror. As if he was spending the whole evening comfortable at home instead of in the lobby of a resort, dodging his coworkers.

"Hey, Dad!"

"You want to explain to me why Mom picked me up and you're not even home yet? Do you have any idea what time it is?"

Not a hello or are-you-safe, but at least he didn't start off yelling. I gulp before launching into an explanation of Nathan's lost keys and little brother. Then I lay out, in excruciating and complimentary-to-me detail, everything I've been trying to do to get home. I leave out that part about scaling the Forest Wheel though. I doubt he'd want to hear about me risking life and limb for cell phone reception.

In the distance, I spot that familiar truck that sold me the overpriced cheese sandwiches. At least I've been making good time on my way back to Kayla's family's tent. I don't dare move from this spot for fear of our call getting cut off.

Dad stays so silent as I speak that I actually check to make sure this tiny bit of reception didn't disappear. His quietness unnerves me. It's like he's letting me dig myself a grave with my words. At least if he was talking back or interrupting me, I'd get a sense of how angry he is. But you can't argue with silence.

"Once I get back to the tent, I'll round everyone up, get those keys, and we'll be on our way home. So maybe two, three more hours, tops?"

There's a pause before a long sigh. "Jana, this is unacceptable. The only reason I didn't drive myself to this conference was because you swore you'd come pick me up after you got home. You and your mom were so adamant about me needing a night out too."

I gulp down the guilt. "I know, and I really tried, but when Nathan—"

"I don't want to hear about what anyone else is doing. You are our responsibility, and you going all the way out there and staying so late?" He gives a heavy sigh.

I catch more than anger in his words: there's disappointment in there, and exhaustion. That hurts even more. This past year, he took on more clients, more work to make up for Mom's shift to part-time and the retirement-threatening realization that Jackie may not be able to manage her own college debt. My face goes hot and I'm glad we're not standing face-to-face having this conversation.

"I tried so hard to get back so I could pick you up. It never occurred to me that Mom would do it. I never asked her to. This night fell apart so badly, and I—"

"Stop. You should have called home the second you knew you'd need a ride. It's after three in the morning. Your mom and I have been worried sick trying to reach you."

"Is—is she okay?"

Dad pauses before answering. "Yes . . . and no. She made it to the resort safely. She was all nerves, so when we got home, she took something so she could sleep. I told her I'd stay up and wait for you. It was really hard for her to get behind the wheel tonight, Jana."

My chest squeezes. Mom isn't well, and I made it worse. *I* did that.

"I—I'm sorry. We thought we'd find Nathan's keys by now

and I'd be on my way home and then over to you. I didn't call because I didn't think I'd need to. And I knew you'd be angry."

"Of course I'd be angry! This isn't the first time we've had this conversation." He yells this time. "But I would've come out there and picked you and your friends up. It may not be what you wanted, but it's what should've happened. Continuing to dodge the hard stuff is not a way to solve anything."

A lump forms in my throat, and it's impossible to reply. That's what I've been doing, isn't it? Dodging the hard stuff: the things I know are coming but can't control or fix. I didn't call them because I knew they'd be angry. I got my own ride to the Orchards because I didn't want to have the kind of blowup with Maddy that we ended up having anyway. And I didn't tell Maddy about Chalmers Design because I know she'll be upset at me for even considering diverging from her roomie plan when she needs me so much. I didn't tell her because I know this could be the real end of us.

But Dad is right. It's not a way to solve anything. I concocted these work-around plans to address everything but the hard stuff. It's made it all worse, letting small problems fester and warp by the second.

Dad's voice is firm when he speaks next. "Look, I don't want to leave your mom at home by herself after the night she's had. But if you don't call home in half an hour and let me know you're on your way, I'm going to have to wake her up so we can drive out there and get you."

"Dad, no! If we have the keys, then you—"

"And I don't care if you're already back in Nathan's car. They are going to pull over and drop you off at a McDonald's on the way, and you're riding home with us. You and I need to have a serious talk, because clearly this message didn't sink in with you the first time. Got it?"

"Yes." A whisper. What is with this man and fast food and serious parenting conversations?

"If I don't hear from you, you're not going to that end-of-the-year yearbook trip to Disneyland either."

I nearly stumble but catch myself before I face-plant in the dirt. Luckily, or not, no one's around to see me almost collapse. "What? That's next month! What does that have to do with tonight?" And how does he even remember that?

The answer comes to me quickly: the family calendar we use to plot out all of Mom's appointments and refills, my work and school commitments, the holidays Dad is planning to be in the office instead of taking a day off, everything. My own creation, turned against me.

"Consequences to your actions, Jana."

"God, don't you think I've had enough consequences?" I spit the words out.

"What's that supposed to mean?"

Something about the Orchards seems to have pried the top off the box I keep all messy emotions locked away in. First arguing with Maddy, and now standing up to Dad? These aren't things that steady, reliable Emotional Support Jana would typically do. But instead of immediately apologizing to placate him, I find myself relieved that that bit of emotion is out in the world, that the box is cracked and can't be patched up easily. I think it's time I finally voice how smothered I've been feeling under the weight of responsibilities I never asked for but took on to make my parents' lives less complicated. Tonight's questioning of everything I've struggled to perfectly preserve might be long overdue. "None of this was my fault, Dad! I've been trying to get home. I never meant for this to impact Mom and you the way it did."

Dad sighs. "Whether you meant to or not, it did."

"Come on, I've followed every other rule, every other time. I've done everything else you and Mom needed me to do. That has to count for something. Why can't you give me any credit for always being the good one?"

There's a heavy silence before he answers. "Good one of what?"

I sigh. "Between me and Jackie, Dad. It's like you're punishing me for stuff Jackie does."

"There's no good or bad kid thing going on here. Your sister has nothing to do with this."

"So then why are you so hard on me when I'm the one always doing what's right? I do so much to help make things easier for all of us, and I can't even get a little slack when something out of my control goes wrong."

I swallow hard. The words have a distinctively Maddy tinge to them, like part of me always recognized the value of what she was saying but the rest of me was too stubborn to admit it. Was it really up to me to make life run smoothly for our family? It's one thing to take on more responsibility around the house; it's another to try to foist everyone's burdens on myself.

Maybe Maddy's right: I need to prioritize myself. And it's not just about my happiness. It's about not feeling unduly guilty for failing to be everything for everyone. Whether I go to Santa Clarita or Chalmers, my family needs to be okay even if I'm not around every second of the day. This always should've been a group project, not a test of how much I can shoulder alone. I've been carrying it all for so long that I can practically hear the yoke bend and crack as I finally dare to put everything down.

When Dad speaks again, there's more of that tiredness in his voice. I've only heard this tone in those eavesdropped conversations between him, Mom, and Jackie. "I know you've stepped up at home. Your mom—I see it. And we appreciate it. It's been hard on all of us in different ways."

"I know, and I'm sorry I made things harder tonight. Look, I'm not running for some big 'best kid ever' award or anything. But it'd be nice to just be treated like I'm as responsible as I've already proved to be, like I'm not one slip away from ruining my life."

"I don't think you're *that* close to ruining your life, Jana. Maybe two slips," Dad says, with a little lightness back in his voice. It seems we're nearing a truce, but it's too early to hope. "It's not just that you let us down tonight. Even aside from me almost getting stuck at the resort and Mom having to drive, we're worried about you. So you need to walk in the door safe and sound in a couple of hours and—"

"I will. I know I messed up, and you know how sorry I am.

But these things happen. I can't turn back the clock and make everyone happy." The moment the words leave my lips, I recognize them as another truth I should've come to sooner. How much time have I wasted trying to juggle everyone else's happiness? But I guess that's what happens when you fill every second of the day with a worry or a task on a to-do list; you don't ever get the time to breathe and ask yourself what it's all for, what you're terrified will happen if you let up for just one moment.

It feels awful to have let things fall tonight, but I don't think I should've been the one carrying it all to begin with. Maybe it's time I let others take on some of the load. "I'll be home as soon as I can: you have to trust me. This time next year, I'll be off at college, wherever that is, and you'll have to trust me then too."

As if the mention of me in college dulls some of Dad's unease, he sighs. "Well, knowing you, you'll try your hardest to fix it. Like how you turned that broken mug your mom loved into a succulent planter." I can imagine him leaning back in the lumpy green recliner in our living room, the room dark, the television volume low so as not to bother Mom. "All right. We can talk about this later, *when* you get here."

I let the tension out of my jaw. It's as close to a win as I'll get right now. This might be the first time he's acknowledged not only how capable I am, but how I'm not Jackie. And it might not seem like a big win to most folks, but to me, it's monumental. It's the start of my road back to being just Jana, to focusing on what makes the most sense for me.

"Okay." It's the only word I can bear to respond with, the only one he'll accept, and likely the only one our spotty, dying cell phone reception will allow.

"Call with an update in a half an hour, Jana."

"No, an hour, Dad."

His tone softens. "An hour."

He hangs up, and I break into a jog.

TWENTY-THREE

SUNDAY, APRIL 24
3:36 am

My cold, muddy feet begin to ache in protest of my rapid pace as I make my way back to Kayla's family's tent. I don't stop. The sooner I can get this night over with, the better. The new deadline I negotiated with Dad is a sliver of a chance at redemption. I need to get home or any small gains from our latest conversation could be obliterated.

Another motivator is that I suddenly find myself with three hundred dollars cash on me, in the middle of a dark campground with people more than willing to come and chat with me unbidden, or to pretend they're friendly bachelorette party goers but actually nefarious thieves.

From a distance, Kayla's family's tent glows from within, as if someone left all the camping lanterns and string lights on, but there isn't any obvious bustling activity inside. Other lit-up tents I pass by have music blasting through speakers, raucous laughter, or even arguing. Kayla's family must be worn out from the long workday at the truck and really did mean it when they said they needed some shut-eye.

But then the youngest member of our group went and stole the youngest member of their group like a continuation of their awful reenactment of *Romeo and Juliet*. In our version, the big twist will be their families killing them with their bare hands for putting them through so much trouble.

Three figures guard the door to the tent, but from where I am, I can't make out who they are. I was wrong in assuming that there wasn't any arguing going on here. These figures are obviously riled up, judging by the tense shoulders, the finger-pointing, the hands on the hips. It's Kevin, Kayla, and—I actually gasp aloud—Everett. I run straight for Everett, not to wrap him in a big hug, but to smack him on the shoulder.

The kid must have a sixth sense for impending punches thanks to that being his primary method of communication with Nathan. He effortlessly dodges me.

"Where have you been, Everett?" It takes all my energy to bring my volume to an angry whisper and not an ear-splitting shriek.

"Exactly what I wanted to know," Kevin says. He has his thick arms crossed over his chest and is glaring down at his little sister. "You know I'm going to tell Papa about this."

The fact that neither Everett nor Kayla looks remotely cowed enrages us more. Did Everett not realize what I'd gone through looking for him? I shake my head. Of course not. There's no way he could've known. Because while he was out slapping stickers on things and making heart eyes at Kayla, he couldn't have realized how my life would crumble in the span of a couple of hours. I barely saw it coming myself.

Some part of my brain corrects me: *that's not entirely true.* Whatever was happening between Maddy and me has been brewing for months, if I'm being honest.

"Hey, are you all right?" Everett asks me. It's then that I realize I've been silent, my face twisted from the tides of exhaustion and emotion I've been damming up.

It's easier to turn this rage at him than to sort through it on my own. "No, I'm not. We needed to leave hours ago. You didn't make getting home any easier, disappearing like that. What were you thinking?"

"We were looking for the keys."

I blink. "You . . . you what?" Whatever I was expecting them to do, it wasn't that. The energy drains out of the arm I was going to try to smack him with again.

"Kayla and I went looking for the keys. Nathan's not in any shape to be going anywhere, and Tyler was still conked out, so we figured we would keep up the search."

"Why didn't you say so when I DM'd you? Your Clippity was nothing but videos of you and those ridiculous stickers. How was I supposed to know what you were actually up to?"

Everett shrugs. "I didn't realize you and Maddy were out searching for us. I thought she'd stay back with Tyler, and you went off to get food for everyone. Also, the stickers are not ridiculous, and I can do two things at once, Jana. It's called multitasking. Gotta keep up the brand, you know?"

Kevin starts to laugh, then quickly stifles it when I scowl at him. He rubs the back of his neck and says, "At least they're back safe. We can argue more about this in the morning, but we've gotta get some sleep: full day at the truck tomorrow. You're opening shift, Kayla."

Kayla's jaw drops. "That's not fair! We have to start prep at nine. I won't get any sleep!"

Kevin heads inside the tent, completely ignoring his sister's protests, but I stay where I am. My mind struggles to wrap around the unexpected discovery that Everett was out doing something productive. But even with his efforts, my frustration at him and at how I spent this ruin of a night refuses to back down so quickly.

"Okay, you might've been out . . . multitasking or whatever, but you were at the bonfire," I say. "You were out partying while Maddy and I were wasting time looking for you!"

Kayla steps in, wrapping her arm around his red-flanneled one. "My security guard friend told us to meet him there after the shift. He was keeping an eye out for the keys for us but turns out he couldn't take anything out of the lost and found after it was logged."

My heart skips a thump. "Does this mean that they finally turned up? The keys are at the lost and found?"

Everett's grin confirms it. "That's what we came back to the tent for. They wouldn't let me claim the keys because I didn't have ID or anything—Nathan is holding it for me."

I raise my eyebrow. "You let the guy who lost our keys crowd-surfing hold on to your important legal documentation?"

Everett shrugs, my point lost on him. He pulls the wallet out of his fanny pack and waves it in front of me. "We can go claim the keys now!"

I'm so relieved I could've jumped up in the air if my legs weren't the consistency of jellyfish roadkill after the miles I've unintentionally walked today. "Finally! Let's go."

"Should we go get the others?" Everett asks. "Nathan's awake, and Maddy's back, but Tyler's still—"

"No, we can get them after. It might take too long to drag the whole team over there." And I have no interest in seeing Maddy at the moment. She headed right back to Tyler after we fought, just as I'd predicted.

Even though my anger at Everett is all but gone after he redeemed himself with this key search, I'm still not in a good enough place with Maddy to purposely seek out her company. I don't even know if this is something we can fix tonight.

A small part of me wonders if this is something we can ever fix. The way we left it earlier, both of us questioned whether our friendship is something worth salvaging. Maybe Maddy's right: maybe what I'm considering the golden years in our friendship weren't some idyllic peaceful time after all. But what does that mean for what lies ahead? Where would we be without each other? The uncertainty is a growing lump in my throat.

"Did you want to stay here and get some rest then?" Everett says. "I can go."

"Nope. No way I'm losing you again." Or waiting awkwardly in the tent with Maddy, someone I desperately need to talk to but would much rather avoid. I hide my anxiety with a wide smile. "Kayla, you're welcome to come if you want, but this guy's put me through enough hell tonight with his disappearing acts. I'm not letting him out of my sight. Now, which way is this lost and found?"

TWENTY-FOUR

SUNDAY, APRIL 24
3:45 am

The Lost and Found tent sits close to the festival grounds entrance. Plastic barricades block the walkway to the stages to prevent any access to the grounds now that the music acts have long since ended. The only tents we can reach are the ticket upgrade tent—because capitalism never sleeps—and the lost and found, like the organizers knew folks would be searching for all manner of misplaced belongings at nearly four in the morning.

Kayla and Everett stroll ahead, chatting quietly with each other. Everett's hands are stuffed in his pockets. In retrospect, I don't know why I thought he was out performing some grand romantic gestures or R-rated antics because he doesn't seem to have even worked up the courage to hold Kayla's hand. It's sweet, actually. And a good reminder that not every guy in this place is a total jerk.

Nathan, for example, is one of the nicest people I know, to the point where he agreed to babysit his minor brother at a music festival. Crowd-surfing and lost keys aside, that says something about his character and the trust within his family. And Tyler has been holding Maddy's purse for her most of the night without a complaint, even when he was propping up Nathan as he maneuvered on his injured knee. Tyler seems like the kind of person who will always try to help—when he's not sidelined by a bunch of weed gummies.

I don't know how to feel about the fact that I was so wrong about Everett though. He's not wholly the irresponsible, viral-fame-seeking skirt chaser I'd pegged him for, and it unnerves me to wonder: If I'm so wrong about him, what—or who—else am I wrong about?

There is no one else waiting at the Lost and Found tent, so we bypass the ropes the organizers zigzagged in front of it to create a line. We walk up to the plastic folding table manned by an attendant. She's a short white woman with dark red hair, a blue "Orchards Staff" T-shirt, and a paper name tag that says "Sandra." She's talking to a tall Latino security guard who looks like he spends hours in the gym and in the barber's chair, getting that precise, clean cut. His name tag is a much more official-looking gleaming brass, with the last name Garcia etched into it.

Sandra and Garcia the guard grumble to each other about getting stuck on the late shift. She brightens and gives us a friendly smile when we stop in front of her. "Hi, what can I help y'all with?"

Everett describes the set of keys, down to the detail about the broken-in-half Lakers key chain, and she lowers her gaze to a clipboard on the table between us. Biting her lip as she concentrates, she flips through the pages and runs her pink-nailed finger down the list of lost items. Finally, she beams a triumphant smile at Everett with an "Aha! Got it. You came by earlier, right?"

Everett nods. "Yup, and I've got my wallet this time!"

"Awesome. Thought you looked familiar. I'll need your ID so I can log it, then I'll get the keys from its cubby." She motions behind her at the set of wire racks loaded with various plastic bins full of sweaters, purses, cell phones, and a mountain of keys.

"Wow," Kayla says, staring at the cubbies. "Looks like you're not the only one locked out of their cars."

I sigh. "Nope. But maybe the only ones who care about being home a good four hours ago."

Garcia the guard laughs. "Man, if my sister tried to come home four hours after my mom told her to, she'd be sent right back to live with our grandpa in Tempe."

"Well, I guess I'm lucky I don't have any semi-faraway family my parents can just ship me off to."

"Consider yourself lucky that a summer manning the family's cell phone repair shop wasn't on your list of punishments then."

I groan, thinking of my dad's threat to keep me from my Disneyland trip. *Disneyland*. The happiest place on earth. What kind of monster takes that away?

"I wouldn't cross that off," I say. "My dad can get pretty creative when he wants to make a point. One time, he got upset I didn't call him immediately when my friend—my ride's car didn't start. In addition to a weeklong grounding, he got Jack in the Box drive-through on our way home and didn't get me anything."

Both Kayla and the security guard wince like they've been burned. "Brutal," she says.

She's not wrong. Watching my dad sip his Oreo shake and crunch on his two oil-dripping tacos was a unique kind of torture. Effective though, considering it's been burned into my brain until now.

I suppose that punishment didn't work out the way he wanted. If Dad was hoping to convince me that I should call him and Mom the second something goes wrong, that was not a lesson learned. All that story reminds me of is how angry Dad gets when Jackie or I break one of our house rules. It's why I try so hard to not give him reasons to be angry, why I try so hard to organize and fix everything myself.

That's not really an effective way of dealing with the hard stuff, as Dad had said, though. It's me finding every intricate detour or tiny loophole, but that can't go on forever. As much as I dreaded that conversation with my dad earlier, there was some good: the tough truths went both ways. I fought for myself, less concerned about destroying things than repairing them, because I needed to be seen for me and my efforts, not for the worries transferred over from my sister and the what-ifs that no one can predict.

Dad seems to have finally understood, at least as much as I could've expected him to over a short call with shoddy reception. But it's a start.

Next to me, Everett continues to dig in his overstuffed fanny pack for his wallet. "Sorry, it's in here, I just need to find it."

"Take your time, hon," Sandra says casually, even though she seems pretty annoyed at the wait, despite the fact there isn't anyone else in line behind us. She stifles a yawn that I have to fight from mimicking, then produces a bright green energy drink from somewhere next to her. She takes a long swig, and I eye that liquid wakefulness jealously.

Everett starts taking out the contents of his fanny pack, slapping his medicated lip balm tube on the table, then a stack of stickers, then more stickers.

Garcia the guard picks one up and brings it to eye level. "These yours?"

Something about his tone—curiosity, but with a purpose—sets an alarm off in my head. Before I can warn sweet, naive Everett to deny it, he blabs, "Yup! Want one? I made a hundred."

The security guard's demeanor immediately shifts from friendly to fierce. "I have a dozen of these our boss made us scrape off wherever we found them. We've been searching for you all night, kid. You're coming with me."

He grabs for Everett's arm then, and, without thinking, I throw myself between them. The security guard accidentally brushes my chest instead before recoiling in horror. He blurts out an "oh my god I'm so sorry! I didn't mean to!" at the same time I yell to Everett, "Run!"

To Kayla's credit, she seizes Everett's arm in that split second and takes off, virtually dragging him behind her. I hear a "but my lip balm!" before I sprint away too. The security guard reaches for my mini-backpack. With a grunt, I hurtle forward and manage to break out of his grasp.

I splash through a puddle, the muddy water leaping up to speckle my legs. I've done more running today than I have all of senior year, and I hate it.

Then I hear the crackle of a walkie-talkie.

"I found the vandal! Teenage male, Hispanic. With two Asian females," the security guard barks. Then he proceeds to give an annoyingly detailed description of us, down to Everett's red plaid shirt, my mini-backpack, and Kayla's distinctive purple hair. "They're heading in the direction of the campground!"

I curse Everett all over again as we cut left and disappear between the tents. I knew I had a good reason to be angry at him.

TWENTY-FIVE

The tiredness of my legs is nothing compared to the piercing ache in my chest over how close we were to getting the minivan keys back. We're finally outside Kayla's family's tent after snaking around the campground twice to lose anyone trying to trail us. I'm bent over, my hands on my thighs as I gasp in breath after breath.

"I'm so sorry, I wasn't thinking," Everett says to me and Kayla.

She squeezes his hand, and for a moment, I hate that I seem to be the only person at the Orchards who is utterly alone. Maybe there was something to Maddy's observation that my pinning lofty expectations on everyone and everything, then quickly finding fault when it all inevitably falls short of what I imagined, is isolating. According to her, it pushed her away. I wonder who else might've come into my life if not for this apparently unfavorable trait I didn't know I had.

Across from me, Kayla's face is scrunched in sympathy as she murmurs something soothing to Everett. She's much nicer than I am. But it's easy to be nice when those keys aren't your own ride home though.

I straighten and glare at Everett. "The keys were right there!" I struggle to keep my voice level despite the urge to scream and throw things. I don't need the inhabitants of any of the other tents nearby waking up and calling in a noise complaint on us. "You and those damn stickers, Everett! How could you be so childish?"

He flinches like I've slapped him. I instantly feel a pinch of guilt. But then I remember what his desire to go viral cost us, and my scowl deepens. I don't want to be angry at everyone all the time, but I find myself here anyway.

"He said sorry," Kayla cuts in. Then she squares her shoulders like she's ready to fight me for him, to defend him the way Maddy did for me against the Goatee guy earlier.

The memory douses some of my fire. I drag in a deep breath to further calm myself. "We're going to have to hide out here until Nathan's feeling steady enough to go and claim them."

"Why Nathan?" Everett asks. "We can just wait until the security guards are away from the lost and found and then swoop in and get those keys."

"They do change shifts at eight in the morning," Kayla says. "I only know because my security guard friend who tipped us off to the keys was complaining that they'd denied his request for that shift. That will be our best bet for going back to the lost and found without getting spotted."

My jaw clenches at the vision of a clock ticking down to Dad's new all-or-nothing deadline. "Eight in the morning? No. I'm sick of waiting. That's all I've done today, look for people and wait. I need to get home."

"Well, my brother can't walk all the way there and back on his knee like that."

"You really didn't leave him a choice there, did you?" I snap.

Everett's face sinks, and I realize then that I'd broken something in this fledgling friendship of ours too. We had fun together earlier in the night, when we were stuck in the Larissa crowd, but all of that dissolved in the acid of my words. I whip my gaze back at the ground to avoid seeing the new distance in his eyes.

I really am doing a stellar job pushing away every single person I came to the Orchards with.

But he doesn't let me off that easily. "You know what? You're kind of mean, Jana. I already apologized."

"Yeah, you don't have to keep piling on him like that," Kayla adds.

"Excuse me, he's the one who royally messed up with his sticker-waving in front of an Orchards security guard." The best defense is a good offense. Throwing the blame right back at him seems the easiest way to avoid facing how much damage I've done.

As I speak, that echo from my conversation with Maddy reverberates again. Not exact words this time, but an inescapable, smothering feeling: the fear that not only what Maddy is saying about me is true, but that other folks are onto it too. And that they're not wrong: that in my drive to control everything, to *fix* everything, I do tend to just focus on how I think everyone else is wrong. It comes off mean. And it's driving people away.

It's hard to miss the truth of that when both Kayla and Everett stare at me like I'm the villain here.

Everett doesn't argue with me this time. He simply purses his lips, unzips the tent door, and enters. Kayla follows, leaving me outside by myself. The wind picks up then. It rustles the fabric of the tent, and I hug my arms close around me to ward off the chill.

Conversation streams out from the gap in the unzipped door, and I'm struck with a solitary sense of the world going on without me. I duck my head and enter too.

Most of the floor is now covered with sleeping bags. Nathan, Maddy, and a groggy Tyler inhabit one corner, Everett and Kayla stand next to them. They whisper among themselves, Everett filling them in on where he's been and what he's learned. I pad closer. Nathan raises a hand to greet me. Maddy doesn't look in my direction.

"How are you feeling?" I ask Nathan.

He slides a half-melted ice baggie off his knee. It's swollen in a way it wasn't before, and even I, with my basic first aid knowledge garnered mostly from ad-filled health websites, know that him traipsing around the Orchards is not a good idea. "Better, I think?"

I try, too late, to hide my pitying look.

He chuckles. "Okay, I know it looks ten times worse. Thanks for your honesty. Everett filled me in on the plan. I unfortunately can't go anywhere though," he says with a kind smile I'm not sure I deserve right now. "You think they'll let you take my ID and claim it for me?"

"Come to think of it, we can probably use our own IDs," I say. "I don't know how they could tie your specific ID to your set of keys, so I suppose anyone can go claim them. I think they're only logging the info of the people who claim the stuff so they don't get sued."

Tyler shifts his weight to rise. "You all have done enough. I can go claim the keys, I just need to—whoa!" He unceremoniously thumps back down, and judging by Nathan's and Maddy's exasperated sighs, this isn't the first time he's done this.

"You're staying here," Maddy says. "Jana can take care of it, right?"

She looks up at me then, and her gaze is blank, almost cold. As if she's ordering a fast-food chicken sandwich instead of asking her best friend to do us all a huge favor.

"I don't think I can. The security guard saw me with Everett and Kayla, so they might be looking for me. If they recognize me at the lost and found, they might detain me or follow me back here and arrest Everett for putting those stickers everywhere. Then we're for sure not going home anytime soon."

"So that leaves Maddy," Everett says, and our collective gaze swivels to her.

"Do you know where to go?" Nathan asks.

Maddy pushes herself off the ground to stand. "No, but I can figure it out."

"Jana can show you, right?" Kayla, ever the nice, helpful girl, chimes in. "I'd offer, but it's not like my brother would let me leave this tent right now anyway. Jana doesn't have to go with you all the way to the tent, but at least you won't need to worry about getting lost. This campground is a maze."

Maddy and I stare at each other. Neither of us wants to be the one to explain to everyone that the mere idea of hanging out together is less appealing than getting our wisdom teeth out.

But damn if I'm going to be accused of not being a team player, in addition to being mean and judgmental. And the sooner we can get the keys, the sooner I can be on my way home and away from all this. I can at least be civil while we get this job done. "Yeah, I can show you. It'll be faster this way. I'll just stay back while you go up to the lost and found itself."

"Fine."

If anyone notices the odd tone of her one-word answer, they don't mention it. All of us must be exhausted and sick of the Orchards enough to want this to work.

"Anyone want to trade jackets or shirts or something? In case they're still looking for me. I don't want to make myself too easy to spot, and a fuchsia bomber jacket is pretty distinctive."

"You're just trying to get my brother's shirt off," Everett cuts in with a smirk.

I feel the blood rush to my cheeks at the joke—I did ask to trade shirts, after all, but I didn't think through the logistics in that much ab-baring detail—and the glare that Nathan levels at Everett could probably set off a forest fire.

"Take my jacket," Tyler says. He squirms to get both arms out of his jacket, and Maddy stoops to help.

In exchange, I shrug off my bomber and hand it to him. Then

I stare at my mini-backpack, which holds three hundred dollars in cash and is also unfortunately eye-catching enough that the security guard mentioned it. I need to leave this with someone.

Maddy had accused me of not liking Tyler, of not listening to her when she spoke about him. But if that was true, how would I remember that he chased a lady down halfway through the bank parking lot when she left her ATM card in the machine? Or that he stood guard at his little brother's lemonade stand when some neighborhood bullies continued to bike past? I know he's trustworthy.

"Would you mind holding on to this for me too?" I ask him. "It's hard to run with. Bobs around everywhere."

Tyler looks at me, his eyes wide, like he's surprised I've uttered so many words to him. The thought stings. I've been nice to him, haven't I? But judging by his reaction and his stammering of "yeah, um, sure. Of course," I begin to doubt my own memory.

"Ready?" Maddy says to me. Another one-word communication, but enough to drag me out of my own head.

I zip up Tyler's jacket, a black-and-cream letterman's jacket for varsity tennis. Style-wise, it's not as cool as my bomber jacket, but it's clean, warm, and doesn't reek of teenage boy body spray like I assumed it would. "Let's rock."

A WEEK AGO

Maddy:

Leaving that cafe when Tyler showed up? So rude.

Jana (drafts—deleted):

Oh, dear me, I wouldn't want to come off rude to someone who clearly texted me as a backup study buddy.

Maddy:

Hello? No snarky comeback?

Maddy:

Okay . . . See you tomorrow.

TWENTY-SIX

SUNDAY, APRIL 24
4:09 am

My gaze swings from shadow to shadow as we head toward the Lost and Found tent. No sign of security guards yet, so it's safe to say that our video-game-based evasive maneuvers earlier worked.

Maddy and I walk a few feet away from each other. A symphony of far-off laughter, nearby whispers, and the chirps of hidden crickets barely veils how uncharacteristically quiet we are. There's something so odd about Maddy in her bachelorette party shirt I almost paid three hundred dollars for and me in her boyfriend's jacket, like the world has turned upside down. And to be honest, it feels like it.

The last time I was hit by this sense of strangeness was when Jackie appeared at our doorstep mid-November. Mere months earlier, she packed up her bags and waved at us from the other side of the airport security check. Then suddenly she was right back in her old room but without the textbooks, homework, or easy smile. It was Jackie, but missing something.

Just like we're Maddy and Jana, but missing something.

Maddy senses it too, because she keeps side-eyeing me.

"Don't do that," I say. Then I tack on a "please" so I don't come off as mean. But it's unnerving, her attempt at not staring while still obviously staring.

"Do what?"

"Looking at me like you're trying to get a sneak peek at my thoughts somehow."

"Well, you could always tell me what's wrong."

A disbelieving snicker escapes me. "Do you not remember having this whole awful fight earlier? You're the one who walked away."

"You don't have to say it like that."

"Why, does it come off mean?"

She goes quiet then. "Never mind. You're obviously in a mood to be upset about something." Then she actually flicks her hair back like a reality show regular.

The way she can just bring this up and set it aside when it's convenient for her rankles me. She can dance from emotion to emotion, forgive and forget—at least temporarily—in a way that I have yet to master. Not that I want to. Remembering is what I'm good at. It's what kept my head above water during Mom's recovery and Hurricane Jackie's return home.

Maddy's flippant attitude makes it seem like I'm the only one hurting. Like I'm the only one who sees a problem when this whole night wasn't a fun-filled carnival for any of us.

"About *something*? How do you not even know what I'm mad

about? I think I made myself pretty clear."

Maddy's face twists then, and it's illuminated by the faint fluorescence of a stadium light in the distance. "I said I was sorry for letting you sleep longer earlier. Sorry for trying to be a good friend."

I almost choke when I realize her apology only covers my extended nap. "You know that's not the only thing."

"So I panicked and invited both you and Tyler to study with me, big deal. Even when I do text or call you these days, you're too busy to respond. Or if, God forbid, I mention Tyler, you find a way to change the subject or weasel out."

"It is a big deal! I dropped everything to come and help you out, and you didn't even let me know I was second string. It's like our friendship is decaying and you don't even care." My eyes prickle with tears I'm desperately trying to hold back. I accused her of being dramatic earlier but I'm the one crying.

When she doesn't respond with an immediate "You're not second string," a tear slips out.

Maddy stops and turns to me. "What are you mad about, really, Jana?" She plants her hands on her hips, impatient. Her hair is a mess, and her bright pink nail polish is chipped. "What did you think was going to happen that didn't?"

Her question makes me pause. "What? Why do you think that's the problem?"

"Because it's always the problem, Jana!" She throws her hands up, frustrated. "We just talked about this, but you don't listen to me. Everything has to be exactly the way you expect it to be. You don't allow anything to change, ever."

"And why is that a bad thing? Surprises aren't always positive." I don't want to bring up my mom and Jackie again, but from the frown that blooms on Maddy's face, she knows this time what I'm referring to. "And finally, things are—were good! I could wake up in the morning and not worry about what fresh problems the world was going to throw at me."

"Things *are* good. We're the lucky ones, Jana. Look at where we are!"

She sweeps her arms out wide like a ringmaster. I can't help but lift my gaze, my shoulders loosening with the movement. Behind Maddy, the darkened silhouette of the Forest Wheel looms in the distance. The wind has moved the clouds up and over the mountains, and the sky is clear. Even with all the lights, there are so many stars overhead, ones we couldn't possibly see from our backyards at home.

"Things are good," she repeats, "but we can't stay in high school forever."

"That's not what I want. I never said I loved my high school life so much I wanted to freeze in it forever."

"Then what do you want?" She drops her arms and her shoulders slump, tired. "Because clearly you didn't get it, and you're taking it out on everyone around you."

Her words are a freight train. My need to fix what I think is broken: it's manifested in the ugliest way tonight. I see it everywhere now. It's in the way Everett and Kayla stared at me like I'd grown two heads, in Nathan's apology for not being able to haul his injured self over to the lost and found, in Tyler's attempts to help even when he's still not over all the edibles in his system.

I tried so hard to control and fix everything tonight, certain that I was the only one truly working at it, the only one who could be relied on to solve our problems. I held on to this idea so tightly that I took my frustration out on the people around me. The chaos of tonight couldn't have been easy for any of my friends, but the way I acted essentially punished them for being real and honest with me. This probably made it so they'd rather not do that ever again.

Which is also exactly how I feel about Dad. When you come to predict a certain negative reaction from someone you care about, you learn to do whatever you can to avoid it. Even if it means dodging the hard stuff and not solving anything at all. We throw patch after patch on it, thinking we've fixed the problem, but it festers anyway.

By the time my thoughts gel enough to speak, almost a minute has passed. Maddy hasn't pressed me or walked away. She stood there, in front of me, that unflattering fluorescent light on her face, waiting for my heart to calm down in a way she must've been certain it would. She has been trying to change my mind longer than anyone, and it took me this long to start seeing some of the truth in her words.

I drag in a breath and catch a whiff of pine in the Orchards air. It's easy to forget that this festival is one tiny blip at the edge of the grandness of the San Bernardino forest.

When I finally speak, my voice is hoarse. "This past year was a mess for me. My grades slipped—that's how bad it was."

Maddy nods in understanding. She'd come over with pistachio ice cream at eleven pm the night before an AP exam because I was stressed over whether I was prepared enough. I'd spent whole weekends studying and had called out sick for a full week of work. But I was prepared enough: I scored a five out of five.

So for me to let any bit of my academic life falter means something must have been seriously wrong: Maddy knows this. Driving Mom to faraway appointments or dragging myself out of bed to let Jackie back into the house in the early hours of the morning had taken its toll on me in a way that I hadn't admitted to anyone—maybe including myself—until tonight.

"But it's gotten better now, right?" Maddy says. "Your mom has almost fully recovered, and Jackie . . . well, Jackie isn't ever going to not mix things up."

A small laugh escapes me. "They are better, and maybe that's part of the problem. I think this annoying habit of mine of micromanaging everything—I think it was my very messy way of preserving that little bit of happiness I found when things seemed to settle down at home."

"That makes sense. You did become really rules-focused. Kind of like your dad. Like more than when you wouldn't sell me that donut at that yearbook fundraiser because I was four cents short."

She smiles fondly at the memory, especially because I eventually brought her a free, somewhat stale leftover donut after the fundraiser ended.

"I think all this sticking to the rules stuff was a way to inject some certainty back into everything. You know what will happen if you follow them, what'll happen if you don't. Everything is black and white, predictable, controllable. And I—I think that made everything worse."

Maddy tucks a strand of hair behind her ear. "You didn't make everything worse. Tougher than it needed to be, maybe."

"Well, can't disagree with that. I—I'm sorry." And that simple apology suddenly lifts a weight off my shoulders, as if it had been sitting there, just waiting to be called forth. "And I'm sorry for what I said at the bonfire. I do like being friends with you; I don't know what drove me to say otherwise."

"I'm sorry too," she says, her eyes crinkling with the beginnings of either a smile or a tear. "Maybe I was being a little—how'd you put it?—dramatic."

"I did say some pretty awful things, so I definitely deserve some of that drama. I'm starting to see how much I shift the blame onto everyone else when things go wrong. Maybe this is something I'm okay with changing."

"You know, you say 'change' like it's a bad thing. It doesn't have to be. Just like keeping things the same isn't always good. Not everything has to be black and white like that."

"So what is it then? Gray? Because I really don't know how much uncertainty I can handle." My Chalmers Design acceptance flits to the top of my mind, and I gulp. She says change isn't bad, but she has no idea how my dreams may upend both our futures.

Maddy shrugs. "The opposite of black and white isn't gray, Jana. It's color. And having things change? It might be painful and unexpected, but necessary."

"Wow, that's . . . actually very poetic of you. That does seem to fit your brand though."

She snorts. "Before you give me too much credit, I read it in one of the self-help books my mom keeps on the coffee table, under all those fashion magazines. But maybe you're ready to live your life in color too."

Her words draw out a genuine smile in me because I can practically see it: the world brighter, more vivid because the constraints I've put on everything have begun to dissolve. It's hard, realizing that you've been wrong. But it's better for me to come to terms with it now than live under that falsity forever, alone.

"But you know, you named all these things that don't make you happy," Maddy says. "You never answered my question on what would."

I close my eyes then and the vision materializes so palpably I could almost step onto that gleaming library tile floor: the product design program at Chalmers that I'd gotten accepted into. That I hadn't told her about. That I'm saying no to, for Maddy.

But if I'm breaking the chains that keep me locked in this predictable but uncompromising life, then I can't hold on to her either. It's not that she's blocking me from going to Chalmers, but it's still hard to move away from someone when they've got their arms linked with yours, when they're constantly talking about how much they *need* you.

When I open my eyes, I see the best friend I've been clinging so hard to these past few months and only succeeded in pushing away. Part of me must have known this friendship was changing or ending and I was afraid.

We've been Maddy and Jana for so long, that being just Jana is new territory.

But Maddy is the one who said change doesn't have to be bad. It can be painful and unexpected, but necessary. And so are the words I force out next. This might break us. But this is the cost of living in color.

"Chalmers. I got into that design program and"—I take a breath—"I know you and I are supposed to go to Santa Clarita together, but I think I want to go."

I brace for anger, for accusation of betrayal at all the plans we'd made together. Because I'm taking this first big step away. I'm the one letting go.

So when the sides of her mouth quirk with a small smile, I'm not sure if she's happy for me or happy she spotted a weapon she can bludgeon me with.

"Jana, that's wonderful. Really. I— You got in, and I don't even think I know you applied." The words sound joyous, but the tone rings a little empty.

I've seen Maddy happy for me before, like when I got a year-book editor position, and this is different. My chest goes tight at what's missing. "It was a last-minute thing. It was such a long shot because their program is so exclusive, and I assumed nothing would come of it."

I talk too fast because I'm nervous that she'll somehow change her mind, that she'll say she's not happy for me after all.

"So, this means no Santa Clarita roomie situation then?"

I tense, dreading a further shift in mood. "No, I guess not. Is . . . is that okay?"

She purses her lips and focuses on some point off in the distance, behind me.

When she doesn't respond right away, that nervousness ramps up again and my own words flow out to fill the silence. "I'll be honest. I'm worried this will be the end of our friendship because we haven't been doing great lately, and we'll be on opposite sides of the country. We made these big plans to go to college together, but if I do this, it's like I'll be the one physically abandoning you. You've gone through so much with your own family, and I still worry about you all the time. What if I'm not there for you when you need me? And what if we drift apart? What if we stop being friends?"

Maddy grabs my hand then, and we stand together in silence, the wind wrapping around us like it's holding us together. I must've voiced something we both fear, and having it out in the open is like facing a specter that's been haunting us for ages. But her holding on to my hand—it's not the kind of grip that makes it hard for someone to break away. It's the kind that asks for reassurance, for one more moment of peace.

"Do you really think that'll happen?" Maddy asks.

"I don't know." And that's the truth. "It makes me sad to think these may be the last moments we have as best friends, you know? Even if we re-created this exact moment next year and returned to the Orchards, it wouldn't be the same. We will never be the same us we are now."

Maddy squeezes my hand, and this small connection feels steady in all the ways we need each other to be. "I think . . . I think that's okay. It's okay for us to drift. Friendships strain and change all the time. Like when Tyler decided to get highlights and I just had to deal with it."

I smile as a mild encouragement at her talking about Tyler to me. She catches my hint and a matching smile paints across her face.

"You're right that it's going to be different," she continues. "And I'm scared too—what would I do without my Emotional Support Jana?" She smiles softly, a blend of joking and complete sincerity. "But no matter what the future holds, we sure as hell had a good run, didn't we?"

She says it like we're breaking up, and there's something about that that tears my heart in half. This is the hard stuff, and I'm facing it, head-on. We both know where this is going, deep down, how challenging preserving anything will be from now on. But this feels like us basically giving each other permission to forge ahead, to take the memories we've made as golden and not once look back with regret.

"We did have a good run."

Maddy lets go of my hand and rubs her goose-bumped arms. Her smile is sad, but it's still a smile. "And haven't I been telling you all this time that you can't get rid of me that easily?"

A tear rolls down my cheek and I catch it on my sleeve—Tyler's sleeve. "So you're not mad, about me wanting to go to Chalmers?"

She shrugs, like what she's about to say doesn't matter. But it does. Every word we say to each other now matters more than any laugh we've shared, any text we've traded in the past year. "No, I'm not mad. How could I be mad when you're finally fighting for yourself, like I've been bugging you to do all this time?"

Her voice goes quieter then. "It does sting that you kept this from me and that we're not going to the same school like we'd planned. But come on, Jana! Chalmers!" She shoves me playfully on the arm, like Everett would've done to Nathan. "There's no way you're not doing this. What kind of person would I be if I let myself get in the way of your dream? I can't do that to you. In fact, if you show up at Santa Clarita in the fall, I'm going to beat you up."

I laugh then, because that line sounds more like the Maddy I know. "You literally would not kill that fly that flew into the computer lab. You insisted on chasing it with a cup to catch and release it. But point taken. Are you going to be okay though? I meant it when I said I worry about you. If I'm not there for you when you need me, then—"

"Then I'll have to figure it out, won't I?" Her gaze drops to the ground then, like she's trying to keep me from seeing all the uncertainty there. "I'll be okay, Jana. You have to choose you. I want you to choose you."

I pull her into a hug then, and it's familiar but also new, like we're different people than we were moments ago. And that's okay, I realize now.

Maddy's voice breaks my emotional streak. "Aren't you glad we're not wearing the same shirt right now? It'd look so weird."

"God, Maddy, be mature for a second," I say with a laugh.

We part just so she can push me lightly on the shoulder again. "Enough of this emotion. Stand aside, Jana. Time for me to save the day."

With a smile at me, my best friend turns the corner and heads straight for the Lost and Found tent.

TWENTY-SEVEN

SUNDAY, APRIL 24
4:16 am

Shrinking into Tyler's letterman's jacket, I post up in the shadows a few tents down, with Maddy in my line of sight. I crouch behind the hay bales that Nathan had perched on earlier, icing his knee and breaking the news to us that the Lost and Found tent didn't have his keys yet. This area smells faintly of vomit, and I'm really trying not to overthink it.

Maddy cruises up to the lost and found like she owns the place and they're just holding something for her, as a favor. She has always been this confident. It's something that I went from admiring to being annoyed by: the way she can walk into any situation and wholeheartedly believe it will work out for her. This doesn't annoy me anymore though. It's this determined optimism that makes me hopeful about this night for the first time in hours.

I scan the surrounding area. That same security guard, Garcia, who tried to grab Everett, paces by the Lost and Found tent. He's no longer chatting up Sandra the lost and found attendant. He's on patrol, sweeping his flashlight back and forth ahead. His other hand hovers by the walkie-talkie clipped on his belt. Maddy strides right by him, and he doesn't give her a second glance once he determines she's not me, Kayla, or Everett.

Even from three tents away, I can see the megawatt smile Maddy switches on once she stops in front of Sandra. It's the same smile she uses at cheer and when she wants something from her dad. Or me. It's why my homework is never safe from her.

The thought tugs at something in my heart: I won't have to worry about her begging at lunch to "just double-check the math homework answers" to avoid another late assignment. This time next year, we'll be in completely different classes, on opposite sides of the country. This image of the future is thrilling and sad all at once, but maybe that's what color looks like: vivid, rich, and sometimes clashing.

"Hi, I'm trying to pick up some keys I lost." Maddy's voice barely drifts over to where I am. I inch to the edge of the hay bale to see if I can catch more of the conversation.

I can't hear Sandra clearly, but from Maddy's sliding out of her ID from her wallet and Sandra's same clipboard flip and scan from earlier, it looks like it's going well. Then Sandra's lips purse and she sets down the clipboard. She doesn't make any move to take Maddy's ID.

"But they're my keys!" Maddy says, her volume rising. "You're telling me I have to sit around and wait for your manager to get here at eight o'clock to release them because they're a"—she does exaggerated air quotes—"'contested item'? All because some random kid tried to claim the same set earlier? Unbelievable."

I bite back the obscenities that bubble up in my throat. Looks like Everett messed us up in more ways than one tonight. Not only with his stickers, teenage love search, and casual disappearing and reappearing, but with this marking of the minivan keys as a contested item. I might be the only one with parents angrily waiting up into the wee hours for them, but I can say with a hundred percent certainty that none of us want to wait around until eight in the morning to pick up keys and see Everett possibly hunted down and held on vandalism charges.

But instead of retreating so we can figure out another course of action, Maddy stays put. What is she doing?

I stamp down the flare of annoyance that starts to rise. I guess I do doubt her a little too often. I need to trust her, even if I can't predict her next move. She knows what she's doing.

Sandra holds her hands out in a conciliatory, calm-down manner, but Maddy has dialed up her angry body language. One hand is on her popped-out hip, and I can only imagine the knit-brow look she's giving Sandra.

"But the keys are right there!" She jams a finger down at the clipboard between them, then points toward the back wall of the Lost and Found tent. "Bin three, bag R, as in 'ridiculous you won't give me my damn keys,' on that bottom shelf. You said so yourself before you mentioned this whole contested business."

Sandra responds with something that looks like "I'm sorry, but," and Maddy isn't having it.

"I can see bin three from here," Maddy yells. "Right next to that plug-in space heater that's probably a fire hazard."

I raise an eyebrow at her escalating volume, and it takes me a moment to connect the dots on what she's doing. She's not so subtly ordering me to get over to bin three and find that baggie marked R.

I spring into action. Sneaking along the side of the tents to stay out of sight, I head toward the back corner Maddy had pointed at. Pausing to let Garcia the guard's patrol route draw him farther away from the Lost and Found tent, I take the last big leaps to drop myself into the dirt behind the tent. I hold my breath, lift up the vinyl wall, and find myself directly behind the metal cubbies sorting everyone's lost goods by bin and baggie.

Which one is bin three? Maddy had mentioned a space heater, so I choose the clear plastic bin closest to it. It's warm to the touch. She's right, this does seem like a huge fire hazard. Inside the bin sit dozens of labeled plastic baggies, with dozens of keys. I lift up the corner of the vinyl wall again and make eye contact with Maddy, who is still berating poor Sandra for Orchards' administrative policies that the woman clearly doesn't control.

I tap my wrist where a watch would be, if I didn't always just use my phone to check the time instead. A sign to Maddy: *this is going to take a while.*

And because she knows me so well, Maddy gives me the slightest of nods, a signal that she'll draw out this distraction as long as she can.

"So this is some big Orchards policy you can't change, is it?" Maddy says, loud enough to cover the sound of the bin contents settling as I pull it toward me and set it on the bare dirt. "Then show me. Show me in whatever handbook they give you guys where it says, exactly, that I'm supposed to be punished because some rando tried to steal my stuff first."

As Sandra sputters an excuse, I dig quietly through the baggies. They're not in any real order, and the first five I inspect are a random assortment of letter-labeled items that don't sport an R, as in ridiculous, as Maddy had hinted. I lift those out and continue my search, but the next five aren't what we're looking for either. There are only twenty-six letters in the alphabet, how is it that hard to find this one?

"What are you doing there? Freeze!"

Every cell in my body freezes at the sound of Garcia's voice. His flashlight sweeps in my direction and the beam hits me square in the face, like I'm already in an interrogation.

The logical part of me reaches for any sort of plausible explanation. But how do you explain an obviously-not-staff someone sitting in the middle of tiny piles of marked, unclaimed lost and found items, behind the tent itself?

The good part about rules is that you know what will happen if you follow them. The bad part is that you also know what will happen if you don't.

"I—I know this looks bad," I stammer.

My brain is tumbleweeds and dust after this night. And there's no way my already exhausted legs are going to be able to outrun Mr. Gym Rat Garcia.

That logical part of me practically shakes its head. *You've lost, Jana. This guard is going to lock you up in whatever passes for a holding cell in this place until the local police show up, then Chalmers and Santa Clarita and everywhere will rescind your acceptances, you criminal.*

My head swivels to meet Maddy's gaze through the gap in the tent flaps then, as a sort of apology that I've screwed this all up. Her eyes, wide with shock at the security guard's appearance, suddenly glint with mischief.

Even if Maddy and I don't make it through college or high school or, hell, even the rest of this god-awful festival, as friends, I will try my best to emulate these long-admired and often irritating traits of hers: spontaneity, with just enough confidence to believe that even the wildest twists will work out in our favor.

"Stay where you are," Garcia yells. He approaches, his hand already on his walkie-talkie. "I've apprehended one of the accomplices of the vandals. She's—"

I don't wait for him to reach me. I'm ready to live in full, wild color.

I grab fistfuls of the non-R-marked baggies around me and, with as much energy as I can muster, throw them into the air.

They soar, sparkling in the fluorescent stadium lights and against the faint stars dotting the night. Garcia and Sandra watch them, Sandra gasping with a strangled sound that I, fellow low-wage worker, can only recognize as oh-no-my-job horror.

As the baggies begin to rain down with all the fury of the storm Maddy and I dodged earlier, I tuck the half-empty bin three under my arm. I force myself to my feet with the grace of a newborn deer just figuring out how to walk and take off to the sound of Garcia ordering me to stop. I glance back in time to see him stumble over Sandra, already on her knees trying to pick up the labeled baggies studding the dirt in my wake.

A hand grabs mine and pulls me faster. It's Maddy, and despite—or maybe because of—the chaos I've just created, she's laughing. We disappear into the night together, speeding back toward the rest of our friends, with a dozen baggies of keys jangling at my side.

TWENTY-EIGHT

SUNDAY, APRIL 24
4:33 am

We explode back into Kayla's family's tent. Maddy dashes over to Nathan and Tyler to rouse them from their cozy, spooning slumber. Meanwhile, I unceremoniously dump the rest of the keys on the floor—to the chagrin of Kayla's family, who grumble and tug their sleeping bags far over their heads—and sift around until I find the elusive Baggie R. Everett and a groggy Nathan both confirm that it's their family's set, complete with that broken Lakers bottle opener key chain.

But our triumph isn't assured until after we leave the Orchards altogether, and we still face a fifteen-minute trek from this tent to the parking lot where Stampy the minivan is parked.

While Maddy forces Tyler to guzzle a water bottle, Kayla helps me scoop up the keys I've scattered.

"You know, if you're not the only ones missing keys, we should probably give these back," she says.

She may be the nicest person at the Orchards. Maybe Everett

was onto something all along. "You're right, but we've got to go. And they probably don't want to see me or my friends strolling back up to the Lost and Found tent."

Kayla considers this, then takes the entire bin from me. "I'll ask Kevin to turn them in. He kind of owes you after using your boyfriends as leverage."

"Um, they're not our boyfriends. I mean, Tyler is Maddy's boyfriend, but Nathan—"

I didn't think it possible, but my rambling and Kayla's misstep make her earthy brown cheeks turn almost berry pink. "Oh, I could've sworn . . . and when he looks . . . um, sorry. Anyway. Kevin can just pretend someone ditched all these keys by the food truck. And by the time he wakes up and gets over to the lost and found, you'll be long gone."

With that last phrase, her gaze drifts to Everett. I'm an expert by now on when I'm intruding into a private moment, so I thank her, then find a way to conveniently disappear while they say their goodbyes.

I take my backpack from Tyler and help him and Nathan totter toward the tent entrance. We glance back at Kayla and Everett in time to see them share a shy kiss. Yes, it's ill-timed, considering we're on the run, and kind of gross because Everett just exudes "weird little brother" to me, but it's also, in its own way, sweet.

While they say their extended promise-you'll-text-mes, I step outside to call Dad, only a few minutes on the wrong side of the new deadline. I spout out a long-winded apology and reassurance that I'm on my way home in a rushed, almost stream of consciousness run-on sentence. Then I turn off my phone.

"You sure that's a good idea?" Maddy asks, noticing the blank screen.

"I know it's not. But my parents can scream at me later." I'm not dodging the hard stuff anymore—just delaying it a little one more time. If this means grounding and giving up that paid-for ticket to our yearbook staff's Disneyland trip, then at least I can look back at how I saw my favorite band ever, with maybe my favorite people ever, and it was worth it.

I'm not my sister, and I'm trusting my parents to remember that after that truce-inspiring call with Dad earlier. But even if our progress hiccups and they slide back into their old worries about their poor, wayward daughters, I don't need them ruining this tiny bit of serenity I've finally found tonight, especially if I'll need both arms phone-free to help ferry our group back to the minivan. This is me choosing me.

Maddy smirks. "You rebel, you."

"Learned from the best."

I force my attention to the path ahead, making our way slowly back to the minivan. A still groggy Tyler leans on Maddy, and Everett holds up Nathan. I naturally lead the way. I've traversed almost every inch of the Orchards these past few hours, so I know the shortest way to the parking lot.

A voice hails us halfway to the minivan. "Hey, you need a hand there?"

I whirl around, expecting the worst, that Garcia and his security guard buddies have caught up with us. But to my surprise, before us, in all their technicolor glory, stand the Newcomers and Goers.

My heartbeat speeds up to drum the rapid beat of the last song of their set. "No. Way."

Keaton, the lead singer, cocks their head. They've changed out of their clothes from the concert and are practically swimming in a comfy-looking, oversize hoodie. "Oh. You sure? Because those guys look like they need to get somewhere." They point to Nathan and Tyler, who must be as wide-eyed as I am right now.

I shake some sense back into my head. "That's not what I meant. The 'no way' was about—" *Stop babbling, Jana.* "Anyway, yes. We'd love a hand. Unless you're busy. Then that's fine too." And I top it all off with a completely unwarranted burst of nervous laughter.

Keaton graciously ignores what they rightfully assume is a star-struck overreaction. "I think we've got a couple minutes to spare while they change the tire on our tour bus."

I blanch but freeze the smile on my face. I dug around for my phone in the wheel well of a bus at the Avocado Stage—the stage they'd played hours earlier. That wasn't their bus, was it? Was there any way my light rooting around somehow caused them a flat?

As if Maddy senses my thought spiral, she interrupts with a cough. "Well, Tyler here is just feeling a little ill, but walking it off will help him. Nathan, on the other hand . . ."

Derrick lopes over to help Everett with Nathan. "What happened to your leg, bro?"

Nathan seems incapable of answering. I figured he's as much of a CoGo fan as I am, and this reaction, as bumbling as mine, confirms it.

Everett responds for him. "Hurt it crowd-surfing at your set."

"Worth it," Nathan blurts out, a tad bit too loud.

Derrick shakes his head. "Then we really owe you our help. Come on, everyone," he says, waving over Aimee the bassist and Byron, the third keyboard player they've cycled through in the past year while founding member Laurie explores a solo career. The band members surround Nathan, edging out Everett, who goes to help Maddy with Tyler instead.

And with a one-two-three-four beat, CoGo hoists Nathan up on their shoulders. The sheer, giddy elation on his face is contagious, and together, we all practically skip back to the minivan.

The sound of the minivan door unlocking is the most beautiful thing I've heard in the past twenty-four hours. It's a bold pronouncement, considering I'm technically at one of this coast's biggest music festivals, graced with the personal presence of my favorite band.

Keaton raises a perfectly manicured eyebrow at our vehicle. "You sure you don't need a ride somewhere too? That thing looks a little dangerous."

And as much as I would *love* to get dropped off by the CoGo tour bus at home, I can only imagine how much that would amplify my parents' rage. Thankfully, Maddy again saves me from myself.

"It's a little worse for wear, but it'll still take us where we want to go. Thanks," she says. "Though one last thing: Can we bug you for some autographs?"

She reaches for my mini-backpack and tugs out my bomber jacket before I can stop her. Derrick digs a marker out of his pocket, and the band members take turns signing my jacket while I valiantly suppress my excited squeal.

CoGo turns to leave, and as Nathan, Everett, and Tyler pile into the van, I perch one arm on Maddy's shoulder, and we wave goodbye at the band that brought us together, time and time again.

Keys in the ignition, the upbeat track from earlier picking up exactly where it left off, and with enough gas in the old tank to get us away from the mountains, we peel out of the Orchards parking lot.

"Best night of my life," Everett says wistfully from the front seat. He has his window open and is leaning out the side, as if reluctant to leave this place behind.

The sun has started to peek over the horizon, turning the sky a glorious mix of pinks and purples. The lasers and fog and pyrotechnics of the night can't even compare with this view.

"No offense, but that's literally the most nonsensical thing I've ever heard you say," Nathan grumbles as he adjusts his rearview mirror. "We're going to need to stop for gas and a new ice pack. This one has melted all over my shorts and it looks like I've peed myself. In front of CoGo too. Ugh."

His brother laughs, earning him an upper arm punch from Nathan, and I laugh too before catching Nathan's eye in the rearview mirror. And maybe it's because he can't punch my arm from where he's sitting, but he smiles warmly at me, a blush crawling up his face, before he turns his eyes back to the road.

Then and there, I silently decide to bring over a #3 hoagie combo, with a strawberry milkshake, to him sometime this week to check on his knee. And maybe I'll take him up on that offer to hang out a little more. Once I submit that deposit to Chalmers Design, we'll be on the same coast this fall, after all.

Poor Tyler, still hopelessly groggy, slouches in the second row of the minivan. I'd draped his letterman's jacket over him after Maddy buckled him in, and he fell back asleep before Nathan had even shifted the van into reverse. I make a note to myself to buy him a new can of Pringles when we stop at the gas station. He might wake with a serious case of the munchies, and a sour-cream-and-onion-flavored olive branch is the least I can do after everything.

In the back row, Maddy and I sprawl out next to each other. I'm cocooned in my signed bomber jacket, and she's still in her bachelorette shirt, with that plastic bag holding her rain-soaked tank top at her feet. She starts to fall asleep too, and her head grazes my shoulder as she fights the inevitable.

I'm struck then with the thought that we'll never have another one of these moments. With her and me, our heads resting on each other in the back of a beat-up minivan, hurtling home at a speed that can't possibly be legal.

We might not even have another big fight left in us. Maybe there'll be a slow pulling away, a lengthening of time between calls and texts and visits, with an easy, one-click like on a social media post now and then as a reminder that at some point, there was an us.

But this realization doesn't make me as sad as I thought it would. This might be our friendship ending, or it might not be, and we need to be fine with it either way.

I will be fine with it either way.

Because as Maddy said, what lies ahead may be painful and not what we had planned, but still necessary. We can't stop ourselves or each other from living in glorious color, from growing, even if it means growing apart. And even if this is the last time we do fall asleep in the back of a minivan together, empty Pringles cans digging into my side, I will always love her for this lesson.

When I angle my head, I can tell she's already asleep.

"Hey," I whisper to Nathan.

He peers back at me in the rearview.

I smile. "Turn the music up. I love this song."

THREE YEARS LATER
January 29

Maddy:

JFK? LaGuardia? Which is closest to Chalmers?

Jana:

Hold on, let me ask roommate

Jana:

She says LGA. What dates?

Maddy:

I'll red-eye Wed March 26, fly out Monday March 31.
Free flight through Dad, owes me for my birthday

Jana:

He's not mad you're missing class?

Maddy:

Um this is MY dad we're talking about, not yours. And we have that Mon off for Cesar Chavez day. That ok, MOM?

Jana:

Ha. Seriously though, bring a coat.

Maddy:

Only if I have room after packing a dozen hoagies. Yay! I've missed you, it's been forever. Maddy and Jana do Manhattan! Pistachio ice cream all around

Jana:

You have to try the mango sticky rice ice cream at this place by campus

Maddy:

WHAT? A NEW FLAVOR? Who are you?

Jana:

I'm living in color, Maddy. Get used to it.

ACKNOWLEDGMENTS

Putting this story out into the world wasn't a solo act,
and I have so much gratitude for the many folks who lent
their creativity and dedication. You're all rock stars.

— AGENT —

Natalie Lakosil a.k.a. Emotional Support
Natalie • Grace Milusich

— THE QUILL TREE BOOKS EXPERIENCE —

Jen Ung, Tamer of Chaos (editor) • Rosemary Brosnan
(publisher) • Laura Mock (designer) • Dave Curtis (art
director) • f.choo (artist) • Mikayla Lawrence (managing
editorial) • Allison Hargraves (copyeditor) • Lana Barnes
(proofreader) • Sean Cavanagh (production) • Suzanne
Murphy (president of the children's division) • Jean McGinley
(associate publisher) • Audrey Diestelkamp (marketing) •
Mimi Rankin (school/library marketing) • Sammy Brown
(publicity) • Kerry Moynagh and the Harper Sales Team
• Tara Feehan (finance) • Laura Raps on contracts

— VIPS —

The Writers (a.k.a. My Saviors), featuring Brittney Arena, Alechia Dow, Koren Enright, Sam Farkas, Jessica James, Rae Castor, Alyssa Colman, Jenn Gruenke, Ashley Northrup, and Kalyn Josephson • GIRLSTRIP, featuring Rai Adair, Jennifer Franz, and Brittani Miller • Kat De Los Reyes • Pauline Villanueva • Rossini Yen • GW Law folks / Sparkle Motion • FALSD • NFALA • Pinay Powerhouse

— HOME —

The Badua Family Singers • Big R and the Little Rs (Rahul, Ruby, and Raja)